Spy
Force
Special

Spy Force Special

Deborah Abela

OXFORD
UNIVERSITY PRESS

OXFORD

UNIVERSITY PRESS

Great Clarendon Street, Oxford OX2 6DP

Oxford University Press is a department of the University of Oxford.
It furthers the University's objective of excellence in research, scholarship,
and education by publishing worldwide in

Oxford   New York

Auckland   Cape Town   Dar es Salaam   Hong Kong   Karachi
Kuala Lumpur   Madrid   Melbourne   Mexico City   Nairobi
New Delhi   Shanghai   Taipei   Toronto

With offices in

Argentina   Austria   Brazil   Chile   Czech Republic   France   Greece
Guatemala   Hungary   Italy   Japan   Poland   Portugal   Singapore
South Korea   Switzerland   Thailand   Turkey   Ukraine   Vietnam

Oxford is a registered trade mark of Oxford University Press
in the UK and in certain other countries

British Library Cataloguing in Publication Data

Data available

ISBN 978-0-19-272714-5

1 3 5 7 9 10 8 6 4 2

Printed in Great Britain by Cox & Wyman Ltd, Reading, Berkshire

Contents

MAX REMY
SPY FORCE
THE TIME AND SPACE MACHINE

For Vera and Poz

CHAPTER 1
DR EVILBRAIN STRIKES AGAIN

Time: 2.45p.m.

Date: Friday afternoon, somewhere in
the future

Place: Spy Force Headquarters

Dr Evilbrain was in the middle of another evil plan to destroy the world and the Chief of Spy Force had his top spy, Alex Crane, on the case as the only one who could stop him.

Dr Evilbrain was the world's greatest mastermind of evil. He was responsible for feats of evil that other evildoers only dreamt of. He was Spy Force's most wanted arch-enemy and they would not rest until the world was free of him.

Not only that, he was just about the ugliest person who was ever popped out into the world.

He had one thick eyebrow that dripped down his brow and into the edges of his eyes, which were small and beady like two rats sniffing for food from inside a dark hole. His nose was a mess of acne scars that looked like someone had taken a piece of the moon and stuck it right in the middle of his face. The ugly stick had been waved so high and long above his head, that on the day he was born, his own mother ran from the hospital and never wanted to see him again. He was so repulsive, mosquitoes wouldn't bite him and mirrors didn't crack when they saw him, they cried out in fear of their lives.

There was only one way to say it.

Dr Evilbrain wasn't pretty.

And he wasn't stupid, either. At least he wasn't stupid after he'd had the operation. He had the most villainous brain that ever slimed its way into a human head.

Literally.

Dr Evilbrain had created the world's first synthetic brain, equipped with hypersmart intelligence and precision evil and knew that with this brain, he'd be smart enough to take over the world. In a complex and very sloppy operation, his assistant, the sinister Count Igor, cut open Dr Evilbrain's head, scooped out his squelchy old brain and replaced it with his new and slimy smart one.

That's when Dr Evilbrain hatched his latest plan.

With his new brain squishing around in his head, Dr Evilbrain developed algae that would, in just twenty-four hours, multiply and choke the world's water supply of its oxygen, killing all living things and making water supplies everywhere poisonous for people to drink.

Human life would have only weeks to live.

(((4)))

For most people, it wouldn't even be that long.

It was up to Alex Crane, the world's greatest mastermind against evildoers, to create an antidote that would kill the algae and stop the deadly countdown to the end of the world.

She'd been working for twenty-two hours straight. There were only two hours left. All she needed was to add one drop of her secret ingredient and get down to the shores of the ocean before the deadline was up.

But only a drop.

Just one more . . .

Kaboom!!

Great sticky clumps of green slime went everywhere. Oozing down walls, across desks, soaking through books and, worst of all, covering Max from the top of her head down to her brand new sports shoes.

She wiped the slime from her eyes and realized she wasn't Alex Crane, Superspy, but Max Remy of Class 6B and her mum was really going to give it to her this time.

A sea of kids' faces traffic-jammed around her, laughing at her new look. Members of Class 6B were not known for their subtlety and they weren't about to change now.

'Hey, brainiac, can't you use a hanky like everyone else?'

'What's the matter, feeling a little green?'

'Guess who forgot to have a bath today?'

The room exploded in a deafening roar of laughter. Suddenly everyone was a comedian. Even Ms Ellen got in on the act.

'OK, class, that's enough. Max has just had a little accident,' she said. But Max could see Ms Ellen was only just managing to hold back her own laugh.

'Even though green really is your colour, Max.'

That was it.

You'd think it was the funniest joke anyone had ever made in the history of the entire world. Max wanted every bird there was to fly over Ms Ellen's head and slime her with their smelly poo. She imagined her teacher running around with her new poo-dropping hairdo, screaming and trying to get it off.

It was as if Ms Ellen could read Max's thoughts because her face turned serious and she lowered her voice.

'Max, one of the most important lessons we can learn is not to take ourselves too seriously.

Otherwise, you'll be sixty-five before you realize you've never had a really good laugh.'

Just then the bell rang.

Phew! Saved from any more of Ms Ellen's cheap women's magazine philosophies.

The class let out a big cheer and Ms Ellen could only just be heard.

'Have a good, safe holiday, everyone, and I'll see you next year,' she called out.

Kids swarmed everywhere, trying to grab their bags and get out of the door for what they'd waited a whole year to happen.

For Max, this meant freedom from the halfwits she had to sit next to.

Adios and see you later. She was out of there, and as far as she was concerned, nothing beat the fact that she wouldn't have to see any of the other kids' lame, laughing faces for the entire summer.

'Ah, Max?'

It was Ms Ellen.

Max's foot was almost out of the doorway.

'Yes?' she replied.

'You're not going to leave without cleaning up this mess, are you?' asked Ms Ellen with her eyebrows raised so high Max thought they'd fly off her forehead.

Max looked at the green slime-covered desk, floor, and walls. Cleaning it up would take ages.

'I didn't think so,' said Ms Ellen, collecting her books and papers. 'Now don't forget to have some fun in the holidays and I'll see you much more relaxed and happy next year.'

It took every ounce of Max's self-control not to pick up some slime and put it through her teacher's roller-curled hair. Instead, she imagined Ms Ellen as a giant bug-eyed monster with horrible breath and cockroaches crawling out of her nose.

'Yes, Ms Ellen,' she said, smiling.

After she'd finished cleaning, Max got her bag and went into the corridor where the other kids were waiting for her.

Especially Toby Jennings and his little fan club.

'So, Max, having a little trouble with your funny bone?'

'Maybe you should get it seen to?'

'Maybe when you were born they forgot to give you one.'

Max ignored them, trying to get to the main door and out of the building as soon as possible.

They wouldn't let it rest. But it was Toby who really knew how to get at her.

'So, Miss Enormous Brain, had a little slime trouble today?'

Max was good at science, but Toby was better at exams and always just beat her. And he let her know it.

'Looks like your second place behind me wasn't a terrible mistake after all, Ms Einstein.'

Max's head was alive with what felt like a hundred snakes wanting to jump out and slither all over Toby, squeezing him to within an inch of his life.

The snakes never appeared, so Toby kept on mouthing off.

'I knew you were the queen of slime, but I didn't think you were into making it,' he sneered.

Now the other kids really let loose.

Max tried to walk past them.

'What's the matter, slime got your tongue?'

Max never understood why Toby Jennings didn't just turn into a toad and fall into the nearest swamp with all the other swamp creatures.

She had had enough. She wasn't going to take this any more. But just as she was about to let him have it, a piece of slime wormed its way out of her hair, down her forehead, and onto her nose.

This was just what Toby needed for his final blow.

'Ah! It's alive,' he screamed. 'The slime's coming out of her brain. It's coming to get us all. Run for your lives! Aaaahhhhhh!'

The corridor burst into a riot of screaming kids falling and laughing and running as fast as they could to get away from Max and her slime brain, as if they had just been told the world was going to self-destruct in five seconds.

Which wouldn't be such a bad idea. At least then Max would never have to come back to this school and all the jerk students who went there.

The corridor was clear in ten seconds flat. Good riddance. All Max had to do was get her bag, walk out of those doors, and she wouldn't have to step back in this place for a whole six weeks.

But there was one thing she'd forgotten.

Her mum.

Max met her on the steps.

'What happened to you?' she gasped. 'What's that in your hair? And what have you done to your new shoes?'

Of course, the shoes. Things always seemed much more important to her mum than Max was.

'What will it take to teach you a little respect for your things, young lady?'

Normally Max would have had a great

comeback. Something funny and sharp. She was pretty good at those. But she was feeling sticky from the slime that was starting to harden and smell as if she'd just fallen down the worst toilet in the world.

Max had to get away from the sniggering she could still hear behind her.

'I don't know, Mum. Let's just get out of here.'

CHAPTER 2
A MILLION MILES FROM HOLLYWOOD . . .

Max climbed in the car with her mum and said nothing. As they drove away she could hear the chanting of 'slime lady' slowly recede behind them as they moved further away from the school.

Her mother sat staring ahead, gripping the steering wheel as if she was trying to squeeze it into another shape. But Max knew the silence wasn't going to last long.

'What's got into you lately?' said Max's mum in her at-her-wits'-end voice.

Max also knew that when a conversation started this way it never got any better.

'Nothing,' said Max.

'Don't tell me "nothing". The last few weeks you've been moody, you've barely said a word, and I can't remember the last time I saw you really smile.'

'Why is everyone so concerned about me being Ms Smiley?' Max exploded.

'Everyone who?' asked her mum.

'Doesn't matter,' said Max and sank down lower into her seat to the crunch of plastic bags her mum had laid out so Max's slimed clothes wouldn't wreck the upholstery.

'Yes, it matters. It's like you don't care for anything any more. You used to be such a happy girl, always off playing with other kids, but now it's like you don't want to have anything to do with anyone,' and here there was a well-timed pause before her mother added, 'including me.'

'Well, you don't have to worry about that much longer,' said Max perking up. 'As soon as Dad picks me up tomorrow I'll be out of your hair for six weeks.'

Max's mother faced the road and although it seemed impossible, gripped the wheel even harder. Her voice softened.

'Actually, there's been a change of plans.'

The way her mother said it Max knew these new plans weren't a good thing for her.

'What change of plans?' she asked suspiciously.

'Your father has been offered a very important film to direct and won't be able to come back to Australia this year.'

Max's dad lived in America and her mother wanted nothing to do with him after he fell in love with a famous actress and moved to Hollywood, where the weather is always sunny and people are tanned and sit around in cafés all day. Even though it sounded like a really boring way to live, compared to spending six weeks in her mother's company it would be heaven.

'But we all agreed that Dad was going to come here for his holidays!' Max cried.

'Sweetie, this is a big opportunity for your father and it was a really hard decision for him. I know it doesn't seem fair . . .'

'Well, if he can't come here, I'll go to America and be with him,' Max said decisively. 'I'm old enough to fly by myself and I'd have much more fun staying with Dad and his new wife than I will staying here.'

Max knew this would hurt her mother, and that's exactly what it did.

'Now, Max, your father's going to be too busy to look after you. You know that when he directs he has no time for anybody . . .'

Max looked away and mumbled into the window.

'If you'd made more time to be with us instead of your dumb job maybe Dad wouldn't have left us in the first place.'

Max jerked forward as her mother pulled over to the side of the road and stopped the car.

Her eyes shifted towards her mother's beetroot-red face that always meant one thing. She was really going to get it now.

'Look, Max, I know it's hard for you to understand but what happened between your father and me was very complicated. I know you think it's my fault we got divorced but there was a lot more involved than you know about.'

'Like what?' asked Max.

'When you're older, you and I will sit down and have a long talk about it, but for now you're too young and you just wouldn't understand,' said Max's mum, softening her voice.

Max looked away. She hated it when her mother treated her like a kid.

'Please, Max, we don't have time to talk now. We have to get you home so you can pack.'

Max turned sharply.

'Pack for where?' she asked.

Her mum took a deep breath.

'For the farm. It's been arranged that you'll spend the holidays with Uncle Ben and Aunt Eleanor. They're expecting us tonight.'

Uncle Ben and Aunt Eleanor! The same Uncle Ben and Aunt Eleanor who lived in the country, a million miles from anywhere? Who spent their days raising sheep and stomping through cow manure? The thought of spending her holidays with this pair of country bumpkins was as horrifying as being locked in a cage with giant man-eating spiders! And as exciting as being strapped to a chair and being made to watch the Oprah Winfrey show for the rest of her life.

Really, really boring!

Suddenly, being with her mother didn't seem so bad after all.

'Why can't I stay with you?' Max pleaded.

'Because things are really busy for me now and I think it would be better if you got out of the city for a while and breathed some fresh country air.'

Max sat staring out of the windscreen at the city. She felt as if she was seeing it for the last time, convinced that if she was made to go to the farm, boredom would take hold of her within days and leave her a shivering, zombied mess.

She hated the country and she hated even more the idea of spending it with two chicken farmers she hardly knew.

Her mother leant over and stroked her cheek.

'I realize this is hard for you, Max, but you know I love you. I've certainly been busy lately and these last few years without Dad have been hard on both of us, but it will get better. I promise.'

Max's mother gave her a quick kiss and started the car.

'We'd better get going,' she said, looking at her watch.

Max wiped the kiss away and crossed her arms against her chest.

Her mum worked in the publicity department of a major TV station and her life was full of dinners, openings, famous people, and parties. It seemed pretty cruisy to Max and as they drove on in silence, she knew she was the one who had the hard life.

CHAPTER 3
THE END
OF THE
WORLD

This was one of the hardest assignments yet for Alex Crane.

She'd been captured and was being driven to the secret hideout of the infamous Camilla La Koole, the most notorious mastermind of poisons the world had ever seen. Camilla's cunning plans saw her befriend the rich and famous and when they least expected it, spray them with her poisons. Each poison was enough to keep the person immobile until she could steal their riches and escape.

And when her victims awoke they remembered nothing.

Camilla was the richest and most clever woman the underworld had ever known, and Spy Force had Alex Crane on the case to bring her evil ways to an end.

Of course Alex wasn't really captured. She'd let Camilla trap her and, armed with a Spy Force micro-recorder in her watch and a piece of Truth Gum, which when chewed forced the chewer to tell the truth, she'd trick Camilla into confessing all.

Just one piece of gum.

Max's head was thrown forward and her pen skidded across her book as the car came to an abrupt stop. A cattle dog had run onto the road and her mother had seen it just in time to stop.

Max stopped thinking of Alex Crane and looked around her. She wasn't superspy Alex Crane in some exotic spy location, she was Max Remy and she was in Mindawarra. A town that had one pub, a Chinese restaurant, a police station, and a general store with a couple of petrol pumps out front. The only person in sight was an old man asleep on the bench at a bus stop that looked as if there hadn't been a bus through for about a hundred years.

This was Mindawarra. Max's home for the entire school holidays.

'According to this, Ben and Eleanor's farm is about three Ks east of here,' said her mum, poring over a map. 'So it won't be long now.'

Long until what? Max thought. Until she became comatose with boredom as she spent the summer watching cows graze? Great.

The sun was just starting to set when they pulled on to a dirt track and, after three dusty, potholed kilometres, came upon a house that looked like something out of a horror film: broken down, creaky, and smothered by evil-looking trees. The only person who could possibly feel at home here was some half-crazed lunatic who'd had their brain removed at birth.

Ben and Eleanor came rushing out to meet them. Max almost got smothered in the folds of clothes as Eleanor swooped on her and gave her a hug. She untangled herself, lucky to escape alive.

Ben stepped towards Max's mother and the two exchanged a brief handshake.

'Hello,' they both said coolly.

Max's mother wiped her hand with a hanky as if to wipe the handshake away. She then mumbled a quick hello to her sister and what sounded like a quiet 'thank you'.

'Would you like to come in for a quick cuppa?' asked Eleanor.

'No thanks. I really should be going. I'm late already.' Then she turned to Max. 'Bye, sweetie. Anything you need just call me. OK? I love you.'

And with that she was gone. A small cloud of dust following her car out of the front gate and back to the city.

Back to the real world.

Eleanor picked up Max's bags.

'Come on, Max. I'll show you to your room,' she said cheerily.

Max followed Eleanor and only just missed

stepping on dog poo before walking up the creaky, dusty front steps.

At the top she turned and looked around her. There wasn't another house in sight. This really was the end of the world and she'd been farmed out like some dumb animal to graze with a couple of hillbillies. Max pictured herself as an old woman walking off the farm, fat from years of eating steak and potatoes every night and watching cows wander around dusty paddocks.

She jumped back as a chicken flapped past her as if from nowhere. She covered her face with her arms as it landed and then cackled as if it was having a good laugh at her.

'You won't think it's so funny when you're next Sunday's lunch,' she snapped.

Max stepped onto the verandah that circled the house and then through the flyscreen door that slammed closed behind her. Inside, she couldn't believe what she saw. She was standing in a long, dark corridor that led all the way through the house to the kitchen at the end. Cobwebs dangled from lights that looked as if they were from the last century. As she stepped carefully forward, she looked into the lounge room to her left and stared open-mouthed at its giant sofas, bare wooden floor, and creepy pictures of really old people propped up on a mantelpiece that looked as if it took all its strength just to stay up. Through frayed curtains, a large window let in streaks of greyish light like frozen lightning bolts. There were bookshelves lining almost every wall and a large glass cabinet that contained some old ornaments, yellowing papers and books left over from the Dark Ages. A tall lamp stood in the corner like a skinny man with a large hat and nowhere to go while a squat table nestled underneath it.

But that wasn't the worst of it.

There was no TV. What kind of a house had no TV?

'Max, I'm in here.'

Max followed Eleanor's voice out of the TV-less lounge room.

Then she saw something she really couldn't believe. Her room. That's what Eleanor called it anyway. It wasn't a proper room but a bed on the back verandah. The 'sleep-out' they called it, and Eleanor showed it to Max as if it was the most special room in the whole place. At least here she'd have a quick getaway in the middle of the night if the whole relic of a house fell down around them.

'I'll leave you here to get settled in. Dinner will

be ready in about twenty minutes,' said Eleanor.

Max looked around the sleep-out.

'Thanks, but I'm not hungry. I think I'll just go to bed early.'

Eleanor smiled, but Max could tell she was disappointed.

'Goodnight then. We'll see you in the morning,' she said and closed the door behind her.

Max wondered what a great spy would do to get out of this situation. How would she plan her escape? In the middle of nowhere and trapped in a house with no TV.

Max changed into her pyjamas and slid into bed. She could hear Eleanor and Ben laughing in the kitchen, that is when they weren't singing off-key and talking at the top of their voices.

She pulled the blankets over her head and thought about her dad in America. She missed him and wondered why he was always too busy to spend time with her. She turned over in her squeaky bed and wished she was at home, with its big-screen TV, cosy lounge room, and bed with soft, comfortable pillows.

Eventually Ben and Eleanor quietened down and the lights in the house were turned off.

Just as Max was about to fall asleep, she heard

a noise. It was like an animal sniffing at the door of the verandah, only centimetres from where she was asleep. The hinges creaked as the door opened slowly. Max held her breath as she thought of who it might be. Maybe it was some terrible monster or a raving lunatic who lived deep in the bush and only came out at night.

In the moonlight Max saw an old cricket bat on the floorboards near her bed. She moved slowly, trying not to be heard, but the squeaking springs of the bed were like a hungry cat that wouldn't be quiet. She reached out and picked up the bat, sitting bolt upright in bed, ready to strike.

Then she heard footsteps. She had to tell herself to take another breath; she was so scared she'd stopped breathing.

Then she saw the silhouette of a large figure and heard the sound of heavy boots trying to be quiet as they stepped towards her.

Closer and closer.

This was it, thought Max. I'm going to die!

A madman had broken into the house and was coming to get her. Max could hardly hear her own thoughts, her heart was beating so loudly in her chest.

She was done for. She could see the headlines

now: 'Girl disappears from farm without a trace.'
For years police would try and solve the mystery of
her disappearance. Her mother would sob and sob
and make sure her make-up was on properly before
the TV news team interviewed her about her lost
child. But what she'd forget to say is that it was her
idea to send Max away in the first place even
though Max had begged to stay with her. If she did
disappear her mum wouldn't have to worry about
cooking her dinner, or coming home early, or Max's
new shoes that she'd wrecked. Life would be great
for her mum. No more Max to worry about, just all
those famous people and a life full of parties.

Then the screen door opened and the footsteps
receded into the night.

Phew! She was safe. For now. But who knew
when the lunatic would be back or if there were
more of them hiding in the bushes, ready to steal
into the night and scare innocent children.

Max got out of bed and sneaked to the window.
She watched the beam of a torch as it made its way
to a small shed. A light was turned on inside the
shed and she could see the black silhouette of a
man. Who was he and what was he doing? Maybe
he was a crazed psychopath creating a devastating
device of evil. Maybe he was no better than Dr

Evilbrain and it was up to Max to stop him before he destroyed the world.

Max climbed into bed and gripped the bat firmly just in case she needed it. She lay there staring at the door and listening to every rustle, hoot, and buzzing sound that filled the night air. The end of the holidays seemed a very long way away.

CHAPTER 4

MUD MONSTERS AND SAVAGE WOLVES

Superspy Alex Crane was being pursued by the treacherous Baron Lichtenstein and his hungry pack of wolves. Alex had uncovered the Baron's scheme to smuggle top-secret Government plans out of the country in a collection of talking dolls and was now running for her life with the Baron and his wolves in hot pursuit. They were gaining fast. Just as Alex was about to pass through the gates of the Baron's estate to safety, she tripped and sprained her ankle. She tried to stand up but the pain was too great. The wolves were gaining on her fast. She could hear the Baron's laugh of victory as they were about to pounce.

Was this the end of Alex Crane? Would the wolves eat her alive? Would Spy Force lose their greatest-ever spy?

Max woke in terror. Someone had thrown something large and woolly over her and was trying to smother her. She struggled beneath the furry weight, trying to breathe, trying to scream, fighting for her life. Maybe it was the heavy-footed man who had terrorized her last night and had come back to kill her. Or maybe it was her weird uncle and aunt who wanted to chop her up and feed her to the chickens. She knew they were crazy. Probably crazy enough to kill.

They weren't going to do away with her that easily, thought Max. She struggled, using all her strength against the smothering weight. Then she felt a long wet slap across her face. What was that? Then she heard a bark.

A dog! It was a dog!

'Get off me!' she screamed. 'I said get off me!'

Max gave the dog one big shove and it landed clumsily on the floor next to her bed. But it thought she was playing and jumped back up on her again.

'Will somebody get rid of this maniac dog before he kills me!' she yelled.

Eleanor came into the room and laughed as she pulled the dog off Max.

'Ralph, I know you're excited to have a new guest in the house but at least let her wake up before you say good morning,' said Eleanor.

Max was furious that Eleanor thought it was so funny. She'd almost been killed! Eleanor wouldn't be laughing if she'd found her lying blue in the face with her eyes wide open, having taken her last dog-smelling breath.

'Sorry about that. Ralph was only trying to be friendly,' said Eleanor apologetically.

'Well, I'd appreciate it if you controlled your

dog so I'm not attacked every morning when I wake up,' Max said sharply.

Eleanor looked hurt.

Max wiped the dog spit from her face and brushed dog hairs off her pyjamas.

'He didn't mean any harm, but I'll make sure he sleeps outside from now on.'

Ralph gave a yelp. Eleanor wouldn't really leave him outside all night, would she? Not after all these years and besides, he hated being alone in the dark.

'Come on, Ralph. Let's leave Max to get dressed in peace,' said Eleanor. Ralph looked away from Max, let out a small whimper and, with his tail sagging to the floor, he quietly left the room after his mistress.

Max threw off the blankets in one angry sweep. Finding her slippers under the bed, she took her toilet bag and dog-smelling self to the bathroom. When she got there, she stood in the doorway with her mouth open as she looked at what was to pass for a bathroom for the next six weeks. It was a small room with one window up high and a small cracked mirror that hung even higher from a crooked nail. Even hardened criminals had it better than this, she thought.

The walls were a floral mess of pale pink and green tiles that looked as if they had come straight out of a magazine from the 1950s. Tiles had fallen off the walls and were piled on a shelf waiting to be fixed. The bathroom cabinet was so small Max wondered that anything could fit in it, and the toilet lid looked heavy enough to break her arm just trying to lift it up. The bath was so deep she thought she was going to need a ladder just to get in and above it the shower nozzle poked out from the wall like a miniature metal weapon left over from the war. Around the bath hung a bright yellow curtain splattered with ducks and rainbows.

Nothing matched, nothing was her height, everything was a nightmare.

As Max tried to get up the courage to enter the room, she thought of her mother. There was a lot about her Max didn't like, but one thing she did have was a sense of style, which Eleanor must have missed when they were handing it out.

'Why me?' muttered Max. She took a deep breath and stepped through the doorway, wanting to wash away every trace of the smelly dog as quickly as possible.

After cleaning up, Max felt better but when she got to the kitchen she met her next horror.

Breakfast!

Eleanor smiled as she saw Max enter the room.

'Just in time,' she said, as she placed before Max a plate of fried eggs, bacon, toasted white bread, and a large mug of tea.

Max gulped hard trying to imagine eating it all.

Unlike the bathroom, the kitchen was a big room with light pouring in from the yard. There were cupboards everywhere. The benches and shelves were cluttered with jam jars, sauce bottles, biscuit tins, recipe books, and canisters with tea, flour, and sugar written on them. There was a spice rack with what looked like every spice in the world and a walk-in pantry that was filled from the floor to the roof with boxes, tins, packets, and containers. The floor was like a giant checkerboard of linoleum and right in the middle was a high wooden table covered with jars of spreads, a jug of milk, cups, a pot of tea, a large loaf of bread, a sugar pot, some cereal boxes, a toaster, knives, forks and spoons, egg cups shaped as miniature Humpty Dumpty characters and, nestled right in the middle of it all, a small vase of flowers. Max's eyes fell on the plate in front of her.

'Thanks, but I'm not hungry,' she said.

'Not hungry? Rubbish,' said Ben, sliding his

toast through the yellow egg goo on his plate. 'You didn't have dinner last night, you must be hungry.'

'It's just that I usually have freshly squeezed juice and fruit salad for breakfast,' explained Max.

'That's not enough to keep a young girl growing big and strong,' her uncle scoffed as he kept eating and Max noticed him give Eleanor a quick wink. 'Besides, you'll need extra energy to work around the farm.'

Big and strong? Work around the farm? Not only was she sentenced to spending her holidays miles from any kind of civilization, but she was also going to be used as child labour. Knowing she had no choice, Max sat at the table, scraped the butter off her toast and made a note to call the child welfare authorities as soon as she could.

Just then the screen door slammed and there stood the gangliest boy with the wildest hair she'd ever seen.

'I've given Ralph a talking to and left him outside,' he said.

Her uncle swallowed the final piece of his egg goo combo.

'Linden, this is Max. She's staying for the holidays and needs to be shown around the place. Think you can do it?' said Ben.

'No problem. What's the weather going to be?' asked Linden.

'Larry's been digging holes like there's no tomorrow, so I'd say we are in for a good drenching tonight,' Ben forecast.

This was too much for Max. Who was Larry and what did digging holes have to do with rain?

Eleanor noticed Max's confusion.

'Larry's our pig. We can tell the weather by how he behaves.'

Linden saw Max needed more convincing.

'He's only been wrong two times before and that was because he had a cold.'

Now Max knew she was living in the Land of the Loonies.

'Right. I'm off,' said Ben, wiping his mouth. He walked over to Eleanor, picked her up under the arms and gave her the sloppiest kiss Max had ever seen two married people give each other. Yuck! She looked away and waited for them to stop.

Eleanor straightened herself out.

'I'll see you all about lunchtime and not before. I've got lots on and could do with some peace around the house.'

Max was sceptical. Lots of work? How hard could it be to scrub floors and feed chickens? At least being with Wildboy would be more interesting than being indoors cleaning out cupboards.

Outside, Linden called Ralph who ran quickly towards him.

'Oh, so the horse is yours?' asked Max.

'No, he belongs to Eleanor and Ben,' Linden explained. 'But he stays at my place two nights a week. He won't be any problem. You won't even know he's around.'

'You bet I won't because I'm going my own way,' said Max, turning on her heels.

'But Ben asked me to show you around,' said Linden.

'I think I can show myself around.' And with that Max was off. She wasn't going to spend any more time than she had to with Farmer Brown Jnr. She'd make her own fun.

But it was later, while Max was in the back paddock, that she found herself in trouble.

She'd been walking through the tall grass cursing the day she was driven to this wasteland. Flies buzzed around her face and up her nose no matter how many times she swished them away, her favourite T-shirt was being snagged by scrubby bush, and burrs stuck their gnarly prickles into her new baggy pants. When she stopped to try and get them out, she found herself ankle-deep in mud.

'Yuck! Swampland. Just what I should have expected,' she said out loud.

When she tried to lift one foot, she sank a little deeper. And when she tried lifting the other, that got her even further into trouble.

Now Max really started to worry. Every time she moved she sank deeper into the brown smelly slime. She tried again to lift one foot out, but this time she became unbalanced and fell forward into the mud. She put out her hands to break her fall, but all she felt were a few sticks and rocks floating in the stinky mess and no solid ground. She was really done for now. What would Alex Crane do in this situation?

'You need a hand?' said a voice behind her.

Max twisted around. Great! Just my luck. I get stuck in some mud and Country Boy and his hound turn up out of nowhere. She could hear him now, laughing at her and calling her the mud queen, just like all the kids at school would have done, making sure everyone within a two hundred kilometre radius knew about it. And making jokes like, 'How does someone get a pat on the head? Sit under a cow.' All the corny ones Toby Jennings would have let fly by now.

'No. I'm fine thanks,' she said stubbornly.

Linden offered his hand.

'Come on. You'll never get out of there without help.'

'I can do it by myself,' Max insisted.

'OK. Whatever you say. I'll be here if you need me,' said Linden.

He pushed his hair out of his eyes and watched as Max struggled with the mud and cow pats and bits of tree and other things that squelched around her. She tried to find solid ground, but only managed to sink deeper into the filth.

The stuff was up to her waist and ponging like mad when she really started to panic.

'Well, don't just stand there,' she yelled. 'Help me!'

Linden picked up a long, sturdy stick and held it out to her over the oozing mess. Ralph stood on the edge of the mud and supervised the whole operation.

'Wow! You're heavier than I thought,' gasped Linden.

'Just get me out of here,' said Max, losing her temper.

When she was freed from the mud pool she looked like a giant chocolate stick.

Linden couldn't help but smile. Max did look pretty funny.

'I'll walk you back to the farm,' he said, trying to keep himself from laughing.

'I can go by myself,' said Max, scraping great clumps of mud from her clothes.

'I was going there anyway. It's almost lunchtime,' offered Linden.

Great! Now she had to walk with him all the way to the farm where he'd laugh as he told her uncle and aunt how stupid she was, getting caught in the mud. Max folded her muddied arms across her even muddier chest and walked a few paces ahead of him.

Some holiday this is going to be, she thought.

'So where are you from?' asked Linden.

What was it going to take for Country Bumpkin to realize Max wasn't interested in any of his chat? She walked on in silence, hoping he'd get the point.

He tried again. 'How come you're spending your holidays here?'

This kid just wasn't getting it.

'Let's just get to the house,' said Max dismissively.

'I was just asking . . .'

Max swung round, put her muddy hands on her muddy hips and really gave it to him.

'Listen, Farmboy, I'm here because I have to be, not because I want to be and just because you got me out of that mud hole doesn't mean I have to talk to you or anyone else if I don't want to. And guess what? I don't want to! In fact, the only thing I really want is the quickest way off this farm. So let's just get back to the house as soon as we can so I can wash this mud from my skin before it soaks into my head and starts eating my brain.'

Linden sighed as he watched Max walk away.

Sometimes girls were hard to understand.

Ralph barked as if he was thinking the same thing.

As Max squelched through the grass she thought about today's spy embarking on a new adventure. And here she was covered in mud in some place that probably wasn't even on the map.

Suddenly Linden and Max heard an enormous explosion. Max flung herself on the ground and covered her head.

'What was that?' she mumbled into the dirt.

Linden stared down at Max as she lay at his feet.

'That's Ben. Working,' he explained.

'Working? What's he doing, blowing up cows?' Max asked.

'Cows?' Linden looked confused.

'Yeah. That's what farmers do, don't they? Work with cows?' Max asked.

This time Linden couldn't hold back and let out a really good laugh.

'A farmer? Ben? He wouldn't know the front of a cow from the back unless I pointed it out to him.'

Max clenched her teeth and felt as if someone had poured hot lava on to her cheeks. She hated being laughed at and she thought she might look a little ridiculous lying in the dirt so she stood up.

'If he's not a farmer, what does he do?' she demanded.

'He's a scientist, of course. So is Eleanor. They *are* your aunt and uncle, aren't they?' asked Linden, frowning.

Max was a bit embarrassed.

'Our families aren't real close,' she explained. 'And if they are scientists, why aren't they working in some laboratory somewhere?'

'They used to, in England. They were part of a team of top scientists working for the British Government, but they left it all behind and came to Australia. They owned expensive cars, were earning loads of money and winning awards with everything they did, but now Ben works in his shed all times of the day and night. I guess working for the Government wasn't all it was cracked up to be.'

So that could explain the footsteps on the verandah last night, Max thought.

'What are they working on now?' she asked.

'Eleanor sends articles to scientific journals and has written heaps of books, and Ben is working on a secret project that could change the face of the world as we know it,' said Linden proudly.

Max had to get this straight. The same Ben who wiped toast through egg goo and the same Eleanor who thought you could tell the weather by the behaviour of a pig were brilliant scientists from England? Things were really turning out to be stranger than she thought they ever could be.

'What's the secret project?' she asked.

'He said he couldn't tell us until he was finished, but he reckons that could be any day now.'

'Can we have a look?' asked Max, still sceptical about what Linden was saying.

'He doesn't like to be interrupted,' explained Linden.

Max wanted to check out what this top secret project was, so she pushed a little further.

'Shouldn't we make sure he's OK?' she asked.

'He'll be fine. Happens all the time,' said Linden.

If Ben really was working on a project that would change the world, Max wasn't going to waste her time falling into swamps. She was going to find out all about it. But first she needed a shower. The flies were beginning to buzz around her in swarms and the drying mud was really starting to pong.

CHAPTER 5
WHAT YOU SEE IS NOT ALWAYS WHAT YOU GET

When Max and Linden arrived at the house there was no one in the kitchen making lunch.

'Eleanor's probably gone to get Ben,' said Linden. 'Once he starts working he can forget the world's still turning.'

Linden paused, staring towards the shed as if he was gazing at some ancient wonder. Max rolled her eyes. After a few seconds, Linden turned to her and realized he must have looked a little odd.

'That's what Eleanor says, anyway.'

'Right,' said Max and walked away. She wasn't interested in anything Farmboy had to say. All she needed now was a hot shower. By now the mud had dried, making it hard for Max to move. She walked down the hall with her legs bowed, as if she'd just got off a horse. She stopped in front of Ben and Eleanor's prehistoric bathroom.

'I bet cavemen had better bathrooms than this one,' she sighed.

She imagined herself back in her own bathroom, turning on the shiny gold taps and running a deep, hot bath with a big squeeze of her mother's smelly and specially imported bath stuff. Then she'd turn on the spa jets and lock the door so she could bubble there for hours without interruption.

'Max?' It was Linden again. What was it about him that just wasn't understanding that Max wanted to be left alone?

'Yeah?'

'Would you like a cup of tea?' Linden asked.

That was another thing about this house. There always seemed to be a pot of tea happening somewhere, as if they spent half their time drinking the stuff.

'All I need right now is a shower, thank you,' said Max, trying to make her voice sound cold so that Linden would go away.

'Okey-dokey,' sang Linden, before he walked away whistling.

The image of the pristine bathroom in Max's head was gone. There was no spa, no smelly bath stuff, just a slab of soap that didn't smell of anything and two ancient taps that screeched like low flying crows as Max struggled to turn them on.

She sighed and would have given her whole CD collection to be instantly transported off this farm and back home.

When she turned off the taps, she could hear Eleanor, Ben, and Linden down the corridor sharing a good belly laugh.

Great! Farmboy had told them about the mud.

Now Ben and Eleanor were going to think she was some klutz from the city, who couldn't even walk straight. Maybe she should just go to her room rather than face the humiliation.

But not before she knew what they were saying about her.

Max tiptoed down the hall to put her ear against the door but as she did, she tripped over a fold in the hall rug and fell forward, crashing through the door and landing face first on the kitchen floor.

'Max, we were waiting for you,' smiled Eleanor.

Eleanor, Linden, Ben, and Ralph all beamed down at her.

'Ben has something important he wants to tell us,' Eleanor added.

Max got up off the floor and sat down at the table. Why did she always find herself on the ground when big things happened?

Ben stood up and made a show of straightening his shirt. Not that it made any difference, it looked old enough for Moses to have worn. He picked up a glass and clanged a teaspoon against it.

'Ladies and gentleman, may I have your attention please,' he said in a very dramatic voice.

Everyone went quiet.

'And may I have a drumroll too?'

Eleanor and Linden banged their hands on the table drumroll style. Ralph gave a loud howl and, from outside the wire door, Larry chimed in with a few loud snorts.

Max stared at them and wondered why Ben didn't just get to the point.

'This morning, Professor Benjamin J. Williams, in his humble yet sturdy laboratory in Mindawarra, Australia, discovered the key to the secret of matter transportation.'

Eleanor and Linden burst into cheers and applause.

'It has a few hiccups,' he went on. 'But I believe with a few simple modifications it will be ready to present to the world.'

Eleanor jumped up and swung her arms around Ben's neck.

Linden jumped up and swung his arms around Max's neck.

'What the . . .?' Max pulled away.

'Sorry, I got excited,' Linden apologized and put his offending hands in his pockets.

Ben and Eleanor meanwhile were in the middle of another long and sloppy kiss. Couldn't they wait until they were alone? It was like sitting through whole episodes of *The Bold and The Beautiful*. I hope they're not going to be like this all holidays, thought Max. Puke city! She had to stop them and get them back to the important bit.

'Can we see it?' she interrupted.

Ben let Eleanor go.

'Sure. Why don't you and Linden make a few sandwiches to take down to the shed and I'll show you how it works?'

Max had never made sandwiches quicker in her whole life. Within ten minutes they were all seated, ready for the demonstration.

The shed was like nothing Max had ever seen before. There were large benches packed so full with stuff that you couldn't see the surfaces. There were wires and panels with dials and switches and lights and tubes and transistors and cords and rolls of wire and jars and boxes of all sorts of bits and pieces. There were tools and manuals and newspapers and torches and tea cups and soldering irons and protective goggles and a miniature replica of Big Ben. The walls were plastered with maps and diagrams and rough sketches of plans, machines and ideas and hats and a few crumpled lab coats and, of course, there were the millions of books that seemed to be in every room of Ben and

Eleanor's house. But tucked away in a corner, only just visible in all the clutter of the shed, Max saw a small shelf with a snow-dome of London and a small photo frame with a young-looking Ben and another man he had his arm around, both smiling at the camera.

Max would never have guessed from the outside that this is what she would find in Ben's shed.

Ben stood next to a workbench where a small object was hidden underneath a cloth.

'And now for the moment we've all been waiting for,' he announced.

Max sat on the edge of her seat, curious to see what was under the cloth.

'But first,' said Ben, 'I want to say something.'

Max's shoulders slumped. Why did he have to drag everything out?

'I want to thank a few people who have been very important in making this happen. First, Linden, who has always been a good friend and whose help around the place has made everything for me and Eleanor so much easier.'

Ben and Eleanor clapped and Linden's face went so red you could use it as a torch to see in the dark.

'Next, I want to thank Eleanor, who has always believed in me and stood by me every step of the way.' He gave a small, crooked smile. 'Even when some of my ideas must have seemed a little kooky.'

Ben leant over and kissed her.

Max groaned. All this mushy emotional stuff was really getting embarrassing.

'And finally, I would like to officially welcome Max. It's been a long time since we've had a visitor and Eleanor and Linden and I want you to treat this as your home.'

All three of them turned towards Max and clapped. She shifted awkwardly in her chair and was probably redder than Linden was. She wanted someone to say something to take their attention off her.

'And now for the moment we've been waiting for. Ladies and gentleman, I give you the key to the Matter Transporter.'

Ben flung off the cloth and on the bench was a small, purple, box-like device. At the top end was a small, round, glass knob that looked like a remote sensor and on the front was an LED screen with a grid drawn across it. Below that was a keypanel, like a computer keyboard, but with three extra keys labelled, *scan*, *activate*, and *transport*. On the side, a long, thin, pencil-like stick nestled into a plastic groove and in the top right corner was a green bleeping light above the word *power*. Ben stood with his chest puffed up with pride and a smile that spread right across to his ears.

'Introducing the Matter Transporter control panel,' Ben cried. 'Max, come over here and you can have the honour of trying it out.'

Max walked over and Ben handed her the peculiar device.

'This light indicates your power supply,' said Ben. 'When it's green, the control panel is in operation, but when it turns red, you know you are running low on power and need to recharge it. You can either leave it in the sun for a few minutes to fully recharge it, thanks to these ultra-powerful solar cells on the back, or simply plug it into the nearest socket using this fold-out, multi-adaptable plug with retractable cord.'

Ben turned the device over and showed Max the line of grey solar cells and small connector cord that he pulled out and which sprang back when he let it go.

'This button at the top is for a micro camera that has two main functions. Firstly, it records images of any place you are in. The image appears on the LED screen. After you have captured the image, you use the plastic rod at the side to draw an outline on the screen around the items you wish to transport, thus defining the limits of the transporter capsule.'

Max was intrigued by the power of such a small machine and was doing her best to take in everything Ben was saying.

'The second function of the micro camera is as a scanner. You simply point the camera at any map, atlas, or street directory, and after pressing the *scan* key, the control panel will, in just a matter of seconds, record all the contents of the map and absorb it into its vast memory. All you need to do then is, using the rod, type the name of the place you would like to transport your goods to. The control panel will work out the coordinates and, just by pressing the *transport* key, do the transporting.'

'What will we transport?' asked Max, eager to see a demonstration.

Ben looked around him.

'This sandwich,' he said, picking up a ham and cheese sandwich. 'Why don't you create the transporter capsule for us?'

Max's eyes lit up. At home she was barely allowed to turn on the TV without asking her mum first and here she was being asked to operate a new, scientific invention that could change the world.

Holding the plastic rod carefully, she drew an outline around the image of the sandwich displayed on the LED screen.

'Excellent! And now let's bring this baby to life,' said Ben, speaking so fast his words ran into each other.

Max held the rod in one hand and the control panel in the other. She took a deep breath and squinting her eyes, brought the rod slowly on to the *activate* key.

There was a quick *zap* sound and then nothing.

'And there she is!' Ben beamed.

Eleanor, Linden, and Max stared.

Ralph gave a confused yelp.

'Well, what do you think?' asked Ben excitedly.

The three of them didn't know what to say. They looked at each other, wondering who should speak first. Eleanor made the first move.

'There's nothing there,' she said softly.

Ben laughed. 'Oh, it's there all right, you just can't see it.'

He put out his hand to touch the sandwich and there was another zapping sound and a quick flash of light.

'What was that?' asked Linden, taking the words right out of Max's mouth.

'It's the transporter capsule,' explained Ben, wanting to get on with the rest of the demonstration. 'An invisible electro-magnetic field that is created around any item you want to transport.'

Eleanor, Linden, and Max stared in astonishment. Ben grinned wildly.

'Now, let's start with something simple and try to transport the sandwich to another position in this room. How about there?'

He pointed to a wooden box near the door.

Max took the rod and typed in the command. The control panel whirred softly as it processed the coordinates of the box.

Ben's voice quivered as he stood beside her.

'Now, press the *transport* button,' he said.

Eleanor and Linden threw each other nervous smiles. They'd seen a few of Ben's attempts at creating a matter transporter before and had watched him sag with disappointment each time it had failed. They crossed their fingers, hoping this time it would be a success.

Max started to think about what she was doing. What if Ben was a complete kook? What if they were all about to witness another of his explosions and they and the whole place blew to smithereens? Or they all ended up somewhere cold like Siberia or the North Pole? Or in hyperspace where no one could ever reach them?

But then Max thought of Alex Crane, Superspy, and knew she'd been in far more dangerous spots and had never let fear stop her embarking on a new adventure.

'Here goes,' she said quietly.

Max pressed the rod on to the key and couldn't believe what happened next.

The shed shook. Smoke started to rise around the sandwich. There was a whirring sound that got louder, like a plane speeding up for take-off. Eleanor and Linden held each other's hand. Then there was a huge crash of sound like an explosion and a blinding white light that seemed to last for ages.

Then . . .

There was quiet.

Smoke rose from where the transporter capsule was supposed to be and when it cleared they couldn't believe what they saw. Or didn't see. The sandwich was gone.

It worked! Ben's Matter Transporter really worked!

With a little hitch.

The sandwich had landed on Linden's head.

Ben took the sandwich and examined it. It looked perfect.

'This is one of the hiccups I was talking about. Sometimes what I transport doesn't land exactly where I want it to, but that can be ironed out. Apart from that, we've done it!'

Linden and Eleanor cheered.

Max just stared at the control panel in amazement, before slowly lifting her head. She had an idea. This little machine could change the world, but, more importantly, it could be the answer to getting her off the farm and back to civilization.

'Can it transport people?' she asked.

'Whoa. Not so fast,' cautioned Ben. 'This machine is purely for transporting matter, not people. It'll be years before the technology will be developed to transport humans safely.'

'But it could happen? One day?' asked Max eagerly, unable to bear the thought of another six weeks stuck in hill-billy land.

'You bet! In fact I know of a scientist living in another part of the world who is working on a machine that will transport people not only through space but through time as well.'

Max stared at the small purple object in her

hands. Could it be true? Could this little device one day transport people through time and space?

'People have been trying for years to discover the secret of this type of travel and so far no one has managed to conquer it,' explained Ben importantly. 'But here in Mindawarra, we've got a little bit closer. And now we need to celebrate! Linden, why don't you and Max go and get the OK from your dad to stay overnight, and Eleanor and I will get the party ready.'

'All right! A party!' Linden shouted.

When Max and Linden left the shed, Max couldn't stop thinking about the Matter Transporter and the fact that in just a short time she could be off this farm for good. Even though she was enjoying the idea of going home, thoughts about the mystery scientist kept pestering her.

'Do you know who the scientist is Ben was talking about?' she asked.

'His brother,' said Linden, as if it was no big deal.

'His brother?' said Max incredulously.

'Yeah. Ben doesn't talk about him. They worked together in England but then they had a big fight and Ben and Eleanor left. They haven't spoken since.'

'Is he the one with Ben in that photo in the shed?'

'Yep. It's a pretty old photo, though.' Linden smiled. 'That's back when Ben had more hair.'

Max ignored the hair comment.

'Do you think his brother might really be close to creating a Time and Space Machine?'

'Well, Ben reckons he's smart enough to do it, but he doesn't want to have anything to do with him. I reckon it must have been a really bad fight.'

Max's head was full of questions about Ben and his brother. Why did they fight? Where was Ben's brother now and how close was he to completing the Time and Space Machine? Or was it a far-off dream that only a few weirdo scientists were interested in?

Either way, Max was sure Ben was being overcautious about the Matter Transporter, which she was sure could become the world's first People Transporter.

And she would be its first passenger.

CHAPTER 6
RETRO GALAXY GUNS AND A LOST BROTHER

Alex Crane had only minutes to save the world from total destruction. The fiendish Clarissa Latham was going to use her Retro Galaxy Gun to destroy Earth's orbit and send it hurtling into the sun if she wasn't handed all the gold that existed. Just before the deadline, Clarissa's bungling assistant, Jimmy the Rat, accidentally leant on the detonator button and the countdown to the end of life as we know it began.

The only way to stop the countdown was to go back in time to Clarissa's hideout and keep Jimmy from pressing the button.

With the seconds ticking by, Alex set the coordinates on the Matter Transporter control panel, pressed the transport button and was hurled at twice the speed of light into Clarissa's hideout. All she had to do was destroy the Retro Galaxy Gun before Clarissa and Jimmy could have their evil way.

Just get to the gun before Clarissa could—

'Max. It's ready,' a voice called.

Max closed her book. She would finish writing about Alex later, for now she had her own spy mission to complete.

When Max went to the dining room she stood in the doorway with her mouth sprung wide open.

The table was laid out with fine silver and crockery and food that stretched from one end to the other. Ben and Eleanor were in their best clothes and even Linden was scrubbed up to look pretty decent.

'You might want to close your mouth. The flies can get pretty bad at this time of year,' said Linden, trying to hold back a smile.

Max did as she was told and shot Linden a look that made him realize his humour was as welcome as a bowl of worms.

Ben pulled out a chair for Max.

'Madam, dinner is served,' he said in a posh accent.

Max looked at the table and wondered how her arteries would survive. At home they only ever ate salads and low-fat meals that wouldn't cause pimples, increase stress, or make you fat. According to her mother, anyway.

But it had been a long time since Max had eaten and she was so hungry she could manage anything.

There was lots of excited talk and passing of plates as Max sat at the table and thought about what to choose. Thing was, though, after she'd scraped the sour cream off the potatoes, piled her plate with honeyed carrots and said no to the pyramid of sausages that came her way, she took her first bite and thought she felt her stomach turn over itself. It was one of the best meals she'd ever tasted and she heard very little of the conversation that filled the kitchen as she took more than she'd usually eat in weeks.

Later, when they'd celebrated themselves out and Linden and Eleanor had gone to bed, Max sat with Ben on the verandah as the rain began to fall on the corrugated-iron roof.

'Here's that rain Larry predicted,' said Ben. 'He sure has a good nose, that pig.'

It was true! Larry was right. Or it was just a coincidence. Either way, it was raining.

Max looked at Ben, who was staring up at the rainy night sky.

Now was her chance. If she handled it right, here was her opportunity to find out more about the Matter Transporter.

'Ben, what would be the worst thing that could happen if the Matter Transporter was used for humans?'

Ben rubbed his hands across his full belly and sighed.

'It's too early to tell, Max. We have to get it right for transporting objects before we start trying it on humans.'

Not happy with that answer, Max tried again.

'But if the sandwich transported in perfect condition, then maybe the same could happen with people.'

Ben smiled.

'I'd love to be able to tell you you're right, Max, and maybe you are, but for now I'd say it is better to be on the side of safety until we work out a few more things.'

Max was convinced Ben was just being extra careful and knew the machine was safe.

As they listened to the rain, Max looked out into the distance. You couldn't see Ben and Eleanor's neighbours from the farm and the town was even further. All there was as far as the eye could see, was blackness. There was a whole world outside this place, thought Max. And Alex Crane spent her time travelling all over it. What if there was a machine that could zap you to places in an instant. Max thought about how different her life would be then.

'Ben, how far away are we from inventing the Time and Space Machine?'

He frowned.

'That's a hard thing to estimate, Max. It could be years away or right under our noses.'

'And you know the scientist who is working on it?' asked Max.

Ben stopped looking at the black distance and stared at the ground.

'Yeah. We were close. Once.'

'What happened?' asked Max.

Ben shifted in his seat and bit his thumbnail.

'We didn't agree on something very important,' he said quietly.

'Do you still keep in touch?'

Max could see a kind of sadness creep into Ben's eyes.

'The last we heard he was living in London and working for the government,' said Ben, taking a deep breath and looking up again as if he was searching for something.

'Sometimes, Max, people have differences that make them feel they can't speak to each other any more,' he said. 'It's sad because he was a great guy and it ate me up that we parted on such bad terms.' Ben let out a long sigh. 'It's been a big day, kiddo. Better hit the sack. We've still got lots of work to do if we're going to make the transporter perfect.'

He stood up and gave Max a kiss on the top of her head. 'It's good to have you here, Max,' he said with a smile. 'I know Linden loves having you around. Someone his own age, rather than a couple of oldies like Eleanor and me. 'Night.'

Max watched Ben as he walked away, his shoulders heavier than when they first sat down. All she had wanted to know was whether the transporter was safe enough to get her off this farm, but after all Ben had told her, why did she feel so bad? She'd never had an adult confide in her like he had. It made her feel special, but also sad.

And she hadn't realized Linden liked her. After she'd been such a cow to him! She'd never had any real friends. Not for long, anyway. She'd moved houses so many times because of her parents' jobs that when she met kids she liked, it wasn't long before she had to say goodbye to them. And so the easiest thing was not to make any friends at all. Saved on all those goodbyes.

She looked in the house and saw Linden asleep in a bed near hers. He was OK. After a little while he might even grow on her. Maybe being on the farm wasn't such a bad thing after all. In the city, all she'd do is stay at home and listen to music and wait for her mother to get in late and barely notice she was there. Whereas here, Ben, Eleanor, and Linden actually seemed to like her.

She thought about Ben and how he was sad about his brother but wasn't doing anything about seeing him again. Max didn't understand it, especially as they could both be working on the Time and Space Machine together.

Then she had a brilliant idea. It was so brilliant she almost yelled out. She was going to use Ben's Matter Transporter to go to London and find his brother, tell him how Ben felt and get the two of them talking. She'd also see if he'd finished the Time and Space Machine and if he hadn't, she'd help the brothers change the world with it.

Max stayed on the verandah for what felt like hours thinking about her mission. She imagined how proud of her Alex Crane would be. It was a long while later that she let out a big yawn and realized how tired she was. Tomorrow would be a great day, but now she was worn out and before she travelled anywhere, she needed to sleep.

CHAPTER 7
MISSION: MATTER TRANSPORTER

The next morning after breakfast, Ben gave Linden a list of things to do around the farm. Cleaning out feed troughs, feeding Larry and Ralph, clipping the front hedges. Farm and house stuff that didn't sound too interesting, but Max needed time alone with Linden.

'I'll help,' she offered.

Ben and Linden looked up at Max as if she'd grown two heads. Ben frowned.

'You sure about that?' he asked. 'It's messy work. Especially after last night's rain.'

'There's nothing wrong with a little dirt,' said Max, trying to look enthusiastic. 'Let's go.'

Linden felt Max's forehead and turned to Ben.

'Feels OK. No fever or anything.'

'Ha ha, Mr Smartypants,' said Max. 'Let's make a move before you kill everyone with your sense of humour.'

Eleanor stood up. 'I'll get you one of Ben's old shirts to wear. And Linden's got a spare pair of overalls you can have.'

Max looked down at her clothes. They were new and she could just hear her mother if she even as much as looked out of the window at dirt.

And then, as if Eleanor had read her thoughts, she said, 'Your mother won't be happy if we send you back with all your clothes caked in mud.' She smiled and went to get the clothes.

So her mother had always been as picky as she was now, thought Max.

After she was dressed, Max strode into the kitchen, ready for action.

'OK, Linden, let's go. We've got lots to do and there's no time to waste.'

She marched past Ben, Eleanor, and Linden and through the door. Ben shrugged his shoulders, as unable as Linden was to explain where Max's sudden enthusiasm for dirt had come from. Linden grabbed an extra piece of toast and followed her.

The more he knew girls the less he understood about them. He decided then and there to give up even trying.

Outside, Linden threw the toast to Ralph, who ate it in one gulp. He picked up a shovel and headed over to Larry's trough.

'You can start by bringing those buckets around,' he began. 'And then . . .'

'There's no time for that,' said Max. 'I have a proposition for you.'

'A proposition?' Linden said, confused. 'It's just a feed trough.'

'I know what it is. I want to find out if you can help me out with a mission I'm working on.'

Linden laughed.

'Are you from some secret spy organization or something?'

'Sort of,' said Max.

Linden turned to Ralph.

'It looks like Max. It sounds like Max, but I think aliens must have come and switched bodies with her in the middle of the night.'

'If you don't want to be involved just say so and I'll find someone else.'

Linden stared at her.

'There's no one else around for miles.'

He had a point.

'OK, then you'll have to do,' said Max, eager to get on with explaining the mission.

But Linden wasn't so easily won over and wanted her to know it.

'Maybe I'm busy and won't have time to help you.'

'Busy?' yelled Max. 'What are you going to be busy with?'

'Oh, this and that,' he said.

Max suddenly realized she was being baited.

'OK,' she said quietly. 'I want to work with you.'

Linden was impressed. Max really did have emotions.

'Sure I'll help. What's the mission?' he asked.

'I want to use Ben's Matter Transporter to go to London and find his brother. Then I can tell him how Ben feels about him and find out how close he is to completing the Time and Space Machine that will make them both famous.'

Linden was impressed.

For a second.

Then he just thought Max was crazy.

'But Ben said the Matter Transporter wasn't ready to transport humans,' he reminded her. 'Who knows what will happen if you try it on yourself?'

'Not just me,' smiled Max. 'You're coming too.'

'Me? Why me?' Linden shouted.

'Well, I can't go on my own. I'll need help. London's a big city and it will take at least two people to find Ben's brother.'

'What if we get killed? What if the machine makes zombies of us? What if we end up floating in outer space for the rest of our lives?' offered Linden, not sure he liked the idea of being transported across the world in a machine that couldn't properly transport a sandwich across a room.

'If the sandwich was transported in perfect condition, I'm sure we could be as well.'

Linden wasn't convinced, so Max tried a different approach.

'And what if we sit here and never try it?' argued Max. 'Ben will never meet his brother again, the world may never know about the Time and Space Machine and we will have passed up an adventure that most top spies only dream about. So, what do you say?'

Linden thought about it. Max sure did have a way with words and he'd never had anything as exciting as this offered to him in his life. Just farm jobs and the odd trip to the city.

'When do you want to go?' he asked.

'Tonight,' said Max.

'Tonight?'

'When Ben and Eleanor are in bed. I figure if we're away overnight, that should be enough time to find Ben's brother, tell him about Ben and get back here before they even notice we're gone.'

'You don't muck around, do you? Are you always like this when you want something?' asked Linden.

'Always,' said Max with a smile. 'Are you in?'

Linden thought about what he was being asked. There was something about Max's excitement that got to him and suddenly he did want to be part of the mission.

'Sure.'

'Great!' said Max. 'Meet me at the shed at eight o'clock tonight. I'll tell Ben and Eleanor that I'm really tired and go to bed early. Then I'll sneak out and meet you. You tell your dad you are staying here again tonight and everything should be set. Here,' she said, handing Linden a scrap of paper. 'I've drawn up a list of some essentials to pack.'

Linden looked over the list. Backpack, torch, penknife, money, ID, string, handkerchief, notebook and pen, warm clothes, raincoat, watch, energy snacks.

'Now give me your jumper and shoes,' said Max.

Linden looked up, not sure he heard right.

'What do you want those for?'

'You'll see. It's all part of the plan.' Max smiled.

Linden wasn't sure what Max wanted the clothes for but he handed them over.

'So, I'll see you tonight?' asked Max.

'Sure,' said Linden, thinking about what was ahead of them.

'Let's shake on it,' said Max.

Linden offered his hand.

'No,' she said. 'The secret spy shake.'

Max touched her nose and ran her hand through her hair.

Linden stared.

'That's it?'

'That's it. The secret shake of spies. Much less obvious than a handshake and being discreet is the name of the game.'

Linden held out his hand slowly, unsure of this new rule, and did the shake.

'Eight o'clock tonight, and wear something warm. It's cold over there this time of year.'

Max walked away feeling excited and a bit scared. Part one of the preparations for Mission Matter Transporter was complete. All she needed now was to put the final details in place and for that she needed Eleanor.

Max went back to the house just as Eleanor was getting ready to go out.

'Eleanor, can I ask you a few questions?' Max asked.

Eleanor was happy to see Max was feeling more at home and put down her bag.

'Sure. What would you like to know?'

'You and Ben once lived in England, didn't you?' asked Max.

'For four years,' Eleanor explained. 'That's where we met.'

'And why did you leave?'

Eleanor went quiet.

'It's a long time ago now. Ben and I were working on a secret project for the government when we found out that not everything we were told was true, and in some cases, was an outright lie.'

'And you left?' Max asked.

'Yep. We decided we needed a big change and moved out here.'

'What about Ben's brother?'

'Ah, you know about Francis?' Eleanor said softly.

'Ben told me. But he didn't say too much,' Max added.

'He never does.' Eleanor smiled. 'Come with me, I want to show you something.'

Max followed Eleanor to a room at the front of the house. She was amazed when Eleanor opened the door and showed her in. There were computers, boxes, and books everywhere. She'd never even known this room existed.

'This is my study,' said Eleanor. 'I don't let too

many people in here, mainly because it's such a mess. In fact, you're the first person other than me to step through these doors in a long while. Now, where is that book?'

Eleanor searched the shelves as Max stared at the walls. All around them were framed degrees, certificates, and awards with Eleanor's and Ben's names on them.

'Ah, here it is. You're also the first person in a long time to see what I'm about to show you.'

Eleanor took a large, important-looking book from the top shelf. She blew across the top and an avalanche of dust flowed across the room.

'It's longer than I thought,' she scowled. 'This is a scrapbook of our time in England. Ben and Francis were very accomplished scientists and famous throughout the scientific world for their work.'

Max looked carefully through the book, which was full of certificates and awards and even a letter from the Prime Minister telling them what a great service they were doing for the world. There were newspaper and magazine articles praising their work, and photographs of them accepting awards and shaking each other's hand with big grins on their faces.

'They look really close,' Max observed.

'They were,' Eleanor said. 'That's why it's so hard for Ben to talk about it now.'

'What happened?'

'When we discovered we weren't being told the truth, we were furious and decided to leave. It was a matter of principle. But Francis thought we were over-exaggerating. He and Ben had a big fight about it and they haven't spoken since.'

'That must have been sad,' said Max.

'It was. For all of us. We were so close and then it ended. It's hard saying goodbye to friends.'

Max thought of the times in her life she'd had to say goodbye and how each time it hurt as much as the last.

'We often think about Francis and wonder how he is,' said Eleanor, staring at the photographs.

Max looked at Eleanor and felt close to her.

'Can I keep looking through?' asked Max, holding the book.

'Sure. I have to go into town for a few things but you're welcome to stay in here as long as you like.'

Eleanor turned to go out.

'And I'll close the door so you can have a bit of privacy.'

There was a study in Max's home but she was never allowed to use it in case she made a mess of her mother's things. Living with Eleanor and Ben was really different from living at home.

'Eleanor!' Max said.

Eleanor stopped at the door.

'Yes?'

Max was grateful to her aunt for all she'd done. The way she treated her, telling her all those private things, everything, but all she could think to say was, 'Thanks.'

'You're welcome. Oh, and before I forget, I'm taking Ben out for a special celebratory dinner tonight. I've asked Linden's dad if he can stay overnight to keep you company. You're very safe around here and Ralph is an expert watchdog. I hope that's OK.'

Perfect! Just what Max wanted so she and Linden could make their getaway even earlier than planned.

'You stay out as long as you want. I'll probably go to bed early,' said Max.

Eleanor closed the door quietly behind her.

Max sank deeper into her chair and slowly turned the pages of the book. Eleanor wasn't kidding. The two brothers really were famous. The newspaper cuttings were filled with praise for all their work.

'Science Brothers Head Top Secret Project.'

'Brothers Search For Key to Time.'

'Brothers Set to Change the World.'

Max came across an interview with the head of the government department Ben, Francis, and Eleanor were working for. Her first big lead. She wrote down the name: the Department of Science and New Technologies and the person in charge, Professor Valerie Liebstrom. But it wasn't until she came across a letter from London that she knew she'd hit the jackpot.

It was addressed to Ben and Eleanor and was from Professor F. J. Williams.

Bingo! Ben's brother. It was postmarked a few years ago but he might still be at the same address, or if not, maybe someone there would know where he lived.

Max wrote down the address, closed the scrapbook and put it carefully back in its place. She then searched for a street directory of London so she could scan it into the control panel. She looked through the shelves of books and, tucked between a travel guide to Africa and a book called *The Complete History of Elves*, she found one. The London A–Z. It was dog-eared and wrinkled with food stains smudged across it and sticky tape plastered all over it to keep it together. Max tucked it beneath her shirt and thought Eleanor wouldn't miss it if she took it with her. All she needed now was to use it to transport Linden and herself to London, where, by this time tomorrow, she hoped to have met Ben's brother, Professor F. J. Williams, and his Time and Space Machine.

CHAPTER 8

FRIED MONKEY BRAINS

AND A

SECRET PACT

Dr Harschtorm smiled as he pulled the lever that lowered Alex Crane towards a pit of writhing, slithering snakes.

'They haven't eaten for weeks and are ready for a grand feast,' he said. 'And you, my dear, are the main course.'

Alex had to think, and fast!

There were only minutes to go before the snakes would eat her alive. Harschtorm sat back, ready for the show, as he ate his own specially prepared banquet. Fried monkey brains cooked within the monkey heads. His favourite.

'Bon appetit, my little ones,' Harschtorm laughed.

If only Alex could reach into her backpack and get out her Hypno Ray Gun, she could blast Harschtorm and his goons, hypnotizing them into raising the lever and letting her go, but not before she dropped her Destructo Pellet, a small pill that would destroy Harschtorm's headquarters in seconds.

Just reach a little further—

'Hi.'

Max jumped in fright and turned to see Linden chewing on a carrot.

'Don't creep up on me like that,' Max cried. 'You scared me!'

'Dad told me you called and asked me to meet you here at seven,' said Linden.

'I know. You scared me, that's all,' said Max, putting her book away.

'Ben and Eleanor gone?'

'Yeah, they left about ten minutes ago,' said Max, her heart still beating from Linden's sudden appearance.

'What were you writing?' asked Linden.

'Nothing. Just scribbling.' Max blushed.

Linden was sceptical.

'Looks pretty involved for just scribble.'

'All right,' said Max, knowing Linden wasn't going to let it go. 'But you have to promise not to tell anyone.'

'Sure.' Linden smiled. 'I'm good at keeping secrets.'

'I'm writing about Spy Force, the super intelligent spy agency that's been set up to capture criminals all around the world, and Alex Crane is their top spy.'

Linden laughed and Max was instantly sorry she told him.

'That's great. I love spy stories,' cried Linden.

Max was wary.

'Do you really?' she asked.

'I know each James Bond story by heart, have watched every *Get Smart* episode ever made, my favourite movie and series is *Mission Impossible* and my dad and I often sit down to watch his video collection of *The Man From U.N.C.L.E.*'

'You really know your stuff.' Max was impressed.

'Can I read some of Alex Crane?' asked Linden.

Max had never shown her stories to anyone.

'Maybe. Some day. But now we have to prepare for departure.'

'Whatever you say, chief.' Linden saluted.

'Max will do.'

Linden smiled as he pulled his jumper over his shoulder. He'd dressed warm, just as Max had told him. He had a big, floppy, hand-knitted jumper and what Max thought was probably his best pair of jeans. Well, at least they weren't full of patches or splattered with mud.

'I was thinking,' said Linden, suddenly looking worried. 'What if Ben and Eleanor come home and find we're not there?'

'All covered,' said Max. 'I stuffed both the beds with clothes, so when they come in to check on us, it'll look like we're sound asleep. I even threw your jumper and shoes around so it looked like a typical Linden space.'

Linden raised one eyebrow. 'Thanks.'

'Don't mention it. Now let's go.'

Inside the shed, the Matter Transporter control panel quietly whirred beneath its cover. Max took the cover off and held the panel in her hands.

'Are you sure you remember how it works?' asked Linden.

'There's nothing to it,' Max replied confidently, but secretly she hoped she remembered all the steps.

Max took the London directory from her backpack and laid it on the bench in front of her. She held the control panel so the camera faced it and pressed the *scan* key.

There was a small bleep before the LED screen lit up with the words *scan complete*.

Max and Linden looked at each other and smiled.

'That seemed to work,' said Linden, relieved that the first part of the process appeared to have gone well.

Max then turned the camera towards them both and captured an image of herself and Linden. Turning the control panel towards her, she saw their image on the LED screen. She used the rod to draw an outline around them both.

'Go easy,' said Linden, feigning a concerned look. 'Don't cut off any of my hair.'

Max frowned, trying to make Linden understand this wasn't the best time for jokes. She took a deep breath as she held the rod above the *activate* key.

'Here goes,' she said as she brought the rod down.

There was the quick *zap* sound and then nothing.

Max and Linden looked around them.

'Did it work?' Linden asked, referring to the transporter capsule.

'I'm not sure. Let's put our hands out and feel around,' suggested Max.

They slowly raised their hands until they were met with a flash of light and another *zapping* sound. A slight tingling sensation spread through their bodies like a wave.

'Found it,' said Linden proudly.

'It worked!' Max almost screamed. 'Now to set the coordinates for London.'

She adjusted them for Cricklebury Lane, London W6. The home of Professor F. J. Williams.

Max knew she was about to do the biggest thing she'd ever done in her life. She was excited, but she'd also never been as scared.

'I guess it's time,' she said softly.

'We should make a pact,' Linden decided.

'A what?' Max asked.

'A pact. Like a deal,' he explained.

'I know what a pact is, but we don't have time,' said Max, eager to get the mission started and avoid any emotional stuff.

'I'm not going until we do it,' said Linden, folding his arms across his chest.

The way Linden said it, Max knew she had no choice. Besides, the sooner she let him get on with it, the sooner they could leave.

'OK. What's your pact?'

'Hold out your hands,' Linden instructed.

Max held out her arms. A zapping sound rang out around as they broke through the transporter capsule's electro-magnetic field. Linden took Max's hands in his and closed his eyes as small sparks flew all around them like fireflies.

Max shook her head. This was not the kind of departure she had in mind.

'If Max should come to harm or get lost or be in danger in any way, I, Linden M. Franklin, will do everything I can to help her and bring her to safety.'

They both stood in silence.

Linden leant forward and whispered, 'You're supposed to say it about me now.'

Great! Just what Max wanted, another mushy moment.

'If Linden should come to harm or get lost or be in danger in any way, I, Max Remy . . .'

She forgot what came next.

'Will do everything I can . . .' Linden whispered.

'Will do everything I can,' Max repeated, then frowned, trying to remember the next bit.

'To help him and bring him to safety,' Linden added.

'Oh yeah, to help him and bring him to safety.'

Linden smiled.

'Good. Now we can go. All aboard. Express Transporter to London leaving in ten seconds,' he announced.

Max looked at her wrist.

'We should synchronize watches. We will only have about ten hours to complete the mission once we're in London if we're going to get home before Ben and Eleanor wake up. Did you wear your watch?'

'Yep.'

Linden pulled up the sleeve of his jumper to reveal a large silver watch that looked as if it had been around a long time.

'Are you sure that's going to work?' Max asked.

'It's my grandad's. He left it to me. I don't use it much, but he said it never lost a second.'

After they'd checked the time, Max held the control panel in front of her. She wiped her sweaty hands against her trousers and adjusted her backpack.

'Here goes,' she said.

This was it! If the Matter Transporter worked, in a few minutes they would be in London. But if it didn't, who knows where they'd end up.

Max took a deep breath and carefully placed the rod on the *transport* button.

The shed shook, the transporter capsule surrounding them started to smoke and a loud whirring sound filled their ears, just like the sound they heard when they transported the sandwich. Max and Linden held their breath as the crash of sound and light exploded around them.

Then . . .

There was quiet.

Smoke rose from where the transporter capsule was supposed to be.

Linden and Max were gone.

Ralph heard the noise from the yard and crept into the shed. He whined when he saw it was empty.

CHAPTER 9
SLIMED!

When Max opened her eyes she couldn't see a thing. She shook her head but still she couldn't see. When she went to move her arms she found they were pasted to her sides but after wriggling them free, she held them up and saw they were covered in . . . rotten meat!

Yuck!

And the smell!

Where was she? What had happened?

She thought hard. The Matter Transporter. Ben's brother. Time and Space Machine.

She looked around and saw she was up to her neck in baked beans, mouldy fruit, scrapings of old spaghetti, fish, and boiled cabbage.

She'd landed in a giant rubbish bin!

Great!

She wiped what was left of a piece of custard pie from her head and felt her body to see if she was OK. Arms, back, legs. Everything seemed fine, and the control panel, even though it was covered in tomato sauce and soggy spinach bits, was still with her and bleeping happily.

She looked over the side of the bin and saw people everywhere. There were street vendors standing over hot iron barrels roasting chestnuts, shoppers in warm coats rushing across streets and just missing being hit by beeping cars, police in funny big hats walking around and sometimes stopping to give directions. The roads were clogged with red double-decker buses, old black taxicabs, and cyclists with courier bags on their backs dodging in and out of the traffic. And on either side the pavements were full of glass cabinets displaying slices of pizza, shops with shoes, clothes, and TV screens playing the same images on each, stands with postcards, shelves of miniature towers and castles, and racks of hats and T-shirts with the British flag plastered all over them.

They'd made it! They were in London! A little soggy, but in one piece and alive! And when she checked her watch, which had also survived the gross landing, all in a matter of minutes.

But then she realized something was missing.

Linden!

Where was Linden?

He must be in the bin! Buried underneath all the slime!

'Linden!' she screamed.

Max searched frantically, pulling up lumps of beef stew, wading through stale pools of soup and dessert goo, picking through half-eaten shepherds' pies and still she couldn't find him.

What if something had happened to him? How would she explain it to Ben and Eleanor? And Linden's father? Maybe this had been a bad idea after all.

He could be anywhere. Literally. Maybe he really did end up in outer space, or in another country or . . .

Max started to panic.

'What am I going to do?' she said out loud. 'Linden and I could have been friends. He was a nice guy and the pact we made, even though it was a little corny, was one of the nicest things anyone has ever said to me.' Max's eyes became teary. 'And I would have done anything to save him if he was in danger. But now . . .'

'Hi.'

Max knew that voice.

She turned around and saw Linden eating a large apple and frowning.

'They don't taste any different from the ones at home.'

Max stared at him and tried to control her voice. He looked warm and dry in his jeans and jumper, and he'd put on a jacket since she had last seen him.

'Where have you been?' she asked.

'I arrived in the hotel across the street and the guy at the desk gave me this apple on the way out,' said Linden, smiling.

'The hotel across the street,' Max said with a shiver, as she started to feel the soggy garbage soak through to her skin.

'Yeah. Lucky, ha?'

Linden stared at Max, as if he only just realized where she was.

'What are you doing in that bin?'

'Oh, just waiting for you.'

'Looks to me like you were slimed by one of the Matter Transporter's "hiccups",' laughed Linden.

Max was trying really hard not to lose her temper.

'Just get me out of here,' she said slowly, feeling like a sizzling firecracker before it explodes.

Linden helped Max out of the bin as it started to rain.

'Great! That's all I need,' she said, looking up at the grey sky.

'At least this way you won't have to have a shower,' Linden joked.

The look on Max's face told him he should cool it with the jokes if he wanted to reach his next birthday.

They ran to a public toilet in a small park nearby, dodging through streams of people who frowned at them as they rushed past. Linden waited outside the Ladies with his hands across his chest to keep warm and tried to avoid the drips spilling from the small sheltered alcove above him.

Max came out of the Ladies in a much better mood now that she had on clean trousers and a jacket from her backpack.

'OK, we're ready to begin the mission.'

Max pulled out her notebook and checked the address. The bin she landed in was right next to the building where Francis lived. Cricklebury Lane, London W6.

'That's the place just over there,' she said, pointing to the building.

They made a dash across the park and came to the front door of what they hoped was Francis's home. There was a security system with a code to enter the building, which meant that Max and Linden had to wait for someone to go in or out before they could sneak in the door before it closed.

They didn't have to wait long. An old lady dressed in a long fur coat and holding an even furrier dog walked out.

'Come on, Poochikins. It's time for your walk, and after that you're off to the hairdresser for a shampoo and trim.'

When Poochikins and the fur lady left, Max and Linden raced forward and caught the door just before it closed. Linden held it open for Max.

'I'm not helpless. I can do it myself, you know,' she said.

Linden looked hurt.

'I didn't say you were helpless, I was just opening the door for you.'

'Well, you don't need to. We've got a case to solve,' said Max as she walked into the building.

Linden stared after her and sighed.

Max walked to the elevator as Linden stopped and looked around the foyer. He'd never been in such an expensive-looking place.

'You'd have to be really loaded if you wanted to live here,' he said.

The elevator doors opened and Max stepped in.

'Come on, let's go,' she interrupted Linden's inspection of the foyer.

On level nine they found flat 907. Francis's flat.

Just as Max was about to knock, Linden stopped her.

'What are you going to say to him?' he asked.

'I don't know. I haven't thought about it yet,' Max replied.

'Shouldn't we have a plan?'

'Do you have one?'

He didn't.

'Just do it and we'll take it from there,' he suggested.

Max swallowed hard and knocked.

They could hear the sound of a chair being moved and footsteps walking heavily across the floor. They both took a deep breath.

The door opened a crack and was stopped by a chain. A pair of beady eyes above a whiskered chin looked down at Max and Linden.

'What do you want?' the man grumbled.

Max was hoping this narky old man wasn't Francis.

'We're, um, looking for our uncle,' Max stammered. 'He lives in this building.'

It was obvious the whiskered man didn't like people knocking on his door.

'What's his name then?' he said angrily.

'Francis Williams.'

The man's eyes opened wide in fright.

'Never heard of him,' he snapped, and slammed the door shut.

Linden looked at Max.

'I guess we said something he didn't like. Let's try one of the others.'

Max knocked on the door of flat 911.

An old lady opened the door and smiled at them.

'Hello there, what can I do for you?'

'Hello,' Max said in her best and most polite voice. 'We were wondering if you wouldn't mind helping us.'

'I'd be delighted. What can I do for you? Are you selling biscuits or something?'

'No, we're looking for our uncle. He lives in this building but we're not sure which flat.'

'I've lived here for twenty-five years,' the old lady said proudly. 'If anyone knows your uncle it would be me. What's his name?'

'Francis Williams,' said Linden.

You would have thought Max and Linden had set a python loose in her flat the way the old lady's face twisted up with fear.

'I don't know him,' she said, her voice suddenly icy.

She began to close the door but Max put her foot in the way to stop it.

'Please. You've got to help us. We're from Australia and it's very important we find him.'

The old lady looked up and down the corridor to make sure no one was listening. 'Your uncle got himself into some terrible trouble,' she whispered. 'And one day some men in suits came and took him away.'

'Why would they do that?' asked Linden, frowning.

A door nearby opened and a man in a suit walked out. He nodded at the old lady and stepped into the elevator. The old lady looked nervous and when the elevator doors were closed she said quickly, 'All I know is that one day he lived here and the next day he didn't. I can't tell you any more. Now please, go away.'

The old lady closed her door and the sound of ten locks being set echoed around the empty corridor. It was obvious she knew more than she was saying. Finding Francis wasn't going to be as easy as she thought, but Max wasn't going to stop until she had done it.

She turned to Linden.

'Something spooked the old lady and the whiskered man when they heard Francis's name, and we have to find out what and why.'

'How are we going to do that if they won't talk to us?' asked Linden.

'We're going to visit the government department where Francis works. And even though I've got a feeling we won't find him there either, maybe we can find someone who isn't afraid to talk.'

As Max and Linden waited for the elevator, a door to one of the flats opened a fraction and two spectacled eyes peered out, watching them. Then the elevator doors closed behind them and they were gone.

CHAPTER 10
THE MYSTERIOUS MAN AT THE TOP OF THE STAIRS

As Max and Linden left the building in Cricklebury Lane, Max took out her notebook and scribbled a few lines.

'This is what we've got so far. Francis did live in that apartment but was taken away by men in suits in a sudden and very suspicious departure that the neighbours are too afraid to talk about. We need to find out what has made them so scared. Who were the men in suits? Where did they take him and why? And finally, where is he now?'

Linden took a mint from his pocket and started sucking it. He had a theory.

'My guess is, whatever is going on it's big and involves some very important people. It may even go all the way to the top.'

He felt like a spy from a 007 film.

Max was impressed.

'I think you're right,' she said.

'Thanks,' said Linden. 'Want one?'

Linden offered Max a mint.

'Thanks.'

The Department of Science and New Technologies was a tall, marble building with statues and carvings in the walls of great scientists throughout history.

As Max and Linden stood in front of it, they

felt as if they were somewhere very important. Max patted down her hair and straightened her jacket.

'If people are scared to talk we have to be careful how we handle this and we have to look and act respectable, so don't do anything that will attract attention.'

Max watched Linden try to control his wild curls.

'Well, try and look as respectable as you can,' she sighed.

'Whatever you say, boss,' said Linden.

'And don't call me boss,' Max snapped.

'Right, boss,' said Linden, trying not to smile.

Max shot him a quick stare and walked up the long stairs of the building. She pushed through the heavy revolving door into the foyer and stood on the polished marble floor. Linden walked in and stood next to her.

'Wow! This is some classy building,' he said.

Linden had hardly been out of Mindawarra in all his life and being in London with all its old buildings and statues was like being in another world.

The front foyer was full of paintings, big carpets, and shiny brass everywhere, from door handles to railings to flash name-plates on long polished desks. There were people in suits hurrying all around them, as if they were all late for important meetings. Two of them nearly trampled Max and Linden as they stared at the high, super-white ceilings that were covered in great dangling chandeliers.

In the centre of the foyer was a man with a small headset on a glued-to-perfection hairstyle and a smile that seemed to have been permanently fixed to his face. He was sitting at a solid round marble desk frantically answering phones, redirecting calls, and saying 'Have a nice day' more often than your average human could have managed in a year. When there was a break in answering phones, Max spoke up.

'Excuse me, we were wondering . . .'

'Good morning, how can I help you?' he asked sharply.

'We're looking for a Professor Valerie Liebstrom,' Max said.

The receptionist's smile fell to the floor in a howling crash.

'Who?' he asked, not sure he'd heard right.

'Professor Valerie Liebstrom,' Max said a little shakily.

'That's what I thought you said,' said the receptionist in a clipped voice, with one eyebrow climbing high up his forehead to show how annoyed he was at her question.

The man looked around him then leant forward, his voice changing from 'How can I help you?' to 'I'm having a bad day and you two are only making it worse'.

'Listen, kids, Ms Liebstrom hasn't worked here for quite some time and if you want to stay out of trouble, you'll have nothing to do with her.'

The man answered a few more calls and was irritated to look down and see Max and Linden still standing there.

They weren't taking no for an answer and Max wanted him to know it.

'Look, mister, I've had a really bad day so if you don't want me to scream at the top of my voice until I break every one of those expensive-looking chandeliers, then you'll hand over the information I'm looking for.'

Linden leant over the desk.

'I'd do it if I were you. She's won competitions back home for this sort of thing.'

'Surely you can't be serious,' the receptionist sneered. 'Now get out of here before I call security.'

Max folded her arms.

'I'll give you five seconds. Linden?'

Linden started counting.

'This isn't going to be pretty,' he warned. 'Five, four, three . . .'

The receptionist was getting worried. These two kids were starting to attract a lot of attention.

'Two . . .'

All around them, people in suits stopped to stare.

'One!'

Max started screaming. A loud, ear-crushing, eye-popping scream. People in the foyer covered their ears. Chandeliers started trembling and clinking overhead.

One of the chandeliers burst into a million pieces, bouncing off the marble floor and sending the suits running everywhere. The receptionist couldn't take it any more.

'OK! OK! Make her stop. I'll give you what you want.'

Max stopped screaming.

The receptionist took a handkerchief from his pocket, wiped his brow, and wrote on a piece of paper.

'Last I heard she could be found at this address, but don't tell anyone I told you.'

Max took the paper and shook the receptionist's shaking, sweaty hand.

'Thank you for your help,' said Max in her

best sugary voice. 'And have a nice day.' She smiled.

As Max and Linden walked out of the building, stepping over the crouching suits who were still holding their ears, a man in a long jacket stood at the top of the stairs and watched them go. He was surrounded by other men, who were bigger than him, wore dark glasses and looked as if they'd never smiled in their whole lives.

The man in the long jacket turned to one of the men and whispered, 'Follow them and find out who they are and what they're up to.'

CHAPTER 11

LASER TUNNELS

ON THE

WAY TO A

NIGHTMARE

Outside the Department of Science and New Technologies, Max beamed as she held out the piece of paper the receptionist had given her.

'This is our next vital clue to finding Francis and the Time and Space Machine. Are we good or what?' she cried.

'That was awesome. Spies who'd been in the business for twenty years couldn't have done better than you,' Linden cried.

Max smiled and shrugged her shoulders.

'Yeah. I guess it was pretty good.'

'Are you kidding, you were great!' shouted Linden.

Max wasn't used to receiving compliments and her face turned bright red. She took out her notebook and started to write down their new findings to hide her embarrassment.

'Let's just go and find the professor,' she said.

Linden realized his praise was maybe a bit much and his face went red too.

And he hated getting embarrassed.

'Good idea,' he said, looking away, but as he did, he thought he saw someone disappear behind a building.

'Max, I don't know what it is, but I've got this feeling we're being watched.'

Max turned around.

'Linden, there are over nine million people in this city. Why would they be watching us?' she asked.

'Well, so far, in the short time we've been in London, we've managed to spook the people in Francis's building and freak-out the receptionist in the Department of Science and New Technologies. And when we were leaving there, I got the feeling that someone was looking at us.'

'You really have seen too many spy films,' said Max. 'We've got the perfect cover. We're kids. Why would anyone think we were up to anything funny?'

'I guess you're right,' Linden said, not really convinced. But he told himself Max knew what she was talking about. They were just kids. The perfect cover, like she said.

Max looked down at the address the receptionist had given her: Hartfield School, Salisbury Road, Bleechgrove E7.

'This must be where she works.'

Linden frowned.

'But she used to be the head of an important government department. What would she be doing working at a school?'

Max took the London A–Z from her backpack as they made their way to the nearest Underground station.

'I don't know, but we're about to find out.'

Alex Crane clung to the roof of the high-speed luxury train and adjusted the earpiece of her Micro Descrambler Watch, listening for what was coming next. Inside was the brilliant Madame Des Arbres, the self-made billionairess, who owned the largest multinational botanical company in the world, and was in the middle of a very secret, high-level meeting with her henchmen regarding the final stages of another evil plan.

Spy Force had uncovered Des Arbres's secret scheme to unleash into the world's forests a virus that would stop trees everywhere from being able to reproduce. Whole countries would be forced to buy her seeds in order to plant more trees, ruining whole economies and making her the richest person in the world.

Alex adjusted the frequency of the Descrambler, which could translate any language in the world, and listened as Des Arbres's French became fluent English.

'If countries don't buy my seeds, whole ecosystems will collapse and they will have no one to blame but themselves.'

Alex heard the squeal of arrogant laughter from Des Arbres, as her final detail of dastardly planning was about to be put into place.

'It will not be long now,' the Descrambler translated for Alex. 'Everything is in order. All we have to do is begin the launch of the planes to all the major forestry sites of the world and spray our lethal Des Arbres Mist all over them to make them mine.'

Des Arbres launched into another annoying cackle as Alex switched off the Descrambler and put it into her backpack. The wind rushed by her like a cyclone as she made her way carefully along the roof of the speeding silver train, clinging to every protrusion and handle she could find as she made her way to Des Arbres's carriage. She had with her Spy Force's newest invention, the Neuro Reversal Spectron. With one zap of this powerful device, she could reverse the thinking patterns of all who came under its spectrum of influence. All she needed to do was reach Des Arbres's window, aim the Neuro Reversal Spectron at her and her buffoons, and the world's forests would not only be saved, but would have Des Arbres as their most devoted greenie, dedicating the rest of her life to saving the trees.

But just then, Alex's foot slipped. She lost her hold and dangled from the careering train like a leaf in autumn. She tried to regain her foothold but the force of the wind pinned her against the train so she was unable to move. As she looked around for something to hold on to, she saw the narrow mouth of a tunnel ahead, hurtling towards her like a hungry giant. She had about ten seconds to avoid certain doom. Would this be the end of Alex Crane? Would she be able to regain her foothold and avoid her fast-approaching demise? Would the world's forests be wiped out by—

The train jerked as it came to a screeching halt. Linden toppppled against Max and collapsed into her lap like a rag doll. Max looked down at him.

'Comfortable down there, are we?' she asked.

Linden pulled himself up and adjusted himself in his seat.

'Sorry, must be that magnetic personality of yours drawing me in,' said Linden, looking away to hide the smirk creeping on to his face.

'You know, if you put as much effort into being clever as being funny, you'd be a genius by now,' said Max, hoping to put an end to the conversation.

'Yeah, but I'd be a bored genius,' said Linden into his sleeve.

'What did you say?' asked Max.

'I wonder what the hold-up is,' said Linden, looking around the carriage and pretending to be interested in what had stopped the train.

Max frowned and went back to her notes.

Linden looked at the people around them. They carried on reading their books or staring at the ceiling as if they hadn't even noticed the train had stopped. Maybe this happened all the time in London and people were used to it.

He turned to Max. She was still scribbling in her notebook.

'So why are you spending your holidays with Ben and Eleanor?' he asked.

Max had been so caught up in their mission she'd forgotten the whole story about her father cancelling his visit, the explosion of slime at school, and the fight with her mum. After all that had happened in the past few days, that stuff seemed like ages ago.

Thinking about it now made Max's shoulders go tense and she turned to Linden with a little more force than she intended.

'What's it matter to you?' she snapped.

Linden was surprised by Max's anger.

'It doesn't matter, I was interested, that's all. You don't have to tell me if you don't want to.'

They sat in silence for a few minutes. No one on the train was moving. The only sound that could be heard was the turning of the page of a book or the occasional cough or snore.

Linden stared at the map of the Underground on the carriage wall and Max turned her pen over and over in her fingers, sorry that she'd been so mean to Linden when all he did was ask a question.

The funny thing was, when Max thought about it, she did want to talk. She hadn't had a chance to tell anyone how rotten the whole thing had made her feel. How she felt as if no one loved her and everywhere she went she made a fool of herself and how she never had any real friends because she was always moving houses and how lonely that made her feel and how most of the time, no matter what she did, she felt life was against her.

'There was no one to look after me in Sydney,' Max spoke up.

Linden stopped looking at the map.

'My dad lives in America and he was supposed to come back home for the holidays but he got this important job and couldn't make it.'

Max looked down at the pen she was turning in her fingers.

'We had some really great things planned too,' she said sadly.

Linden reached into his pocket for a mint and offered it to her.

'Who do you live with in Sydney?' he asked.

Max screwed up her face. 'Ms Popularity.'

Linden was confused. 'Who?'

'My mother,' explained Max. 'She's the head of publicity for a big television network and spends most of her time running after famous personalities at dinners and parties and launches of new TV shows. But if you ask me,' Max said sarcastically, 'there's not much personality to be found.'

Max had been talking really fast and getting excited. She stopped and let out a small laugh.

'She probably finds these people more interesting than me,' she said softly.

Linden saw that Max had a tear in her eye.

'If they all had brain transplants maybe,' he said.

Max laughed but what Linden said made her want to cry more. It was nice. She looked away, not wanting him to see her face. Linden put his hand on her shoulder, but she pulled away from him, took a handkerchief out of her backpack and blew her nose.

'I must be getting a cold,' said Max into her hanky.

Max hated crying in front of other people but she did feel better now that she'd said all that. She knew not everything she said was exactly fair but sometimes things her mum did weren't fair either.

The train lurched forward with a jolt as it slowly started up again. The sound of the wheels on the track beneath them resonated throughout the carriage.

'How about your mum?' Max asked, wanting to change the subject. 'What's she like?'

Linden looked out the dark window of the train as it rocketed through the Underground tunnel.

'She died two years ago. Cancer,' he said quietly.

Max froze. She hadn't known. No one had told her. What do you say to someone whose mother has died?

Linden stuck his hands under his legs as if he suddenly felt really cold.

'It's OK. Dad's great. He's more quiet these days than he was before but he's a really good dad.'

Max shifted in her seat. She'd never been told anything so important in her life and she couldn't think of a thing to say. Not one thing.

'I miss her. Especially at nights when it's quiet and I can still hear the sound of her voice saying goodnight and telling me to dream of great things.' Linden smiled. 'She always used to say that.'

Max stared at Linden as he looked at the lights of the tunnel flash by like shooting lasers.

The train slowed down and the squeal of brakes echoed around them.

Linden stood up.

'This is our stop,' he said.

Max followed him to the door of the carriage and stood by him in silence. She wanted to make him feel better like he'd made her feel better. She remembered the pact they'd made and went to put her hand on his back, but the doors opened and he stepped off the train.

They were quiet all the way to Hartfield School as they walked past streets with boarded-up shops and thick wire fences across dirty window fronts and flashing neon signs saying 'Fish and Chips'. There was an old, stone church with bars across the stained glass windows and cracks in the pavements where kids had scribbled with chalk to play hopscotch. They passed high buildings with grey cement walls and washing hanging on strings from poky little balconies, and crossed streets at traffic lights where the cars, buses, and trucks were piled up against each other in an endless stream. Linden had never seen so busy a place in his whole life and wondered if it ever slowed down.

When they reached the school, they stood in front of the gates with their mouths open. If Valerie did work here it was a long way from the flashy foyer of the Department of Science and New Technologies.

The school was like your worst nightmare: a concrete and brick tangle of buildings that looked as if they'd been there for decades and no one had bothered to look after them. Everything was grey and crumbling as if it was going to fall down any minute and the really strange thing was that there wasn't a single tree to be seen. Anywhere.

Linden screwed up his face.

'Kids really go to school in a place like this?'

Max checked the address again.

'I guess they do,' she said.

Suddenly, an old man grabbed them by the shoulders. Max and Linden screamed.

'So you thought you'd get away with it, did you? Sticking your noses in where they're not welcome. Well, I'll fix that,' he growled.

Max and Linden shook with fright. Maybe they *were* being followed. Maybe someone *really* didn't want them to find Francis. The man looked about a hundred years old and had the meanest face they'd ever seen. And from the way he grabbed their shoulders, it seemed he meant business.

CHAPTER 12
A DARKENED CORRIDOR AND MEN IN DARK SUITS

Max and Linden struggled under the tight grip of the old man. Whatever it was he thought they'd done, he was really angry.

'I'm sick of you kids thinking you can do as you please. I'm going to teach you a lesson you'll never forget,' he threatened.

What was he talking about? Where was he taking them? Max was scared but she was also furious at being handled like this.

And she wasn't going to take any more.

She gave Linden a wink and with a quick turn, sank her teeth into the old man's arm. He let out a scream loud enough to bring down the crumbling school buildings.

Linden followed Max's lead and bit into the man's other arm. His grip loosened and they twisted away, leaving him to nurse his two injured arms.

'Bloody kids. When are you going to learn that you're the ones missing out when you skip class?'

Max looked at him.

'We don't go to this school,' she said. 'We're from Australia.'

The old man looked confused and Max couldn't help herself.

'Australia, it's a big island down south,' she explained.

'I know where it is,' the old man said grumpily. 'I'm the Geography teacher.'

He rubbed his sore arms and mumbled, 'I guess I made a mistake. Sorry. What are you doing here?'

Linden straightened his jumper.

'We're looking for a friend,' he said. 'Professor Valerie Liebstrom.'

The old man started to laugh.

'That's rich. So you think she's a professor, do you?'

He kept laughing.

Max was losing her patience.

'Can you just tell us where she is?' she said curtly.

'I'd do it if I were you, mister,' Linden warned. 'Back home she's known as Jaws.'

Max shot Linden a look that told him to stop. Linden tried to cover his smirk but didn't do very well.

The old man stopped laughing and pointed to one of the buildings.

'She's in there. End of the corridor. Turn right.'

As they walked away they heard the voice of the old man behind them.

'Professor. That's rich. That's really rich.'

Max and Linden had to use all their force to open the heavy, creaking door of the building where they were supposed to find Professor Liebstrom. Max turned to Linden.

'Jaws?' she asked.

Linden could see Max wasn't happy.

'It was a joke,' he explained. 'That's something funny that people laugh at.'

'I know what a joke is,' Max snapped, looking down at her watch. 'We just don't have time for joking.'

Linden frowned. When was having a laugh a waste of time? Max was really in need of an injection of humour.

It had been almost three hours since they had arrived in London. With only seven hours left, they needed to work really fast to try and complete their mission.

Inside the building they could hear the muffled echo of kids talking. There was one light flickering overhead and blackened paint peeling off the walls of the corridor like giant strips of liquorice.

Linden was spooked.

'And that old man was wondering why kids skip class,' he said.

Max squinted through the darkness. She could just make out the shape of a door.

'That must be it.' She pointed.

Just then, the loud clanging of a bell swept through the corridor. Max and Linden covered their ears as doors burst open and kids came flying at them from everywhere. They fought their way through a sea of faces to the door at the end of the corridor. It was partly open and a dusty stream of light spilled out of what looked like a science lab.

'Dr Frankenstein would have felt right at home here,' said Linden.

Max frowned.

'OK, OK. No jokes,' Linden said. 'But it's not going to be easy.'

Max knocked and pushed the door open wider. Inside was a small woman in a long white coat, walking between lab benches and gathering beakers, test tubes, and Bunsen burners onto a metal trolley.

'Excuse me, are you Professor Liebstrom?' she asked.

The woman looked up and smiled.

'No one's called me that for a long time. And who might you be?'

Linden and Max were relieved. This was the first person in London who hadn't freaked out when they asked a question.

'I'm Max and this is Linden. We're from Australia and we're looking for Francis Williams.'

The woman's smile dropped.

Max froze. Maybe the professor *would* freak out after all, now she knew who they were looking for. Valerie Liebstrom was their last real lead and time was running out if they were going to get back to Australia before Ben and Eleanor woke up. They couldn't blow it now.

Linden knew this too and tried to think of something to convince Valerie it was OK to talk to them.

'We don't want to get you into any trouble,' he began. 'Max's uncle is his brother and we're trying...'

'You know Ben?' she asked.

Max and Linden were wary.

'Yeah,' they both said slowly.

Valerie smiled and a faraway look came into her eyes as if she was remembering something from a long time ago.

'Ben and Eleanor,' she whispered. 'How about that?'

Then she snapped out of her reverie and looked worried.

'Has something happened to them?' she asked.

'No, they're fine,' Max burst out. 'Ben has created a Matter Transporter and knows that

Francis has been working on creating a Time and Space Machine. We know that you once worked with the three of them and Ben and Francis had a fight and don't see each other any more. But Ben really misses his brother so we've come to find him.'

Valerie's eyes brightened.

'And you used the Matter Transporter to get here?' she asked excitedly.

'Yeah. It works!' Linden cried. 'It's not perfect yet, but Ben's close.'

Valerie had that dreamy look in her eyes again.

'So he did it,' she said quietly.

Max looked at her watch.

'Yeah, but we don't have long before we have to leave. Can you help us find him?'

'I can try,' she said.

'Mum, are you ready to go?' asked a voice behind them.

Linden's eyes widened when he turned and saw a girl standing at the door. She had dark, curly hair and big brown eyes that looked out at him through a pair of pink glasses. He straightened his jumper and walked over to her.

'Hi, I'm Linden.'

Max felt a strange twinge as she watched Linden speak to the girl.

'This is my daughter Ella,' smiled Valerie. 'And this is Max and Linden from Australia. They know Ben, Eleanor, and Francis.'

'Australia? How cool. I've always wanted to go to Australia,' said Ella.

Linden's smile reached so far up his face it nearly crashed into his ears.

'Yeah, me too.' He blushed as red as raspberry cordial. 'I mean, yeah, it's a really cool place.'

Max was going to be sick. Since when did Linden say 'cool'?

'We'd better get going,' said Valerie, grabbing her bag. 'I know where Francis used to live just a few months ago. We can try there and talk on the way.'

Walking to the car, Max couldn't help feeling a little weird when she saw Linden and Ella together. Linden was laughing as if Ella was telling the funniest jokes in the world. Valerie had given them all some fruit from her bag and they were sharing theirs as they walked. Max ate hers in silence.

In the car, Valerie told them the story of how Francis and Ben fell out.

'Ben and Francis were working on a top-secret project for the government, which was being supervised by me. They were going to make a Time and Space Machine like Ben told you. They were close too, until Mr Blue came on the scene.'

Max frowned.

'Who's Mr Blue?' she asked.

'A very suave man the government hired to be in charge of that project and others Ben and Francis were working on. He was supposed to sell the machine overseas and make sure England was the first country to succeed in creating it because there were other countries working on it too.'

Linden leant forward from the back seat.

'What happened?' he asked.

'It turns out Mr Blue didn't have the best interests of the country at heart. He told Ben and Francis that the machine and the money they made from it would be used to help people in England and in other countries less fortunate than ours, but he really wanted the money to go into his own private funds and some dubious nuclear projects.'

'Not only that,' Ella added, 'Mr Blue was making lots of money for himself from selling government secrets all over the world and was planning to sell the secret of the Time and Space Machine when it was finished.'

'Does he still work for the government?' Linden asked.

'He has one of the highest positions in the country next to the Prime Minister,' Ella explained.

'He is also very clever at covering his tracks,' said Valerie. 'We've been trying to expose him for years, but he's not only clever at planning evil schemes, he's also brilliant at hiding any evidence that they exist. But when Ben found out about Mr Blue's lies, he quit and asked Francis to come with him.'

'And Francis didn't go?' Max guessed.

'Francis is a scientist and wanted more than anything to continue working on the Time and Space Machine. He didn't want to believe Mr Blue had lied to them and thought Ben was overreacting.'

'That was when Ben and Eleanor came to Australia?' Linden asked.

'They left as soon as they could,' Valerie added with sadness in her voice.

'And Francis stayed?' asked Max.

'Not for long. He discovered Mr Blue had lied and he confronted him. Mr Blue told Francis that if he refused to work with him, he'd make sure he never worked in the field of science again. Francis was shocked. He thought what he was doing was good but instead he was just part of Mr Blue's terrible plan. By then he was far away from the two people he loved most, Ben and Eleanor.'

'And that's when he disappeared,' Ella added. 'Without a word.'

'With the help of a few men in suits,' said Linden to Max, remembering what the old lady had told them.

Max and Linden felt sad about the story of Francis and Ben's split. Max really wanted to find Francis now so she could tell him how much Ben and Eleanor wanted to see him.

'And what about you?' Linden asked.

Valerie sighed as if it was really hard for her to tell them.

'Soon after Francis left I found out everything. I resigned and told Mr Blue I was going to tell the whole world about what he was doing, but before I could, he ruined my career and credibility. He had drawn up some scientific results that were full of flawed work and told the papers and the TV that I was misusing government money and science for my own advantage. He invented a whole lot of evidence against me. He then called me a disgrace to the scientific community and they believed him. After that, no one would listen to anything I had to say.'

Ella looked sad as her mum told the story and Linden took her hand. Ella smiled and blinked a tear from her eye.

'I was kicked out of the department,' Valerie said, 'and stripped of my credentials. Nobody believed me when I tried to tell the truth. Mr Blue was very thorough and the only job I could get was as a lab assistant at Hartfield School.'

Max looked at her.

'Well, we believe you and we're going to make sure the world knows the truth about Mr Blue,' she said.

Valerie smiled as she parked the car.

'Here we are,' she said.

Max and Linden looked out of the window and stared in surprise at the scene around them. The street was full of potholes and lined on either side by grey, crumbling apartment buildings surrounded by broken brick fences overgrown with weeds and bins overflowing with rubbish.

'It looks a little more run down than when I saw it last,' said Valerie.

Max and Linden looked at the building she pointed to. It stood among the others like a tired old man, worn out with the effort of trying to stand up.

'Let's go in and see if we can find Francis,' said Valerie, trying to fill her voice with a positive note.

As they got out of the car, a black BMW pulled up in silence nearby. Behind its heavily tinted windows sat two men wearing dark glasses and black jackets. One of the men whispered into his mobile phone.

'We've found them, boss. It won't be long now until you have what you want.'

CHAPTER 13

THE TIME AND SPACE RETRACTOR METER

Max stepped into the building where they hoped to find Francis and she turned around to see Linden holding the door open for Ella.

'Thanks, Linden, that's sweet,' Ella said.

Sweet? That's worth throwing up on, thought Max.

Valerie led them to the elevator but standing in front of it was like standing in front of a giant bear in hibernation. There were no lights working and not a single crank of steel or cables to be heard.

'Looks like we have to do the five floors on foot,' she said.

Max cringed with the thought that Linden would probably offer to carry Ella up.

On the stairs, Linden and Ella were talking quietly.

'When do you have to go back to Australia?' Ella asked.

'We have to leave in a few hours,' said Linden.

Ella was disappointed.

'Can I give you this?'

She handed Linden a small white machine.

'What is it?' he asked.

'It's a communication, tracking, and recording device,' Ella said proudly. 'Mum made it so she and I can always be in contact with each other. Just press this button here and a communication signal will go directly to us.'

'That's great! Will it work all the way from Australia?' Linden asked.

'Mum says it could work from the moon. So we can talk to each other every day.'

Big deal, thought Max, who was listening in to what they were saying.

Linden beamed and for a second Max thought he was actually going to give Ella a kiss.

She couldn't stand it any more.

'Linden, can I talk to you?' she asked.

Ella knew something was wrong and stepped past Max to walk with her mum.

'Linden, if we're going to find Francis, you're going to have to keep your mind on the job and not go all gooey-eyed over some girl.'

'I wasn't all gooey-eyed. She gave me this,' he said, holding out Ella's present. 'It's a communication, tracking and . . .'

'I saw what was happening. You can chase girls when we get back to Australia. For now we've got an important mission to complete, or have you forgotten that?' Max snapped and walked on ahead.

Linden muttered to himself, 'Maybe if you

were a little less stressed out we could finish the mission *and* have a good time.'

Max swung round.

'What did you say?' she asked.

'I said it's a shame the elevator isn't working because it's a hard climb,' Linden said, smiling.

Max was sceptical but spun round on her heel and walked on.

On level five, Valerie found the room she was looking for. The corridor was dark and there was a strong musty smell, as if no one had bothered to open any windows for years.

'This is it,' she said, looking doubtfully around at the papers and rubbish littering the floor.

She knocked on the door.

They waited but heard nothing.

Valerie knocked again and this time they heard the crash of crockery followed by an angry snarl and mumbled complaining.

'Stupid, half-witted, ridiculous . . .'

Valerie pulled Linden, Ella, and Max behind her.

They jumped as they heard footsteps clumping towards them. Then there was a thump against the door and a gruff voice shouted, 'What do you want?'

'Francis? Is that you?' Valerie was shocked. It sounded like Francis, only older and very angry.

The voice yelled back, 'Who wants to know?'

'It's Valerie Liebstrom, and I've brought some people to see you.'

There was a pause before the angry voice yelled again.

'Well, I don't want to see anybody, so why don't you all just turn around and go back to where you came from?'

The hall went quiet and Max looked at Valerie.

'Maybe if he knows Ben's my uncle, he'll listen to me,' she said.

Max stepped closer to the door.

'Mr Williams, my name is Max and I've come all the way from Australia . . .'

Before she could finish, Francis shouted again.

'Are you still there? I thought I told you to go away?'

Valerie put her hand on Max's shoulder.

'Maybe we should leave,' she said.

But something in Max fired up and she suddenly lost her patience with this rude man and wanted him to know it. She and Linden had come too far and done too much to find Francis and now they were here, she wasn't sure he was even worth it. If this was how their mission was going to end, she was at least going to tell him what she thought.

'Now you listen here. You may be sick of the world, but there are some people who'd like to talk to you. If it was up to me I'd have nothing to do with you because you sound like a mean and cranky old man, but Ben and Eleanor do care. But if that's the way you want to treat . . .'

'Ben and Eleanor?' the voice barked, but this time less loudly.

Max and Valerie looked at each other.

'They're my uncle and aunt and I just wanted . . .' Max began.

'Well, why didn't you say Ben was your uncle instead of just raving on?' Francis interrupted.

Ella, Linden, Valerie, and Max stared at the door as the hall echoed with the sound of bolts being drawn. They had no idea what to expect and stood back apprehensively, waiting to see what this man looked like. When the final bolt was released, the door opened with a tired creak and the shadow of a man appeared from the darkness of the flat.

'Well, don't just stand there,' he said. 'Come in.'

They filed in slowly and when Francis flicked on a small lamp, the whole place took on a dim, blurry focus. The flat was just one small room which was the kitchen, bedroom, and lounge room all in one. On the floor near the lamp was a broken tea cup, which Francis stepped over as he lowered himself into a large, dusty-looking armchair. There were piles of yellowing newspapers everywhere and frayed curtains covering the windows. The fireplace was filled with soot and ashes below a mantelpiece strewn with cups, papers, unopened mail, and apple cores. In the corner was a small, unmade bed, scattered with twisted blankets and discarded clothes. In the kitchen area, the table was covered with sauce bottles, cups, plates, salt and pepper shakers, and gooey leftovers from breakfast. Dishes piled in the sink like a crooked tower about to topple over. There was a small fridge with a broken handle and next to this, garbage bags sat like obedient pets, waiting to be taken out.

Max and Linden stared with open mouths. They'd never seen such a mess.

'You might as well sit down,' offered Francis gruffly.

When Valerie and Ella sat on the two-seater sofa, a small cloud of dust ballooned around them. Linden perched on the armrest next to Ella and sneezed.

'Bless you,' she said, smiling up at him.

Max rolled her eyes and moved away from them to sit on a wobbly kitchen chair near Francis.

She studied his face as he stared at the floor. In the photos he was young, handsome, and smiling, but in person he was a small, bony man who looked more like a ghost. Everything about him was grey. Grey hair, grey skin, even his eyes were grey. He looked like someone whose hard times had sunk into his skin and stayed there.

Valerie was the most shocked.

'How have you been, Francis?' she asked, trying to make her voice sound calm.

'I've been better,' Francis hurrumphed.

He played with a piece of wool dangling from his frayed jumper and his trousers hung around him as if they were from a past when he was a much bigger man. He kept his head down as he spoke to Max.

'So what did Ben have to say?' he asked softly.

'That he misses you and is sad you don't talk any more.'

Francis kept looking down.

'He said that, did he?'

'He also said you were close to inventing a Time and Space Machine,' said Max.

Francis looked up.

'That's all in the past now,' he said sharply.

Linden moved forward on the armrest. 'Ben has

created a Matter Transporter and that's how Max and I got here.'

'He did?' Francis asked, unable to hide his increasing curiosity.

'And we thought you'd like to come back to Australia and finish the Time and Space Machine with him,' said Max.

Francis looked down at his hands.

'I'm finished with science,' he said curtly.

Max looked at Valerie. How were they going to convince him to come with them?

'Francis, you love science,' Valerie said. 'And your brother needs you.'

There was a pause before Francis spoke again.

'When we were kids, Ben and I were very poor. Our dad ran out on us when we were young. Some nights we were so cold we slept in the same bed to keep warm. It was on one of those cold nights that Ben and I made a pact that we would always stick together and we would make something of ourselves so we'd never be poor again.'

Francis wrung his hands in front of him as if he was trying to keep them warm.

'Mr Blue offered us money we'd only ever dreamt of and a chance to save lots of kids from ever having to be cold or hungry. I thought we had it all. We had money, we were helping the world and we were together. But the money made me blind to what was really going on. When Ben told me the truth about Mr Blue, I didn't want to believe it. If I did, I'd have to give up everything.'

Francis sighed. 'I took someone else's word over my own brother's,' he said sadly. 'That's something you can never forget.'

'But Ben *has* forgotten it,' Max almost shouted in excitement. 'He really wants to see you again.'

Francis smiled.

'We were very close to making the machine work.'

'Great, let's go,' yelled Max, standing up.

'There's only one thing,' Francis interrupted. 'There's one vital part of the machine we need. The Time and Space Retractor Meter.'

Max and Linden frowned.

'When I left the Department of Science and New Technologies, I destroyed all the files and components of the machine except for that.'

Francis smiled as if he was savouring his favourite dessert.

'Mr Blue has been after it for years. He's offered me everything he could think of, but there's nothing that would make me work with him again, ever.'

'Where is it?' Max asked.

'It's in a locker at Victoria Station.'

Ella and Linden jumped up.

'Let's go and get it,' they said.

They all stared at Francis as he made up his mind. Max gulped hard, hoping he'd agree to come with them.

'As long as all the windows in the car are wound down. I get car-sick,' explained Francis.

'All right!' shouted Ella and Linden.

Francis picked up a crumpled coat that was draped on the back of his armchair as the others made their way out to the corridor. He turned to Max, trying to find the courage to ask what was bothering him.

'You're sure Ben wants to see me?' he asked nervously.

'He said it eats him up that you two parted so badly,' said Max.

Francis smiled and looked as if he was going to cry. Max hated to see people cry. It was just too much emotion for her to bear. She said quickly, 'We better get going.'

Max walked with Francis down the five flights of stairs.

'Aren't you afraid Mr Blue is still after you?'

Francis laughed as he pulled his coat around him against the cold.

'Mr Blue has long finished thinking about me,' he said.

'How can you be sure?' asked Max.

'He has spent years having people follow me. He had my every move watched to make sure I didn't tell the world about him and to find out if I was still working on the Time and Space Machine.'

'But why didn't you ever go to the police about him?'

'When it came down to it, it was just his word against ours and because he moved in some pretty important circles, people were never going to believe us against him.'

Francis ducked his head as he stepped into the car. He looked awkward as he fumbled to do up his seat belt. Max leant between the front seats and did it for him. He turned and gave her a crooked smile as if he knew everything was going to be all right. But something bugged Max. After what she'd heard about Mr Blue, she wasn't sure he was the kind of person who gave up so easily.

CHAPTER 14

HIRED THUGS AND A SECRET PARCEL

Alex Crane wedged herself into the small passageway just outside the entrance of the Galactatron V that was orbiting somewhere between Mars and Jupiter. On either side of her she could hear the talking of the evil and foul-smelling Blastaroids who were guarding the Galactatron's entrance. One thing Alex had learnt about the Blastaroids was that, even though they were known as some of the most evil, cruel, and repulsive henchmen in the Galaxy, they also had a weakness for incessant talking. Once they started talking, they just wouldn't shut up.

Inside the cabin HQ was Captain Clearstink Glump, the mastermind of one of the most dastardly plans to ever face planet Earth. He had decided during a brief visit to the planet that not only did he like Earth, but that it would look good in the front yard of his home in Galaxy 423 on the far side of Spectre 7. All he had to do was knock Earth out of its orbit, much like a marble out of a chalk circle, and he would have his wish. He was in the middle of toasting his certain victory with a tall glass of Viridion Blast, a mixture of ice-cream and melted chocolate he discovered during his Earth visit, as Alex affixed the Orbit Thruster onto her belt. All she needed to do was adjust the settings of the Thruster which, if she got it right, would eject the evil ship from Earth's galaxy and place a force field around it preventing it from ever entering again. Once the process had begun, she would have sixty seconds to leave the ship and be collected by the Spy Force Space Probe which was circling nearby, or she would be flung from Earth for ever.

'Good luck, Crane. We'll be standing by for your pick-up,' Spy Force Probe Deck radioed into her earpiece.

'We are just minutes away from being rid of Clearstink for ever,' replied Alex.

She heard the continual chatter of the foul Blastaroids near her as she entered the final numbers of the code.

'Bye-bye, Clearstink,' she whispered. But as she pressed the detonator, a double reverse thrust from the ship's engines forced the Orbit Thruster from her grasp and she tumbled onto the floor in front of the large, evil-smelling feet of the Blastaroid guards. They hovered over her, laughing and shouting all sorts of unintelligible things as the seconds melted away for her to make her getaway.

What was she to do? How was she to get away from these intergalactic stinkbombs? The Galactatron V was about to be thrown out of

Earth's galaxy for ever and she was their newest passenger. Was this the end of Alex Crane? Would she ever get away from the incessant chatter of the Blastaroid baboons? Would she—

'Hahaha!'

Max held her pen in the air above her notebook and tried to block the laughter out of her head. They were in the car on the way to Victoria Station and Linden and Ella hadn't stopped talking about what they could do when the Time and Space Machine was finished.

'We could go to Alaska or Antarctica or Andalusia.'

'Or we could travel back in time to the land of the pharaohs or the dinosaurs or King Arthur and his knights.'

Linden rolled his eyes. 'It'd make history lessons a lot more interesting.'

Ella nodded. 'History isn't my favourite subject, either.'

Then they went on and on and talked about favourite films, insects they'd collected, and books they'd read while Francis and Valerie talked about old times and how much they'd missed each other.

If this goes on much longer, Max thought, I'm going to be the first eleven year old in the world to spontaneously combust from too much mush.

Max looked out of the window at the London streets. It was winter and the pale light reflected off the decorations that hung everywhere. Then Max remembered. It was Christmas in a few days and she suddenly realized she missed her mum and dad. This Christmas was supposed to have been the first one they'd spent together since she was three, and now she wasn't going to spend it with either of them.

Max looked around at the others in the car.

How could someone be in a small space with four other people and still feel as if they're all alone!

'Here we are,' said Valerie with a quiver of excitement in her voice. 'Why don't you all hop out while I park the car and I'll meet you at platform six below the clock?'

Francis, Linden, Max, and Ella got out of the car, waved to Valerie and made their way through the afternoon crowd.

Francis looked nervous.

'There are so many people,' he said shakily. 'Makes me wonder why I live in the city.'

Max moved closer to him and took his hand. If Francis had been a hermit for the last few years, seeing so many people all at once was going to be pretty freaky.

Francis looked nervously at her. He clasped her hand tightly as he wiped a handkerchief across his brow.

Around them the busy station was flooded with announcements of late trains, cancellations, and trains about to depart. There were signs for doughnuts and platforms, and advertisements for new perfumes and holiday destinations. But worst of all there were people everywhere. Ticket inspectors, police, schoolkids, and business people, and they were all in a hurry.

'Make sure we stay close together so we don't lose each other,' Francis shouted above the noise.

Ella slipped her hand into Linden's.

'There are more people here than I've seen in my whole life,' said Linden as they were jostled in a dark sea of business suits and long coats.

'It has changed since I was here last but I think the lockers were over there,' yelled Francis as he led the way through the crowd.

'Ouch!' yelled Max.

Francis turned round.

'What happened?' he asked.

'Some big guy in a suit just stood on my toe,' said Max huffily.

Francis put his hand on Max's shoulder.

'We're nearly there,' he said.

Max scowled and thought about what they'd been through in the last few hours. She'd been slimed, had doors slammed in her face, was almost strangled by a crazed Geography teacher, and now she was being trampled by a stampede of people who were twice as big as her.

Max forced her way between two suits in front of her and found herself with Ella, Linden, and Francis standing in front of a wall of lockers. Francis stared at one locker in particular.

'This is it. Thirty-two. My favourite number.'

Max was elbowed in the head by someone rushing to catch a train.

'I know this is an important moment, but can we open the locker before we all get squashed to pulp?' she said, rubbing her head.

'Sure,' said Francis taking a chain from around his neck. He fitted the key in the locker and turned it. With no effort at all, the door opened.

Francis removed a small leather pouch and carefully took out something wrapped in a white cloth.

Ella and Linden looked at each other in excitement.

Max stood on her toes to get a better view.

Francis unwound the cloth to reveal what they'd all been waiting for. The Time and Space Retractor Meter. A small, shiny chrome disc with what looked like some kind of voltage meter and flashing lights.

Francis beamed in recognition as if he was seeing an old friend for the first time in years.

'This is it. The secret of time and space travel.'

Max turned to congratulate Linden and saw him giving Ella a hug. She looked away until she felt Linden tap her on the shoulder.

'We did it, chief! Mission Matter Transporter has been successful.'

Max smiled. They had done it. They were good spies after all.

Francis rewrapped the Time and Space Retractor Meter and put it back in the pouch.

'Now let's get to platform six to meet Valerie before we get trampled,' he said.

All four of them began to make their way through the crowd, but it seemed there were even more people now than when they'd first arrived.

What happened next was so quick that afterwards, Max and Linden had trouble remembering what really went on.

Max could hear Francis's voice shouting for her but she couldn't see him through the crowd.

'Max, where are you?'

'I'm here,' she yelled. But it was no good, Francis couldn't hear her above all the noise.

Max began to feel scared. London was a huge city, much bigger than Sydney, and she was frightened of being separated from the others.

'Linden! Where are you?' she called.

'I'm over here!' Max heard Linden's voice but she couldn't see him either.

Just then, a fat man in a brown jacket pushed past Max and she just managed to see the back of Linden's head.

'Wait for me,' yelled Max. But with all the noise no one could hear her. She was hemmed in by so many people that all she could see were different coats and jackets moving past.

'Hey! Get off me!' yelled Max, as one coat engulfed her like a net around a fish. 'Get *off* me!'

Then suddenly everything went black and the ground fell away from under her feet. She was moving through the crowd much faster than she was before but her feet weren't touching the ground. She was being carried!

She struggled underneath the coat but was held

so tightly she couldn't move or make a sound. Then she felt herself being dropped onto a seat and the muffled sound of someone yelling out something as though they were in a great hurry.

Max was in a car and she was being driven away.

Away from the station.

Away from Linden.

Away from the Time and Space Retractor Meter.

Then she realized the horrible truth.

She was being kidnapped!

CHAPTER 15

MOBILE PEOPLE MOVERS

Max woke with a start and felt sore and tired and confused.

'Where am I?' she said out loud.

She was in a large comfortable bed with her jacket and clothes folded neatly on the end. She looked down and frowned when she saw she was in a pair of pink flannelette, cloud-covered pyjamas. The room was like a cartoon-coloured adventure world. There were beanbags, toys, slides that twirled from the ceilings, whole shelves of lollies and fruit and three drinking fountains sticking out from the wall with Raspberry, Lemonade, and Orange Juice written on top of them.

'What is this place?' she whispered to herself. 'And where's my backpack?'

Frantically, Max looked around her and saw the pack sitting on a table next to her. She picked it up, and after going through it, was relieved to see everything was still there, including her notebook.

Then she remembered.

She'd been kidnapped!

Not only that, there was someone asleep in a bed across the room! She put her backpack on, stood up, took a large, round, rainbow-coloured lollipop from a shelf nearby and tiptoed over to the other bed. She wasn't going to be kidnapped without letting them know how much trouble she could be.

She stood by the bed and held the lollipop high.

'OK, you kidnapper, take this!' she cried.

Max brought the lollipop down just as the person in the bed rolled over and only narrowly avoided being hit.

'Hey, what are you doing? Can't a person get a little sleep?' someone said from under the blankets.

Max knew that voice.

'Linden? Is that you?' she asked.

'Who else do you think it is?' he mumbled.

'I thought you were a kidnapper.' Max shrugged, holding the lollipop against her chest and feeling a little guilty.

Linden threw the covers off his face.

'A little relaxed for a kidnapper, don't you think?'

'Sorry,' Max apologized.

Linden sat up.

'I could have been killed by a giant lollipop. I was hoping for a more glamorous ending to my life,' he said.

Max put the lollipop down and rubbed her forehead as she sat on the bed next to him.

'I feel like someone's been using my head for a football.'

'Yeah, me too,' said Linden. 'Whoever grabbed us must have given us something to knock us out.'

Max suddenly looked worried.

'Who do you think they are? What do you think they want with us?'

'I'm not sure,' said Linden. 'But from what Francis and Valerie said about Mr Blue, I'm sure he's involved somehow and that it's no accident it happened just as we found the Time and Space Retractor Meter.'

Max took out her notebook and tried to think calmly.

'OK, here's how it stands. We're trapped in a house, location unknown. We've been kidnapped by strangers, separated from the only people we know in this country and,' Max looked at her watch, 'we've got about three hours left before we need to be back in Australia.'

'Not only that,' said Linden, looking down at his clothes in horror, 'I'm wearing bright blue pyjamas with toy trains on them.'

Max glared at Linden.

'I hardly think what you're wearing is . . .'

Max was interrupted by the door opening. A woman dressed in a smart suit walked in.

'I'm Ms Peckham,' she said gently with a friendly smile. 'I hope you both had a good sleep. Mr Blue would like to see you now.'

Max was furious. She leapt off the bed.

'He would, would he? Well, I'd like to see him too. I've got a few things to tell him.'

Linden tried to reach for Max's sleeve to tell her to calm down, but she stepped away from him and stalked out of the room. Seconds later she reappeared, remembering she had no idea where she was, and glowered at Ms Peckham.

'I guess you'll have to lead the way,' she said.

'Certainly, but I suggest you put your slippers on first. It can get cold on the marble floors,' said Ms Peckham as she picked up two pairs of slippers.

One pair were shaped as fluffy yellow ducks while the other pair were two baby bears.

Linden sighed. 'This is going to do nothing for my reputation as a man of fashion.'

It was hard to know who Max was more angry at, Mr Blue or Linden. Unfazed, Linden put on his slippers and backpack and did everything he could not to catch Max's eye.

Outside the room there was a small humming

machine that looked like a mini hovercraft waiting for them.

Max and Linden stared.

'This is our Mobile People Mover. Or MPM. It's really quite safe,' smiled Ms Peckham. 'And it is a bit of a way.'

Max and Linden looked at each other. They weren't sure whether to trust her but knew they had little choice. Max shrugged her shoulders and stepped into the MPM. Linden followed and they held on to the sides not knowing what to expect. Ms Peckham got in after them and with a gentle whirring sound, the MPM took off and sailed across the floor and up to the high ceilings like a small glider.

'This is awesome!' said Linden.

The MPM sailed through brightly lit corridors filled with sensors that opened and closed doors as they approached. Television screens as flat as paper were hung every few metres along the walls and robotic arms moved out from the walls to do everything from water plants to open and close curtains. There were also vending machines snugly nestled into walls, containing everything from lollies to hot snacks, drinks, and even games. At the end of one corridor, they glided into a large, glass-roofed area that resembled an overgrown greenhouse with trees, birds, and, amazingly, a waterfall.

'This is Mr Blue's nature reserve. If you look closely enough you'll see a giant panda and her baby,' said Ms Peckham proudly. 'Mr Blue is a great lover of animals and is one of the few people to successfully breed them in captivity. He is on the verge of completing a series of experiments that will hopefully bring pandas back from the brink of extinction.'

Animal conservation! This didn't sound like the evil Mr Blue Max and Linden had been told about.

The MPM then turned and headed for the lip of the waterfall.

Linden yelled, 'Watch out! We're going to crash!'

Ms Peckham smiled at them and said, 'Hold on.'

Max and Linden grabbed on to each other and closed their eyes.

Max shouted, 'I know it's a bad time, Linden, but there's something I want to tell you.'

'What did you say?' Linden yelled back.

'There's something I want to tell you,' Max

shouted again, as the thundering wash of the water came closer and closer.

'I can't hear you,' Linden cried.

But it was too late. Just then Max and Linden screamed as the MPM headed straight into the waterfall.

CHAPTER 16
VATS OF GREEN JELLY AND A ZILLION TRILLION MILLION DOLLARS

When they came to a standstill, Max and Linden opened their eyes and saw Ms Peckham standing on a shiny metal platform next to their hovering MPM.

'I told you it was perfectly safe, and here we are,' she beamed.

Max and Linden realized they hadn't died in the waterfall and tried to take in their new surroundings. They were high above the ground in a giant metallic room that looked like a darkened aircraft hangar. Behind Ms Peckham was a large, silver door that seemed to be vibrating with a pulsing light. There were no walls, just the door with a camera fixed above it, a platform and a seemingly endless abyss on either side. Nothing else could be seen except a window of light above them, which they assumed was the back of the waterfall they had just navigated.

'But how . . .?' began Linden.

'With this,' said Ms Peckham, holding out a small electronic device. 'Just before we passed through the waterfall, I activated the hydrogen atoms in the water so that they stood aside. That's why we aren't wet, to answer your question.'

Linden's mouth fell open. 'Come in,' said Ms Peckham, gesturing towards the door.

As Max and Linden stepped out of the MPM onto the platform, the camera followed their every move. Ms Peckham put her palm against the door. The light coming from it pulsated strongly before it opened, as if it had read her palm print as some kind of identity pass.

Max was impressed but tried as hard as she could not to show it.

'This Mr Blue has got a lot of explaining to do,' said Max, as she waited for Ms Peckham to lead the way.

Linden moved close behind her.

'Max, can you do me a favour?' he asked. 'We are talking about an evil mastermind here. Can you not say anything that's going to upset him?'

Max kept walking.

'As if I'd do that,' she said, raising her eyebrows.

'Follow me,' said Ms Peckham, still beaming.

Max wondered how anyone could smile so much.

As they followed Ms Peckham through the door and down a dimly-lit, metal passageway, Max leant close to Linden.

'Do you still have that recording device Ella gave you?' she whispered.

'It's a CTR.'

'Whatever. Have you got it?'

'Yeah. It's in my pack,' Linden replied.

'Switch it on,' said Max. 'We might need it later.'

Linden felt around in his pack and turned on the CTR.

They reached another door that again opened when Ms Peckham placed her hand on it. Inside was what looked like a brightly-coloured amusement park. There were TV monitors and video walls everywhere, and all the latest consoles and games, including some neither Max nor Linden had seen before. Lining the walls were shelves containing the largest selection of videos they'd ever seen, including all Linden's favourites.

'There's *Batman*, *Indiana Jones*, *Mission Impossible*, old and new versions.' Linden walked over to them. 'I could stay here for ever.'

'Well, we don't have for ever,' said Max, grabbing his wrist.

A bright red chair swung round to reveal a smiling man sitting behind a large wooden desk staring at them. Two familiar-looking men stood at his side.

'Sorry about the unusual invitation to my home,' the seated man said in a smooth TV-advertisement voice. 'It may have seemed a little abrupt but it was necessary for everyone's safety.'

He picked up a plate from the table beside him and held it out to them.

'Raspberry doughnut?' he asked.

Linden's stomach rumbled at the sight of the doughnut and Max put her hands on her hips.

'What I'd like is an explanation,' she said. 'Starting with who you are.'

'Of course, first things first. Please, have a seat,' he offered.

Linden's face fell as the man put the plate back on the table.

Before Max could protest, he pressed the button of a remote control device on the arm of his seat and two very comfortable chairs rolled across the room from behind them, gently forcing them to sit down.

Max and Linden looked at each other, puzzled.

'Did those chairs just move across the room?' asked Linden.

'I think we have enough to think about without asking that,' said Max.

The man took a chocolate bar from his pocket and unwrapped it.

'I am Mr Blue,' he announced, taking a bite of the bar.

Max's and Linden's eyes widened. He was much younger than they expected and looked like a regular guy, not someone who broke up families and wanted to control the world.

Linden looked longingly at the raspberry doughnuts and the chocolate bar.

Mr Blue smiled.

'Sorry for my rudeness. Maybe you'd like something a little more substantial?'

Mr Blue clapped his hands. Two chefs in tall white hats walked through the door carrying steaming plates of food, which they placed on the desk between Max, Linden, and Mr Blue.

Linden nearly fainted from the smell of it.

'Roast lamb and vegetables,' he whispered. 'My favourite.'

Max looked down at her plate and saw her favourite dish, Thai vegetable curry.

How did he know what they liked?

Linden tried to resist, but he hadn't eaten properly in ages. He grabbed his fork and was about to swallow his first mouthful when Max stopped him.

'It might be poisoned!' she warned.

Mr Blue laughed softly.

'I see you need a little convincing. Let me reassure you.'

Mr Blue took a gold fork from his pocket and tasted both dishes.

'A little too much salt on the lamb, but otherwise they are both perfect.'

Linden and Max couldn't wait any longer. They dug in.

Max pointed her fork at Mr Blue.

'So are you going to tell us why you kidnapped us?' she demanded.

Mr Blue smiled.

'I think the word *kidnap* is a little harsh. I just wanted to show you my wonderful home.' He paused. 'And ask you a few questions.'

Max put down her fork while Linden kept eating.

'Well, I have a few questions of my own, like what were your plans for Francis, Ben, and the Time and Space Machine?'

'My plans were very honourable, I assure you. With the Time and Space Machine we'd be famous all over the world as saviours of humankind. We'd be able to go back in history and stop wars before they happened, go into the future and find cures for diseases and make the world a better place.'

Mr Blue paused and smiled at Ms Peckham and his bodyguards.

'Or at least that's what I told Francis and Ben,' he laughed.

Max disliked Mr Blue more and more with each word he said.

'What are your real plans?' she asked.

'To become the richest man in the world by selling the machine to whoever wants to use it.'

'Even if they buy it for bad reasons?' asked Max.

'What they do with it after it is theirs is none of my business, my dear,' said Mr Blue with another smile.

'And what do you want with us?' asked Max.

'Oh, Max, I think you're clever enough to know that.'

Max froze.

'How did you know my name?' she asked, her brave front slipping a little.

'There are a lot of things I know about you, Maxine Anne Remy. I know your dad lives in America and couldn't be with you these holidays and that your mum works long hours fussing over famous TV personalities all day instead of you.'

Max and Linden looked at each other.

'And Linden, you live in Mindawarra on a farm with your dad, you love Ben and Eleanor like your second parents, and you lost your mother to cancer two years ago.'

Suddenly Max and Linden lost their appetites.

Mr Blue examined a fingernail on his right hand as he continued.

'And do you want to know the best part? I know you're going to help me find the Time and Space Retractor Meter because you don't want anything to happen to the families you love so much, do you?'

He looked up sharply at Max.

She was shaken but didn't want to let Mr Blue know.

'So you really are the slime-bag we were told you were,' she snarled.

Mr Blue looked offended.

'Now that's not very nice. It's just business, Maxine.'

'It's Max and I'm not doing business with you!' she shouted.

Linden looked worried.

'Max, be careful,' he whispered.

Mr Blue's smile dropped. He looked carefully at Max so that she felt uneasy and shifted in her seat.

'You and I have a lot in common, Max. We're not the kind of people who give up easily,' he said in a quiet voice that had a scary edge to it.

'For years I have been trailing Francis to get the

Time and Space Retractor Meter, but it seemed nothing I had would tempt him to help me. Until now.'

Mr Blue stared at Max and Linden as if they were two freshly cooked chickens and he was savouring the moment he would devour them. He clicked his fingers and the men in suits moved closer.

'Take them to the Jelly Room and see if that won't convince them to co-operate. And make sure Francis Williams knows where they are.'

Max was furious. She hated being pushed around by anyone and even though she was facing one of the meanest, most powerful men in the world, she wasn't about to let him have it all his way.

'I'm not going anywhere until I've changed,' she declared, crossing her arms against her chest.

'Max, be careful,' Linden cautioned out of the corner of his mouth.

'I'm sorry?' Mr Blue asked quizzically.

'I'm not going anywhere until I've changed back into my own clothes. You can do the tough-guy act all you like but your brain's completely turned to mush if you think I'm going anywhere dressed like this.'

Linden saw Mr Blue's eyes light up with anger,

as if someone had lit two little warning flares in them.

'Maybe we could just go as we are,' suggested Linden, thinking that if Max didn't stop, they were going to end up somewhere a lot worse than the Jelly Room.

Max stared at Mr Blue as he stood before her with his eyebrows raised. No one had ever spoken to him like this and here was an eleven-year-old girl doing just that. As much as she annoyed him there was something about Max Mr Blue had to admire.

'Fine, Maxine. You may change, but it won't make a scrap of difference to where you're going. Take them away.'

Max and Linden struggled as they were carried outside and back to their rooms. Then they were led down a long corridor and into an elevator that seemed to take for ever to stop. When the doors opened, they were herded into a round room with a huge vat of green jelly in the centre.

'The MPM was a much smoother way to travel,' said Linden as he was jostled forward by the guard.

In the Jelly Room, the guards made them sit on a small metal plank so that their backpacks leant against each other. They tied their hands behind them with thick rope that they then circled around both their waists. The plank was hoisted up so that they were suspended high above the vat of jelly.

Mr Blue walked in, his hands clasped behind his back.

'Have you ever eaten green jelly?' he asked calmly.

'I never was a big fan,' said Linden.

'This jelly has been found to absorb a formula of ours more readily than other foodstuffs, which enables us to control the thoughts of the young children who eat it,' explained Mr Blue. 'Could have lots of advantages in the future. Children are such unpredictable creatures. But back to the jelly. It has a soothing feel at first but after a while it's like you're being eaten by the blob and you just sink.'

Max stared Mr Blue in the eye.

'Let me tell you what is going to happen,' he continued.

'Do you have to?' said Linden, not sure he wanted to hear the gory details of his imminent demise.

Mr Blue smiled.

'Oh, but it's my favourite bit. In ten minutes, you will be lowered slowly towards the jelly. In half an hour the jelly will begin to sink into your shoes, then rise to your trousers then up to your jumpers and to your necks, soaking into your clothes and leaving a pleasant yet strangely sticky feeling all over you. Then, a short while after that, you will be swimming. And if Francis doesn't respond to my call, a short while after that you will be a permanent fixture of green.'

Mr Blue and his guards laughed and turned to leave.

'I'll let you think about that,' Mr Blue called over his shoulder as the door closed behind him.

Max looked down at the jelly and started to breathe quickly.

'Linden,' she gasped.

'What?' he asked.

'I'm afraid of heights,' she whispered.

'The best way to stay calm is don't look down. And think about something else,' said Linden. 'Like whether the recording device worked. If we got all that Mr Blue said to us, we can use it to finally convince the government he is evil. You just have to try and get it out of my bag. It's in the side pocket.'

He wriggled around so that Max could get a better angle to reach for it. She twisted her hands in the rope, moving closer and closer to the side pocket.

After a bit more manoeuvring, she had it. She held it carefully so as not to drop it in the jelly.

'Is it working?' she asked, holding it out so Linden could get to it.

Linden strained his neck hard so he could see the CTR in Max's hands. He wriggled his fingers to the buttons and after rewinding the tape, pressed *play*.

'My plans were very honourable, I assure you. With the Time and Space Machine, we'd be famous all over the world as saviours of humankind. We'd be able to go back in history and stop wars before they happened, go into the future and find cures for diseases and make the world a better place. Or at least that's what I told Francis and Ben.'

'It worked!' Linden said excitedly.

'That's great,' said Max, who accidentally glanced at the jelly again.

'Max, are you OK?' Linden asked.

'Yeah,' she said. 'Except we're going to die!'

'Will you stop looking down!' Linden cried.

Max looked up but she was still breathing fast.

Linden thought hard about how he could make her calm.

'If you could get rid of any vegetable in the world, what would it be?' he asked.

Max scowled.

'What?'

'If you could get rid of any vegetable in the world, what would it be?' Linden repeated.

'I don't know,' she said, thinking Linden had lost it.

'Nobody likes every vegetable. Even you. Now, what would it be?'

Max thought about it.

'Cabbage,' she said, breathing a little slower.

'I'd get rid of brussel sprouts,' said Linden. 'I've never seen the point of those and I have to have a dad who grows them.' Linden went on, 'If you won a zillion trillion million dollars what would you do with it?'

'Buy the biggest bar of chocolate I could,' said Max quickly.

'Chocolate? But you're a health freak,' said Linden.

'I know, but when I'm worried I like to eat chocolate,' explained Max.

Linden tried to think of another question.

'If you could change one thing about yourself, what would it be?' he asked.

Max thought about this one.

'Anything?' she asked.

'Anything,' said Linden.

Max thought some more.

'I'd have a mother and father who both lived with me,' she said in a much calmer voice.

'Yeah, me too,' he said quietly.

Max and Linden looked at each other and smiled.

'Max, what was it you wanted to say to me before we went through the waterfall?'

'Oh, I just wanted to say . . .' Max began, but she was interrupted as the suspension bridge suddenly jerked downwards.

'What's happening?' she shouted, panicking again.

'We're being lowered towards the jelly,' cried Linden.

Max screamed.

'We're going to die!'

CHAPTER 17
A DEAL WITH THE DEVIL

In his office, Mr Blue sat with Ms Peckham and his bodyguards over cups of tea.

'Not long now and I'll have the vital component I need to create history,' smirked Mr Blue. 'Once the Time and Space Machine is finished, everyone will want it and we'll become the richest people in the world. Governments will want it to build economies and win elections, prisoners will want it to escape to safety in another era, rich people will want to take exotic holidays. I don't care what they use it for, as long as I make lots of money.'

Mr Blue, Ms Peckham, and the bodyguards laughed while on the wall behind them, a monitor displayed the scared faces of Linden and Max as they were being lowered towards the vat of green jelly.

Ms Peckham's mobile phone rang.

'Hello?'

There was a pause while Ms Peckham listened.

'Send him up,' she said and turned to Mr Blue. 'Not long now until the past, present, and future of the world is ours.'

The door opened and Francis entered the room.

'How wonderful to see you again, Francis.'

Mr Blue stood up and held out his hand.

Francis didn't move.

'Where are Max and Linden?' he said, his face looking stern.

'They're busy for the moment, which gives us a chance to catch up and talk about old times,' said Mr Blue.

'I didn't come here to talk, I came to get Max and Linden,' said Francis. 'They have no business with you!'

'Oh, but they do.' Mr Blue added with a smarmy grin, 'Let me show you.'

Mr Blue pointed to the monitor where Francis saw Linden and Max dangling less than a metre above the jelly and getting lower each minute.

Francis lunged at Mr Blue but the bodyguards stepped in front and held him back.

'They haven't done anything! What do you want with them?' yelled Francis.

Mr Blue sat down in his chair and took a sip of his tea.

'Oh, I think you know that, Francis,' he said. 'You're going to hand over the Time and Space Retractor Meter or Max and Linden will be on tonight's menu as dessert.'

Francis tried to wrestle free from the guards but they were too strong for him.

'You only want the machine so you can use it

for your evil scheming ways,' he shouted.

'Evil is in the eye of the beholder,' said Mr Blue with a sickly sweet smile.

Francis stared at the monitor, not knowing what to do. He had to save Linden and Max before they drowned in the vat of jelly, but he also knew if Mr Blue got his hands on the Time and Space Retractor Meter, the world would never be the same again.

Mr Blue turned to the bodyguards.

'Take him down to the Jelly Room where he can enjoy the show up close. Maybe that will convince him to help me.'

The guards dragged Francis away.

'You'll never get away with this, Blue!' Francis shouted.

CHAPTER 18
A VERY SLIMY END!

'We're going to die!' screamed Max for what seemed like the tenth time.

'Don't you have anything more useful to say?' asked Linden, sick of hearing her predict their end.

'Not when we're going to die!' Max yelled.

She'd really lost it this time, Linden realized, as their shoes reached the top of the green jelly. It couldn't end like this. Not after they'd come so far and got so close to completing Mission Matter Transporter.

Again, he struggled to think of what they could do.

Why not use the CTR to call the top security forces in England so they could rescue them? But he didn't know the number or how they would find Mr Blue's hideout.

He did know Ella's number though!

'Max?' asked Linden.

'We're going to die,' sighed Max, watching the jelly seep into her favourite pair of blue sports shoes.

'No we won't, I've got an idea,' said Linden. 'We can get Ella to rescue us.'

Max stopped panicking and turned her head towards Linden.

'Well, isn't she just great?' said Max sarcastically.

'What is your problem with Ella?' demanded Linden.

Max thought hard.

'She . . . she . . .' Max floundered.

'Well?' asked Linden.

'She flirted and wasted our time when we had important work to do.'

'You're jealous!' Linden said.

'Me?' Max laughed. 'Jealous?'

'Yeah, and the sooner you get over it the better because the jelly has reached almost up to our shins.'

Max looked down, saw the jelly soaking into her jeans, and forgot all about Ella.

'We're going to die!' she called out.

Linden pressed the button on the CTR that sent a signal to Ella.

He waited a few seconds before a signal came back and he heard Ella's voice.

'Linden, where are you?' she asked frantically.

'We're at Mr Blue's hideout,' said Linden.

'It works!' shouted Max. 'That's great!'

'Are you OK?' asked Ella, sounding worried.

'I've been in more friendly places,' said Linden, trying not to let on they were about to become giant jelly babies.

'We just need to talk for a few minutes to give the CTR a chance to get a reading of where you are,' said Ella.

'We want you to do something first,' said Linden. 'We've got a recording of Mr Blue that will prove to the world he is a fake. Is there any way we can get it to you?'

The jelly soaked up to Max's and Linden's knees as they listened to Ella's instructions.

'Each recording is saved as a document,' explained Ella. 'Enter the number of the document and using the main menu press *transfer*.'

Linden did what Ella said and the communication device hummed as it transferred the recording.

'Got it!' Ella cried.

'Take it to the top security forces as soon as you can and we'll finally stop Mr Blue in his tracks,' said Linden. 'Has the reading of our location come through yet?'

'Nothing. Mr Blue may have put some kind of magnetic force around his hideout to stop detection by devices such as radars and the CTR,' said Ella.

'At least we've got him on tape,' said Linden.

'Yeah. Mum and I will get it to the right people as soon as we can. Then we'll see you soon,' she said hopefully.

'We'll be gone,' said Linden sadly.

'Oh,' said Ella, unable to hide her disappointment.

'We've got to get back to Australia. But I'll talk to you when we get there,' Linden added.

'I'll miss you,' said Ella.

'Me too,' Linden replied quietly. 'Bye.'

Just then the door opened and Francis, with his arms held behind his back, was hustled into the room by the two bodyguards. Linden quickly turned off the CTR and tucked it into his pocket.

'Francis! You came!' shouted Max.

The bodyguards stood over Francis.

'When you're ready to help, just press this button here and the kids will be saved,' said one of the guards, pointing to a large red button on the wall.

'It's all up to you, Mr Professor,' they sneered as they left the room.

Francis was shocked to see how deep in the jelly Max and Linden were.

'I'm sorry I got you kids mixed up in this,' he said. 'We have to find a way of getting you out of here.'

Max's face brightened, knowing exactly what Alex Crane would do in a situation like this.

'That depends,' she said as the jelly squelched up to her waist. 'Are you ready for a big trip?'

Linden smiled excitedly, knowing what Max was thinking.

'We could use the Matter Transporter to take us to Australia.'

Max looked at Francis.

'That's if you want to,' she said quietly.

'That way we escape from here, keep the Time and Space Machine from Mr Blue and get back to Australia before Ben and Eleanor wake up,' cried Linden.

They sank deeper into the jelly as Francis's face grimaced in trying to decide what to do.

'Only we have to go now,' said Max.

Francis saw the jelly rise still higher.

'Let's do it!' he said.

'Do you have the Retractor Meter with you?' asked Max.

'It's somewhere safe,' Francis replied, pointing to the sole of his left shoe.

Linden and Max beamed.

'Now for the control panel,' Linden said.

Max instructed Linden over her shoulder. 'See if you can reach into my bag and get it.'

Linden managed to do as she said and manoeuvred the panel out, holding it so Max could see.

'How does it look?' he asked nervously.

The red light beeped faintly.

'The signal's really weak,' said Max.

She looked at Francis. 'Do you think it will work?'

'If Ben has made it following our plans, it will be fine as long as the jelly hasn't short-circuited the initialization panel,' said Francis.

Max, Linden, and Francis looked worried.

'We have to try,' said Linden.

Max's fingers wriggled towards the rod at the side of the control panel.

'Can you hold it out a little more?' she asked Linden. 'I can't quite see the screen.'

Linden forced his hands to stretch as far as the rope would let him towards Max. An image of the room appeared before her on the LED screen and she did her best to draw an outline with the plastic rod around her, Linden, and Francis.

'Done,' she said breathlessly. 'You might feel a bit of tingling when you make contact with the transporter capsule, but you'll be fine,' Max explained to Francis.

She moved the rod on to the *activate* key. There was a small *zap* sound and a quick flash of light. Francis held his arm out in front of him as sparks ricocheted around him. His eyes brightened.

'Ben, you did it,' he said quietly.

Linden held the control panel above the rising jelly. Max tried not to panic as she used the rod to type Ben and Eleanor's address in Australia.

'See you all when we get there,' she said.

'Happy flying,' said Linden, trying to smile, but worrying that transporting all three of them with a weak power signal was probably very risky.

'Ready? Three, two, one.'

Max took a deep breath and brought the rod down onto the *transport* key.

The room shook and filled with noise. There was the whirring sound that got louder and louder, echoing off the walls of the Jelly Room. Max and Linden closed their eyes as the jelly wobbled around them and swirled across the room in green flying bits.

There was an explosion of sound and light.

And then they were gone.

Ms Peckham's eyes widened as she stared at the monitor.

'Mr Blue, I think you should see this,' she said.

Mr Blue walked over to the monitor. He was smiling.

'Have they finally decided to give themselves up?' he beamed.

'Not quite,' said Ms Peckham shakily.

Mr Blue looked at the monitor and the smile fell from his face like a brick.

'Where are they?' he asked, his voice shaking with anger.

'They just,' Ms Peckham struggled to find the right word, 'disappeared.'

'Disappeared!' shouted Mr Blue. 'They can't just have disappeared!'

He turned to the two bodyguards, who shrugged their shoulders.

'Find them!' he barked. 'Or you'll end up in something far worse than a vat of jelly!'

Mr Blue's face went beetroot red as the guards backed out of the room.

'If Francis and those kids have escaped, this will not be the last they hear of me,' he said to Ms Peckham. 'The day they met me will haunt them for ever!'

CHAPTER 19

HOME SWEET HOME

'Boy, you really panicked back there.'

Max opened her eyes and saw Linden and Ralph standing over her.

'Where am I?' asked Max, frowning and trying to remember what had happened.

'Same place as me,' said Linden. 'On Ben and Eleanor's farm. Only I landed on a few bails of hay and you landed in Larry's feed trough.'

Max looked around her.

'Urghh! Why is it me who always has the smelly landings?'

Linden smiled. 'Ben really needs to iron out those hiccups before you land in too many more stinky situations.'

Max wasn't impressed.

'Just help me out,' she said.

Ralph barked and licked Max on the nose.

'Not you. I said Linden.'

Ralph whined.

'Max is excited to see you, Ralph,' said Linden sarcastically. 'She just has a funny way of showing it.'

Linden helped Max out of the trough.

'Do you still think we're going to die?' Linden asked.

Then Max remembered where they'd escaped from.

'I know I seemed a little worried back there,' she stammered, 'but I always thought we'd get back safely.'

Linden frowned at Max as she tried to pick bits of Larry's food and green jelly from her hair and clothes.

After all they'd been through, he still didn't understand girls.

Or at least this girl.

Then Max remembered something else.

'Where's Francis?' she asked.

Linden turned round.

'Somewhere very cosy if you ask me.'

Max followed Linden's eyes and saw Francis asleep in a rocking chair on the verandah.

'Should we wake him up?' asked Linden.

'No. I've got a better idea,' said Max with a smile and she walked towards the house.

'I hope it involves breakfast,' said Linden to himself.

Later, after they'd washed away the green jelly and changed their clothes, Max and Linden stood in the kitchen and heard Ben and Eleanor's bedroom door open.

'Here they come!' whispered Max excitedly.

They could barely stop shaking with excitement as Ben and Eleanor walked into the kitchen.

'Well, what do we have here?' asked Ben, squinting against the early morning sunshine that was flooding the room.

Max and Linden beamed.

'Hash browns, fried eggs, bacon, toast, tea, muesli, yoghurt, fruit salad and freshly squeezed orange juice,' said Max proudly.

'What did we do to deserve this?' asked Eleanor.

'We just wanted to tell you that we think you're really cool,' said Linden.

Max rolled her eyes. He was probably going to say that everything was cool from now on.

'But that's not the only thing we have for you, right, Max?' asked Linden.

'Right! Stay there, I'll be back in one moment,' said Max as she went outside.

'I hope it's not something too big. I don't function very well before breakfast,' said Ben with a smile.

Linden flung the screen door open and Max reappeared.

'Linden and I have someone we want you to meet,' she said.

Francis stepped forward and Ben's smile melted away as if he'd seen a ghost.

'Francis? Is that you?' Ben asked quietly, thinking his eyes and the sun were playing tricks on him.

'It was the last time I looked in the mirror,' Francis answered. 'But a lot has happened over the last few hours.'

Ben looked at his brother and a smile spread across his face like jam across toast.

'It's good to see you, Francis. Now come here.'

Ben gave him a big hug. Then Eleanor hugged Francis and Ben hugged Eleanor and everyone got pretty teary.

Including Max.

Linden looked at her.

'You're not crying, are you?' he asked.

Max wiped her eyes.

'No. The sun's making my eyes water.'

Linden smiled at her.

'You're really something, Max Remy. And you know what? I think we make a good team. Next time you have a spy mission, I'm your man.'

Max felt as if she wanted to cry even more.

'It's great to see you, but how did you get here?' said Ben to Francis.

Francis looked at Max and Linden.

'Why don't we talk about it over breakfast,' he said. 'It's a long story.'

Francis, Max, and Linden told Ben and Eleanor everything that had happened. Landing in London, finding Valerie and Ella, riding on the Mobile People Mover, sinking in the vat of jelly, and meeting Ms Peckham and Mr Blue.

Ben wasn't happy about Linden and Max using the Matter Transporter, especially after he'd told Max it wasn't ready to transport people. He also told them what they did was dangerous and they could have been hurt, but he couldn't stay angry with them. The transporter had worked and, for the first time in years, Francis was back with them.

'Let's make a toast,' said Ben, raising his orange juice. 'To Francis, who I waited too long to see again.'

'To Francis,' they all said as they clinked their glasses.

'And to Linden and Max, two of the bravest kids I know,' said Ben proudly.

The glasses were clinked again as Max and Linden looked at each other and smiled.

There was a lot to catch up on and as everyone talked and laughed and listened to each other's stories, Eleanor put her arm around Max.

'You're a very special person, Max Remy, you know that?' she whispered. 'Life around here will never be the same again because of you.'

Max blushed and thought about what had happened since she came to the farm. She looked around the kitchen with everyone talking and laughing and eating, and realized she felt more at home here than she had anywhere else in her life.

When they had finished, Max and Linden suddenly felt exhausted and almost fell asleep at the table.

'I think it's time for our two top spies to get to bed,' said Ben.

Max and Linden dragged themselves up from the table.

'Do you think you and Francis will finish the Time and Space Machine now?' asked Max.

Ben and Francis looked at each other.

'We'll have to talk about that. For now you two get some rest,' said Ben. He gave her a big hug and said goodnight.

When they were in their beds, Max turned to Linden.

'Linden, you're right, we are a good team and I wouldn't want to work with anyone else. I also want to tell you what I was going to say before we went through the waterfall.'

Max took a deep breath.

'I've never had a best friend before, but now

I've met you I know what it's like. The pact we made before we used the Matter Transporter was one of the nicest things anyone's ever said to me. And even though I don't say it very often, you're really OK, you know, for a boy and everything, and I hope we stay friends for a really long time.'

There was a pause.

'Linden? Did you hear me?'

Max stepped over to Linden's bed and lifted the blankets off his face.

He was sound asleep.

Max smiled.

'Maybe I'll tell you another time,' she said.

Max yawned and climbed back into bed.

She dreamed of spies and missions and Alex Crane, Superspy from Spy Force.

CHAPTER 20
A CALL FROM SPY FORCE

Eleanor stepped onto the back verandah and called out, 'Max, Linden? Where are you? Why am I even asking?' she mumbled. 'Like I don't know the answer to that myself.'

Eleanor walked down to the shed and knocked on the door.

Nothing.

She knocked again.

Still nothing.

'Sometimes I wonder if they even remember I'm here,' she said.

She turned the handle and slowly pushed the door open to see Ben, Francis, Linden, and Max leaning over a small contraption with buttons, dials and knobs, and flashing lights.

'Max and Linden, there's a letter for you,' said Eleanor, handing it over. 'And it looks important.'

Max took the letter and opened it.

Her eyes widened.

'It's from Spy Force!'

'What?' Linden asked. 'I thought you made that up?'

'So did I,' Max exclaimed.

'What does it say?' asked Ben.

Max read out loud.

Dear Max and Linden,

On behalf of Spy Force, the Secret Government Security Agency, we would like to extend to you our gratitude for helping to uncover the illicit activities within the Department of Science and New Technologies. Your service to this country and the world has been invaluable.

Yours truly
R.L. Steinberger
Administration Manager,
Spy Force

'Wow!' said Linden. 'There really is a Spy Force!'

'And they seem to think you've done a pretty good thing,' said Francis. 'I wonder where Mr Blue has ended up?'

'Somewhere far from us, I hope,' said Eleanor.

'The world would be a better place if he just disappeared for ever,' said Ben.

'I don't think there's much chance of that,' said Max. 'Mr Blue doesn't give up easily.'

A ringing sound came from Linden's pocket.

'It's the CTR,' said Linden, his hands bolting into his pocket like lightning.

Max, suspecting it was Ella, rolled her eyes.

'Really, now how can you tell that?'

Linden missed the sarcasm and excused himself as he walked outside to take the call.

'Ella, hi!' Max heard him say.

Max folded the letter before putting it into her pocket. All the excitement she'd felt before melted away as she listened to Linden's voice, which was a combination of pauses, laughter, and excitement as he talked about the Time and Space Machine and how it was nearly finished, the letter from Spy Force, and other things Max couldn't quite hear because he turned away and lowered his voice.

Eleanor saw Max's face fall and attempted to cheer her up.

'Who would have known we'd have a famous spy in our house?' she asked.

Max tried to smile but she was too busy listening to what she could hear of the rest of Linden's conversation.

When Linden finished he came back inside the shed.

'That was Ella,' he said excitedly.

'Who?' asked Max, as if she didn't know.

'Ella,' Linden replied. 'She got a letter too and guess what else? The tape was enough to help Spy Force finally prove Mr Blue is evil. He quit his job saying he wanted to spend more time with his family, but he was really sacked and Valerie reckons the government kept it quiet because if they told the world what he'd been doing they'd look really stupid.'

'Well, you two should be very proud of yourselves,' said Ben. 'People have been trying to stop Mr Blue for years.'

Linden looked at Max and smiled.

'I guess Mission Matter Transporter was a success?'

'Yeah, I guess it was,' said Max.

Eleanor looked at her watch.

'Max, we're going to have to get ready. Your mum will be here soon to pick you up.'

Max had forgotten. Today was her last day on the farm.

She looked at the Time and Space Machine and then at Ben and Francis.

'I guess you'll have to finish it without me,' she said sadly.

'You'll be the first to know as soon as we get it working,' said Francis.

Max smiled and felt a tear in the corner of her eye.

'I'll help you pack,' said Linden.

In the house, Linden sat on Max's bed as she started picking up her stuff.

'Do you think you'll come back and stay sometime?'

'I don't know,' said Max. 'Would you like me to?'

'Sure,' said Linden. 'We haven't had a summer this exciting for years.'

'Do you think we might get to do another mission together?' asked Max.

'Yep!' said Linden confidently. 'Now that Spy Force has our names we'll be called to help out in other missions for sure.'

Max smiled as she folded clothes and squeezed shoes and books into her bag.

There was a pause before Linden said, 'And I wouldn't want to work with anyone else.'

Max blushed.

'Neither would I,' she said.

Linden could feel his face go red too. Then there was another awkward pause as he twisted the tassels on the end of Max's chenille bedspread.

'Max?' he asked. 'Can I ask you something?'

'Sure,' she said.

'How do you know when you really like someone?'

Max kept packing and avoided looking at him. She tried to remember what she'd heard from her mother and things she'd read in books and seen in films.

'You feel like you're walking a metre off the ground all the time. You can't concentrate on anything and you start saying weird kinds of things like someone else has taken over your brain.'

'That's exactly how I feel!' said Linden.

Max blushed again, but this time she was sure she was redder than she'd ever been. She turned to face her bag, refolding some clothes she had already packed.

She remembered the first time she'd met Linden and how he looked like a real wildboy. Who'd have thought she would be talking about liking each other six weeks later.

'Ella's really cool!' said Linden, smiling and thinking about the last time he saw her.

Max stopped packing.

'Ella?' She frowned.

'Yeah, she's really amazing. She said to say hello to you too.'

Max looked away and pushed her pyjamas into her bag before zipping it up.

'That's great,' she said.

They heard a horn beep and a car drive into the yard.

'That must be Mum,' she said quietly.

'I'll miss you,' Linden said.

'You'll get over it,' said Max, trying to smile.

'Hey,' said Linden. 'That was a joke.'

'Yeah,' said Max. 'I'm thinking of being a comedienne when I'm not spying.'

Linden and Max smiled.

Outside, she heard the slam of a car door and stilted voices buzzing like flies as her mother desperately tried to find something to say to her sister. All the while Max knew she was itching to leave as soon as possible and was wondering where on earth her daughter could be. Her mum could talk to most people as if she'd swallowed a dictionary. Words just poured out of her in one giant flood. But when it came to her own family, they dried up like dust in her mouth, making her look really uncomfortable.

'Max, I'm here.'

Max thought it would be about three and a half minutes before she ran out of small talk. A bit of a record for her mum under the circumstances.

'Gotta go,' said Max as she picked up her bags and her folder of writing.

Outside, her mother was looking at her watch as Max walked down the steps. Something inside Max burned when she saw this.

'Oh, there you are, sweetie,' her mother said. 'We have to get a move on because I need to be back in the city for an appointment.'

Her mother gave her a quick kiss on the cheek and loaded her bags into the car.

Max sighed. Nothing much has changed, she thought.

Ben, Francis, and Eleanor walked towards them and stood nearby.

'Thanks for looking after Max. I hope she wasn't too much trouble,' said her mum.

'None at all,' said Eleanor. 'Would you like to come in for some lunch?'

Max's mother looked at her watch again and seemed as anxious as if someone had dropped a jar of ants down her long, velvet skirt. 'I'd love to but we've got to fly.'

Typical, Max thought. She never has time for anyone except herself and her work.

She turned to Ben and Eleanor.

'Thanks for the best holiday I've ever had. I'll never forget you,' she said.

Ben gave her a hug.

'You have to promise you'll come back whenever you can,' he said.

'And don't leave it too long,' said Eleanor, brushing Max's hair from her face and giving her a kiss.

'Besides, you'll have to come back to see the machine when it's finished,' said Francis.

As they hugged, Francis whispered in her ear, 'I was a very unhappy man until I met you and Linden. Thank you.'

'OK, sweetheart. Let's go,' said Max's mum, trying to hurry her along.

Max ignored her mother and walked over to Linden and Ralph.

'I've got something for you,' said Max.

She opened her folder and handed Linden a small book entitled, 'The Adventures of Alex Crane, Superspy. Chapter One. Mission: The Time and Space Machine'.

Linden smiled.

'It's all about us and the mission,' Max explained.

'Thanks.' And for once Linden didn't know what else to say.

'Max?' said her mother with rising impatience in her voice.

'Bye, Ralph,' Max said, and patted him on the head. 'My master's calling.'

'Another joke,' said Linden. 'You should be careful, this could become a habit.'

Max got into the car and watched Ben, Eleanor, Francis, and Linden wave goodbye.

She thought about the summer, the mission, and the people she'd met. Toby Jennings, school, and her home in Sydney seemed another galaxy away. She looked at the farm getting smaller and smaller as the dust rose up behind her mother's sports car.

I'll be back, she thought.

Linden sat on the verandah and started reading.

The Chief of Spy Force congratulated Alex for another mission successfully completed.

'Thanks to you, Mr Blue is safely behind bars and the world can rest easy that he won't be able to have his evil way any more.'

'I don't think that's the last we'll hear of him,' said Alex knowingly. 'Mr Blue's as cunning a criminal as I've ever met.'

'For now, you deserve a well-earned break,' said the Chief. 'And Spy Force is happy to send you anywhere in the world for a two-week rest. Just name the place.'

Alex thought hard.

'How about Australia?' she said. 'I've never been there: the beaches, the sun, the islands.'

'I'll get someone to organize it right away,' said the Chief happily.

Just then the Chief's secret phone rang.

'Yeah?' he answered.

There was a pause.

Alex watched as his face became serious.

'OK, we'll get right on to it.'

The Chief hung up the phone.

'How about London instead? Mr Blue has escaped.'

MAX REMY
SPY FORCE
SPY FORCE
REVEALED

For Todd

A letter from Max Remy, Superspy

OK, listen. I'm only going to say this once. Just in case you missed what happened last time. My name is Max Remy. I'm eleven, I live with my busy mother while my dad is a famous film director who lives in America with his young actress wife. I hate school, especially the slime-brained Toby Jennings who enjoys making my life a complete misery. To get away from him and the other jerks I have to share this planet with, I've invented Alex Crane, a secret spy who works for the international intelligence agency called Spy Force.

The whole story started when I was parcelled off to the country last summer to stay with my hick aunt and uncle. But guess what? They weren't the chicken farmers I thought they were, but world famous scientists working on a Time and Space Machine! Trouble was, to finish the machine, Ben needed to find his brother, Francis, whom he hadn't spoken to in years because of a fight they had while working together in London.

With my new friend Linden, I used the machine to travel to England where we found Ben's brother but also met this evil guy, Mr Blue, who wanted to steal the Time and Space Machine for himself to use as part of his sinister schemes to rule the world. Soon, though, we ruined his plans and saved humanity from certain doom.

But guess what? When we arrived back in Australia, we got a letter from Spy Force thanking us for our bravery. From Spy Force! And I thought I'd just made them up.

Anyway, that's all I have time to tell you. Any other details, you'll just have to read the first book.

Now, let's get on with the story.

CHAPTER 1
A FOUNTAIN OF YOUTH IN THE SKY

Alex looked out of the open exit of the small twin-engine plane as it swooped above the dense treetops of the Amazon jungle. The thick canopy of green hurtled beneath them like an enormous ocean, each treetop another wave in a vast flurry that seemed to last for ever. They were flying so close Alex was sure that if she ran a hand along the leaves, she could have scooped up the dew that was sprinkled over the jungle like a giant handful of liquid gold. She fixed her eyes on the landscape below and thought to herself, whoever was responsible for making the world was showing off when they made this part.

Suddenly the plane lurched sideways as it struck a pocket of turbulence. Alex's head hit the cold metal wall with a thud as the giant of a man who was in charge of the mission launched another tirade against the pilot.

'Where'd you get your licence from? The back of a cereal box? My three-year-old nephew could fly this plane better than you. I've heard they've trained chimps that could outdo your aviation skills.'

Alex was impressed. She'd been dealing with Blue's thugs for years and 'aviation' was the longest word she'd ever heard from any of them.

The pilot's face remained unchanged. He'd

heard all about this guy from the other pilots and had already filled his ears with cottonwool so that none of his cursing could filter through.

The suited tough adjusted his seatbelt tighter around his waist before pulling out a floral handkerchief and wiping his brow. The short, fat guy sitting next to him stared.

'Floral?' he smirked.

'It was a present from my daughter.' The tough guy said it like a warning, his nerves making him more edgy than usual.

He'd been nervous since the trip began and if Alex's guess was right, the pilot was as skilled as they came and was getting great pleasure out of the occasional and 'unexpected' turbulence the plane was experiencing.

Just then, the short, fat guy buried his head in his lap and filled another sickbag with vomit. Alex thought she saw the faintest of grins on the pilot's face.

She adjusted the miniature parachute on her back and crawled across the metal floor of the cargo plane between wooden crates that were stacked like bowling pins. Taking out her laser knife, she carefully broke the reinforced seals on a few of the crates before she found it. A small humidifier case that, if she was right, was packed with exactly what she was looking for and it was her job to get her hands on it before the case reached Blue.

Alex had boarded the plane in a place called Manaus on the banks of the Amazon River. Well, not quite 'boarded'. She 'sneaked on' while Mr Blue's thugs were busy working out new ways to yell at the locals who were about to fly them into the jungle's deep and mysterious heart. On top of their fear of flying, the thugs were also nervous about their destination. It was said to have been cursed for any white person who entered. Stories had been told of only three known attempts to defy the curse and how each of the trespassers had been struck down by a hideous rash that slowly encrusted their skin before they slipped into a deep and fatal coma.

Alex was taking a big risk going on this mission, but it was a risk worth taking in order to thwart Blue's latest villainous operation. Blue had heard about an ancient plant that grew in the Amazon and had remained secret for thousands of years except to a few locals. The *Tropaeolum majorium,* or Fire of Life, was a small, innocent-looking plant with a large orange flower that, when combined with a few other green leafy fronds and put through a precise fermentation process, produced an elixir to preserve life for eternity. A veritable fountain of youth. The locals who drank it had been alive for hundreds of years but no one looked over thirty years old. Anyone with half a brain, even a quarter of a brain with slight malfunctions, would know that the potion would revolutionize the world, but would also lead to massive overpopulation and, what's worse, having to put up with Blue longer than any planet could bear.

After finding out about the plant by some sneaky, covert scheming, Blue tricked a few locals into selling him the plant, paying them a fraction of what he stood to make. He also made a few grand promises he had no intention of honouring once he'd got what he wanted.

Thump! The plane hit another air pocket as Alex carefully took the humidifying case from its crate. She knew she was holding something precious, something nature and history had protected for centuries and that if Blue got his hands on it, she was letting down all of that. She looked through the small, glass window in the side of the case and saw it: the leaves and the orange flower. She had to succeed.

The plane hummed beneath them as she

carefully placed the case in her backpack, secured the straps and crawled back to the exit hatch at the side of the plane. Checking her parachute one more time, she readied herself to unhook the rope that was strung across the exit, when the plane struck another jolt of turbulence. Alex lost her grip and was flung into the aisle of the plane in full view of Blue's thugs. Their eyes only just managed to stay in their sockets. First from fear and then from the shock of seeing her.

The bigger thug looked at the crates and saw they'd been tampered with. His eyes then slowly moved towards Alex like a shark silently swimming towards its next meal.

'I think you might have something that belongs to us,' he said in a voice dripping with quiet menace.

Alex sprang towards the exit and in one smooth move, unhooked the rope. She stood on the edge, said a small prayer to whichever god may have been listening and jumped. But as she did, a strap on her backpack caught on a metal railing, leaving her dangling high above the trees. If she fell, it would mean certain and messy doom.

The thug moved towards her as if she was an annoying insect he was about to crush. A smile crept onto his lips. Alex struggled to release the strap but it was no good, with all her weight hanging from it, she'd never succeed.

The thug curled one arm around the metal railing while the other held a knife ready to cut Alex free from the backpack and from the living world, leaving the plant to become the unfortunate property of Blue. He worked the blade across the straps as Alex looked down at her feet waving above the jungle and contemplated her possible last moments of life. Just then one strap was cut. Her body was flung sideways through the air and slammed into the plane. A small blue package jolted free from her pocket and silently grew smaller beneath her as it disappeared into the jungle. The thug, despite his fear of heights, laughed a measly, itchy laugh.

'Bye-bye, Ms Crane. I doubt even you could save yourself this time.'

Is this the end of Alex Crane? Will she free herself from the plane and Blue's thugs? Will she be able to save the *Tropaeolum majorium*? Will she escape in time to—

'Aow!'

Max rubbed the spot on her head where the small blue box had crashed into it. It lay a few centimetres beyond her feet and was no doubt flung at her by some giant brainhead with nothing better to do with their intelligence than prove to the world they didn't have any. She looked at the box and read the message on the side: 'Personality delivery for Max Remy'. She rolled her eyes. It was a wonder the entire school didn't self-combust from an overload of humour.

Max scanned the school playground to see who the culprit might be.

Suspects No 1, 2, and 3: Anthony, Richard, and Andy. Also known as the Three Stinkos, not because they smelt, even though that was up for debate, but because they once let off a stink bomb during assembly when Veronica Preston was receiving her 'Oh You Are So Great At Everything Award'. (Or something like that.) It was pretty funny, except the whole school had to stand in the hot sun as the stink got worse and listen to the principal lecture them on why the world would be a better place if they all liked each other. Why do adults do that when they know kids hate it?

Suspect No 4: Russell Allen, or Suss Russ. He

was a bit of a loner who spent a lot of his time doing weird things like arranging small pebbles on the ground to look like famous musicians. He'd then call kids over and say, 'Guess which rock star that is?' Some people said he collected other strange things too, like shoelaces, and that he even had one from some dead prime minister from the 1920s. Weird.

Suspects No 5 and 6: Antonia Balldalucia and Brigita Stevenson. Max knew they didn't like her since she accidentally spilt her chocolate milk all over them on the bus one hot afternoon. They never believed it wasn't deliberate no matter how many times she said it. They just glared at her as the milk spread into long brown stains on their uniforms and looked oddly like a map of Italy. After the forty-minute bus trip, the maps had curdled and their walk home was accompanied by the cries of hungry cats. Max spent most of her time trying to avoid standing near them while she was holding any kind of liquid.

Prime suspects: Toby Jennings and Co. There they were sitting on the steps of the main hall like they owned the place. All they needed were a few suits worn over some fat stomachs and they would have resembled overstuffed businessmen carving up the world like a Sunday roast. The first time she'd met them, she'd just arrived at Hollingdale (Max's third new school in five years) and she made the mistake of accepting an apple they offered her. She thought they were just trying to be nice but when she took a bite, her teeth sank into the middle of a plump, unsuspecting, and cleverly placed worm. Toby and his mates had dug a long, thin hole into the apple, slid the worm in and corked it up with a small piece of the fruit. Max had to rinse her mouth out for one hour with Mr Fayoud's mouthwash before she started feeling normal again. Sometimes, out of nowhere, she still got the taste of worm in her mouth. These suspects were definitely not to be trusted. Ever.

Other suspects: the rest of the playground.

Max's shoulders slumped. Anybody could have thrown the box.

Just then the bell chimed its awful shopping-centre drone. Like Tinkerbell caught in a time warp. Ms Peasley, the principal, had it installed rather than a clanging bell because she said it fostered a more harmonious school environment. She actually said that! Where do these people get these ideas from? It might as well have been signalling the end of civilization, Max thought, as she prepared to face another two hours with some of the world's undiscovered animal kingdom.

After she'd packed away her lunchbox, she picked up the small blue box and tossed it in the closest bin before going to class.

CHAPTER 2

A MYSTERIOUS GUEST

AND AN

OFFICIAL INVITATION

From: Max Remy

To: lindenfranklin@loonmail.com.au

Subject: Things

Dear Linden,

Just got your email. Thanks! Everything here is pretty normal . . . normal for my life anyway. Toby topped the class again in science yesterday and you'd think he'd just won the Nobel Prize the way Mrs Grimshore was going on about it. Dad is still making that big film in LA. And get this! He was having lunch the other day when he met Steven Spielberg. He said he's a nice guy, too. He doesn't get a lot of time to answer my email, but that's OK. Dad's always really busy. He sent me this great top that I'm wearing now. He has the best taste. Mum got this promotion which means she's even more manic than ever, so most of the time she hardly even notices I'm here. Oh and she's got this new obsession with wheatgrass. Every morning she grinds up this bunch of green grass and makes us both drink it. I'm not kidding. She grows it on the windowsill and it looks just like normal grass. I'm not sure what she thinks it's going to do apart from make me gag and sprout small saplings from my tongue. She said she read that it will make us live longer or get younger or something. I'll just ride this fad out until she finds another one. But she better make it quick, I don't know how much more paddock food I can stomach.

'Max, honey? It's time for dinner.'

Great! The food guru has just called. Maybe if I stay quiet, she'll forget I'm here. She's good at that. I've written another Alex adventure I'll attach. See what you think. She is on assignment in the Amazon. Why can't my life be like hers? Do you think Spy Force will ever contact us again? I still keep the letter they sent us in my pocket. Mum put it through the wash once so it looks a little crumpled, but you can still read it.

'Max? Did you hear me? Dinner is on the table.'
    Max sighed and stopped typing.
    'Coming!'

Sorry, Linden, gotta go. The wicked witch is calling. I'll talk to you tomorrow. Say hello to Ben and Eleanor for me.

Max paused as she tried to think of a way to sign off. She decided to keep it simple.

From Max

She logged off and shut down the computer. She missed Linden. He was the only one who could make her laugh. Even if his jokes were dumb. Before she met him she was happy not having any friends. She'd made heaps before but just when she was happy, her mum and dad would decide to move again and she had to say goodbye to them, so it was easier not to make any in the first place. But with Linden, it was different. She didn't have to see him all the time to know they were good friends.

She leant into the cactus on her desk.

'Think yourself lucky you're not a human and you don't have a mother making your life a misery.'

Max stood up and opened the door on to the landing at the top of the stairs. She stopped when she heard voices coming from the kitchen. There was her mother's voice talking at a million miles an hour like she normally did, and someone else. A man. Her mum never mentioned anyone coming to dinner and she hadn't heard the doorbell ring either. He must have come home with her. Why didn't her mother get that she liked to be warned when someone else was going to be here? Was that too much to ask?

She tiptoed down the stairs, listening hard and trying to work out who the man was. She crouched low and put her ear against the kitchen door. Her mum was going on about some new show that was starting on TV and how it was going to stop the world, blah blah blah, and whoever the mystery man was, was agreeing with her like she was telling him the secret of life no one had ever stumbled on before.

This was going to be too much. If Max had to sit in a room listening to this all night she was sure she was going to explode. She wouldn't be able to stop it. Her whole insides would splatter across the walls and floor and down the front of their designer clothes and overdone expressions.

Then, just as Max was turning around to creep back up the stairs, the kitchen door swung open and her mother only just stopped herself from tripping over Max's crouching body. What she didn't stop was her glass of red wine from spilling all over Max.

'What on earth are you doing on the floor? Didn't you hear me call you for dinner? And look at your new shirt. How am I ever going to get that stain out?'

Now this scenario could have run a few ways. Some mothers, distraught that they had almost trampled their only beloved child, would have bent down and kissed them repeatedly as they became overwhelmed by the near fatal tragedy. Others may have swept their precious daughter snugly into their arms while they apologized for ruining a brand new shirt that had been given to them as a present. And others may have just felt really bad as they offered a simple and quiet apology.

None of these ever happened in Max's house.

She looked down at her shirt and only just managed to hold back a blood-curdling scream when she saw it was totally ruined.

Then Max's mother remembered she had a guest and forgot all about the new shirt.

'There's someone in the kitchen I'd like you to meet,' she said, suddenly sounding all bright.

'Now?' Max was horrified. How could her mother even think of her meeting anyone when she was dripping with wine?

A head then appeared from behind the door.

'Hi. I'm Aidan. I've heard heaps about you, Maxine.'

Anyone clever enough would see there were a few problems here. First, no one, but no one, ever called her Maxine. That is one of those really important laws of nature you must never forget, like, 'remember to breathe or you will die'.

Also, as he made this monumental error against nature, he held out his hand. Max lowered her eyelids to give him a half-eye stare. She'd never heard about this Maxine-calling nobody before and she certainly wasn't about to make physical contact with him. He looked away awkwardly as his hand slowly made its way to a pocket for safety.

Aidan? I've never heard of any Aidan, she thought. And how come he knows about me? Because from his bad clothes and the fact that he's about thirty years younger than my mother, I know all I want to know about him.

There was an uncomfortable pause as nobody knew what to say. A trickle of red wine dribbled from Max's head down her face, adding another stain to her shirt.

'I'm going to get changed,' she said.

'Well don't be long, sweetheart,' Max's mum said with a nervous giggle. 'Dinner's getting cold.'

If Max had been given a choice of being banished to the coldest regions of Siberia or facing a dinner with her mother and whoever this Aidan was, she'd have known what would have been worse. But since Siberia was out of the question, she changed her clothes and made her way back downstairs.

'Aah, there you are,' said her mum in a sickly sweet voice that was like having your head dunked in a barrel of honey. 'I've kept your dinner warm for you.'

Sweet voice, nice gestures. Max wanted to know where her real mother was.

There was another awkward pause as her dinner was placed in front of her.

'So how was school today?'

Now she really knew this wasn't her mother. She never asked about school.

'Fine,' she said, trying to eat as fast as possible so she could escape to somewhere saner.

Awkward pause number three. This meal was going to be worse than Max thought. The ticking of the clock above the fridge got louder and louder.

'Well,' said her mother, which never meant good news for Max. 'I thought it was about time you and Aidan got to meet.'

Her mother looked at her as if it was Max's turn to speak but she didn't know what to say, so she kept eating instead.

'Aidan is my boyfriend.'

Max dropped her fork, sending bits of spaghetti worming all over her lap. Boyfriend? What boyfriend, she thought. I've never heard Mum mention a boyfriend before. When did all this happen? People her age don't have boyfriends. They're too old for that kind of thing.

Max was picking spaghetti strands from her lap and wondering why the world just got so crazy. Her mum continued talking.

'So I thought it would be good if you two got to know each other.'

You know those times when everything seems to stand still and every second passes as if it's an hour? When you want to jump up and get out of where you are but you're stuck and it seems as if you'll be there for ever? This was one of those times.

'I've got homework to do,' said Max as she wiped her mouth on her napkin and stood up.

As she closed the kitchen door behind her, she heard her mother say, 'I think that went quite well, don't you?'

That's how it was with her mother. Everything was measured as having gone well or badly. She thought most of what Max did was bad and if things went her way, then everything was going well. It was at times like this when Max missed her dad more than anything.

Upstairs, Max closed her bedroom door, changed into her pyjamas and prepared to stay there all night. Emailing Linden or writing another Alex Crane adventure would make her feel better. She turned on her computer and discovered she'd received an unusual email. It was marked Top Secret and came with a list of instructions and questions before she could open it.

Secure file

The following email is to be opened by M. Remy. Any person other than M. Remy found to have accessed this file will be subject to the full force of the Protection of Privacy Laws Act of 1926.

Please answer the following security questions before the attached email can be opened:
Name?
Date of Birth?
Address?
First names of only uncle and aunt?

If the questions are answered correctly, you will receive the accompanying mail. Failure to answer the questions correctly or within two minutes will lead to the neutralization of this message.

Linden, thought Max. He was always joking and mostly this annoyed her but after what had happened downstairs, she needed all the cheering up she could get. Max answered the questions and hit *send*. She waited eagerly for his reply, but instead, something strange happened to her computer. A series of numbers and letters hurtled up the screen like bugs caught in a wind tunnel. Finally the bugs stopped and the screen went blank.

Max stared at her computer not knowing what to do next when the following words appeared:

Security clearance granted. Email to follow.

Max knew Linden was clever with computers, but she'd never seen him do anything like this before. After two minutes exactly, the email alert appeared before her. Max moved the mouse across the pad and opened it.

From: R. L. Steinberger
To: maxremy@emailaus.com.au
Subject: Meeting

Dear Max,
This is a top secret email that will be deleted completely from your system within one minute of its arrival. We request your company at Spy Force Headquarters on

20 April of this year. Further details will be forwarded to you once we have received your acceptance.

Regards
R. L. Steinberger
Administration Manager,
Spy Force

Clever, thought Max. She was impressed but was going to let Linden know she was on to his games. She hit *reply* to his new phoney email address.

From: Max Remy
To: rlsteinberger@spyforce.com
Subject: Too funny

Very funny! You must be exhausted now from being so witty.

Fond regards
Not Easily Amused

She waited to hear back from Linden.

From: R. L. Steinberger

To: maxremy@emailaus.com.au

Subject: Meeting

Dear Max,

Confused about your previous email. Are you able to attend the meeting?

Regards

R. L. Steinberger

Administration Manager,

Spy Force

Max frowned as she read the email again. Maybe it wasn't from Linden. He knew not to stretch a joke too far with her. But could it really be from Spy Force?

She wrote an email to him using his usual address just to be sure.

From: Max Remy

To: lindenfranklin@loonmail.com.au

Subject: Mr Funnyman

You might be clever. Security clearance? Meetings at Spy Force? I thought the Administration

Manager of a major intelligence agency would be based somewhere a little classier than Mindawarra?

Max waited a few moments until a reply came back.

From: Linden Franklin
To: maxremy@emailaus.com.au
Subject: What Funnyman?

Max,
I think maybe you've been sitting too close to your computer and it's starting to fry your brain. What's this about a Spy Force meeting?

Max sat back and tried to think of a witty reply, but before she had a chance, another email came through.

From: Linden Franklin
To: maxremy@emailaus.com.au
Subject: Spy Force email

I got one too! It just arrived. A secure file. Is it really about a Spy Force meeting? What do you think they want to talk to us about? Do you think they want to send us on a mission? What are we going to tell them?

How are we going to get there? This is going to be the wildest thing ever!

Max read Linden's reply three times and each time her eyes got wider and wider as the truth sank in. The first email was from Spy Force! What did they want? Max and Linden hadn't heard from them since the end of last summer when they received a letter thanking them for their help in uncovering Blue's crooked scheme. Maybe they wanted help with a secret mission. Maybe the world was in great danger and only they, Linden and Max, could save it. Whatever it was, Max was ready. And no matter what it took, she'd get to that meeting on 20 April.

Her heart beat against her chest as if it suddenly didn't have enough room to keep beating. She thought about what to say in her reply. About how she was poised on the brink of possibly the most important meeting she'd ever have in her life. About how she'd probably offended a member of Spy Force. About how if only she could keep her big mouth shut . . .

'Ha ha ha.'

The laughter from downstairs cackled around her room like a squawking crow had been let loose near Max's head. It was full of coy, girlish giggling and macho try-hard bellowing that sunk into Max's shoulders like quick-drying glue, cementing them into what felt like hardened armour. She looked towards the door, wishing the laugh back downstairs and out of her life. She didn't care how much her mother was trying to impress fashion boy, she wasn't fooled one bit by his smarmy ways. He was as interesting as dry grass on a hot day and if her mother couldn't see it then she was in desperate need of a major spring-clean of her senses.

Max put on her headphones and wrote back to Spy Force.

From: Max Remy
To: rlsteinberger@spyforce.com
Subject: Meeting

Dear Mr Steinberger,
Sorry about my previous email. I thought you were someone else. Linden and I would be happy to accept your invitation to Spy Force. We await further instructions and details.

From Max Remy

She then emailed Linden and said she'd accepted the invitation for both of them and would get in touch when she heard more.

And this time she knew how to sign off.

From Max Remy, Superspy.

Blah blah blah blah blah blah blah blah blah blah blah blah blah blah blah blah blah blah blah blah blah blah blah blah blah blah blah blah blah blah.

CHAPTER 3
FIRE DRILLS AND A MAD STRANGLER

Sometimes life has an annoying way of trying to be as difficult as possible and Max was just about to be landed in the middle of one of those times. Hoping for a quiet, painless day at school with as little to do with the other students as possible, she arrived the next day as the fire siren was screeching around the schoolyard like a sick rooster gone mad.

'Brrurrp! Brrurrp! Brrurrp!'

'Great. A fire drill,' she mumbled to herself as she walked through the school gate. She saw two teachers race out of the staffroom with bright yellow fire hats that kept falling down over their eyes. One teacher was looking through the fire manual trying to work out which exit she was supposed to direct the students through to escape the imaginary fire that was engulfing their school. If it was up to Max, she'd let the whole place go up in a huge technicolour bonfire that all the fire manuals in the world wouldn't be able to stop.

'Just what we need,' she said under her breath. 'To be herded around like cattle while the fire wardens, who just five minutes ago were ordinary teachers, direct us to who knows where as the sun beats down making sure we get a good dose of UV rays and my life flashes before my eyes in one giant wasted blur.'

'Talking to yourself, Max? You know that's one of the first signs of madness. Any day now you'll start seeing your very own imaginary friend.'

Toby Jennings. Of course. When days started badly, you could pretty much guarantee he'd be there to make sure it got even worse. Max was never in the mood for Toby and today was no different.

'I'm sorry,' she said, determined not to let him get away with being a jerk. 'You must have mistaken me for someone who actually cares about what you have to say.'

'Now, Max. I'm just worried about your welfare,' said Toby in his best fake sympathetic voice. 'That's why I've organized this little outing, so you and I can share some quality time together.'

So Toby had set off the fire alarm. She should have guessed it was him. Being in school was bad enough, but at least in class she could be distracted from the world of losers she was surrounded by with her books and computers. Why couldn't Toby find someone else whose life he could make miserable?

'My welfare would be a whole lot better if I didn't have to share this planet with you.' Max flicked her head back and walked towards the fire warden who was directing students across the street. Why, she wondered, did her life at Hollingdale seem like some terrible and mysterious punishment for a crime she never committed?

Despite doing her best to get rid of him, Toby followed closely behind Max, eager to get in another jab of his brain-dead wit. But he didn't have to. As Max reached the fire safety area, she tripped up the kerb and fell face forward onto the grass in front of the entire school. She covered her head as the contents of her bag flew into the air before raining down on top of her. Now this alone would have been embarrassing enough, but Max had fallen near a leaking hose which had turned the surrounding grass into a kind of lumpy, green and brown milkshake. Max lay in the oozing mess with her eyes closed, knowing no matter how she looked, it wasn't going to be pretty.

As the first peals of laughter drowned out the fire siren, she opened her eyes and things instantly got worse. Worse than she ever could have imagined.

Toby had found her Spy Force book and was getting ready to read it out loud.

'Well, well, well. What have we got here?' he announced to the audience of laughing faces that were gathering around him.

Max wiped mud from her face and said in as threatening a voice as she could, 'Give me that book now.'

'Now, Max,' Toby said in a sarcastic voice that made her want to scream. 'You and I both know that's not going to happen. Remember? I'm the bad guy and you're the one who I have to pick on. That's the beauty of our relationship—it's so simple.'

Max could feel the anger inside her heating up like a stick of dynamite about to explode. She imagined herself on the end of a giant plunger, loading Toby headfirst into a cannon that would send him all the way to the other side of Australia in one soaring blast.

'Now where were we?' he asked the kids standing near him who were happy to be entertained during something that was usually really boring. 'I know, I was just about to read something from Max's secret spy book.'

Max cringed as she lay in the mud. A wall of legs and feet gathered closely around so that none of the teachers could see her, penning her in and making it impossible for her to get up.

Toby began to read as if he was a narrator at a very bad and overacted school play.

The rope dug into Max's and Linden's wrists as they were tied to the suspension bridge high above the vat of slimy green jelly. The evil Mr Blue's laughter rang out around the chrome-grey room as he told them of their fate. A slow, sticky doom awaited them and if they didn't give him the secret code to the Time and Space Machine, they would find themselves on the night's menu as dessert. Would this be the end of Max Remy, Superspy? Would Spy Force, the secret spy organization she worked for, be able to save her? Would she be able to thwart the sinister plans of the evil Mr Blue? Would the world be for ever doomed to live without her?

'Oh no!' Toby stopped reading from the book and looked around him, getting more melodramatic by the second. 'This is terrible! What are we going to do? The world won't cope without Max Remy . . .' and the next part he said as if he was enjoying every syllable, 'Su-per-spy.'

Never before in her life had Max so badly wanted to disappear. She wished now she had her uncle's Matter Transporter control panel, so she could zap herself as far away as possible from the crush of faces leaning in and laughing. Some of the kids were laughing so hard they were crying. Others had to hold their stomachs from laughing so much.

'I hope lying in the mud wasn't your secret weapon for outwitting the evil Mr Blue?' asked Toby as if nothing was ever going to shut him up. 'Because I can give you a hint, it's not going to work.'

He relished the laughter that swirled around them like a whirlpool and made him feel as though he was leader of the world. He got ready to read another piece. Max watched him turn the pages and knew she had to get the book off him fast. She lunged forward from where she lay and grabbed the book at the top and bottom. Toby held onto the sides and pulled it back towards him. Max wasn't going to let go until she had her book back and was surprised at how strong her anger made her feel.

'Give it back!' Her teeth were clenched as she pulled the book towards her.

'No! Not until I've read out a bit more of your amazing spy adventures,' he wheezed as he tugged the book against his chest.

That was when Max found herself doing something she'd never done before. She hadn't even had time to think about it before she realized she was surrounded by excited faces screaming, 'Fight! Fight! Fight!'

Mr Fayoud pushed his way through the students and pulled Max off Toby.

'And just what is it you think you're doing?' he shouted. His face was twisted into a purplish mix of anger and shock.

Max looked at Mr Fayoud's oversized face leaning into her and knew she had no explanation. She rubbed her hands together which seconds before had been around Toby's neck. This time she was in for it. She was never going to be able to explain what she'd done. She could hardly explain it to herself.

Toby ran his hands over the deep red marks on his neck.

'I don't know what I did, sir,' he said, putting on his best pathetic act. 'One minute I was standing here obeying the fire drill, the next she tried to strangle me.'

Max's mouth fell open. She looked at Toby and then down at her book. The cover had been torn off in the fight and was lying in the mud.

'You two can both go to Ms Peasley's office. I'm sure she'll have a few things to say to the pair of you about bullying and violence. As for the rest of you, the fire drill is over. Form two lines and follow your fire warden back to your classes.'

There was a general moan of disappointment as everyone realized this was probably as exciting as the day was going to get. Mr Fayoud walked behind Max and Toby as they made their way to Ms Peasley's office. That was never a great experience, mostly due to the floral wall hangings she painted herself out of a cheap monthly magazine. The place was full of them and other puke-inducing stuff like embroidered signs that said, 'A school that learns together loves together', and cushions on an old sofa that were shaped as love hearts. The entire place should have been condemned as a health risk for having so much phoney love it could choke someone.

Either way, being marched to the principal's office was never a good thing no matter how much stuff it had in it. Max held her breath and prepared herself for the worst.

●

CHAPTER 4
TWO-HEADED PRINCESSES AND A WORLD FULL OF STRIFE

Alex Crane took a deep breath as she faced one of the most fearsome monsters of her life. It writhed before her like a hungry ogre, ready to feast on anything in its sight. Only this was no ordinary, foul-smelling ogre but the two-headed perfumed princess of the fabled land of Taraxakum, which, like Atlantis, was believed to be completely mythical. That is until Spy Force uncovered a time slip that had for centuries kept Taraxakum hidden from the world and which the fragrant princess was using to steal precious energy reserves to power her overly aromatic land.

Taraxakum was once a prosperous land but when the princess ascended to the throne after her father had been eaten by a freakishly big fly, she declared that all the land's energy be employed in the making of perfumes that would be sprayed across the land in a constant sprinkle of delicate rain. Even the simplest of Taraxakumanians could see that the princess was missing a couple of floors in the brain department, but as she was the ruler, her orders were to be obeyed. This soon resulted in the running down of the economy and an extraordinary oversupply of sweet-smelling stuff. She also decreed other ludicrous laws. Flowers were to be strewn at ten-minute intervals throughout the capital and she had three Taraxakumanians with her at all times to throw rose petals at her feet so she walked across an unending bed of colourful scents. Slogans were to be written across the sky reminding people to love each other. Schmaltzy, hideous, idiotic, mind-numbing, trashy—

'Max, are you listening to me?'

Max had been doing her best to avoid listening to Ms Peasley for the last twenty minutes by thinking about another Alex Crane adventure. Why couldn't she just disappear into Alex's world for ever? She was sure she wouldn't be missed and life would be a lot more pleasant than it was right now.

And it was about to get much worse.

'Yes, Ms Peasley.' She frowned, trying to look as if she'd heard every word.

Being in Ms Peasley's office was as painful as Max expected. Toby stood next to her in front of the flower-filled desk, rubbing his neck and acting in pain and as innocent as he could. There was a small trickle of blood from a scratch on his brow but apart from that Max was sure Toby had never felt better in his life. Especially now that she was in such trouble.

She couldn't tell what was more annoying, Toby's lame attempt at acting or Ms Peasley's speech about how 'the world is a place full of strife and turmoil and how it was up to each and every one of us to do our part to fill it with love'. She said lots of other pukey stuff too that sounded as if it came straight out of one of those corny self-help books displayed at supermarket checkouts. Books like, *How to Make the World a Better Place in 10 Easy Steps*. Max tried not to listen to most of it for fear her brain would seize up in protest and never want to work again.

After the positive-guide-to-life sermon was over, Max was sent to sit in the corridor and did her best to block out Ms Peasley's sugar-sweet voice that was still ringing in her ears like a lovesick mosquito. She was picking a piece of dried mud from her hair when through the congealed strands she saw her mother marching down the corridor towards her to pick her up. And to see Ms Peasley so they could have 'a word about Max's behaviour'.

The way her mother's footsteps echoed off the walls, it wouldn't have taken a genius to see she wasn't happy. From the other end of the corridor she looked quite small, but each footstep made sure that soon she'd be towering over Max like a crazed giant with a sore head.

Max looked above her at the Gold Clock of Peace (it was actually called that) hanging from the ceiling by gold tinsel and realized class was just about to finish. This was going to be embarrassing. Not only because the whole school was going to witness Max's mother in one of her tirades but because that same mother was being followed by Aidan! Now everyone was going to know her mum was going out with someone who was young enough to be her son!

Why does everything in my life have to be so hard? thought Max, and almost in answer to her question, the school chime echoed around them like an invisible, cloud-like cotton ball bouncing against the walls.

'Great,' Max whispered into her muddy uniform.

As the corridor filled with the multitude of arms, legs, and eyes that poured out of every class like a volcano, the once small image of her mother now loomed over her like a huge storm cloud about to burst.

Which it soon did.

'Have you anything to say for yourself for having me dragged away from a very important lunch so that I can spend my time listening to how you've been misbehaving?'

The excited titters of the other kids flew around Max like sparks from fireworks. This was going to be even better than they expected.

Max's mother stared at her with eyes so wide they looked like two bugs under a magnifying glass. Aidan finally caught up with Max's mother and stood like a stuffed dummy behind her. Max sank as low as she could on to the bench, wishing she could disappear into the polished wood as her mother's dressing-down was only just getting started.

'And why every time I come to pick you up from school do you seem to be covered from head to toe with slime or mud or some other repulsive goo?'

What was Max supposed to say to that? She'd had a few 'accidents' with slimy substances in the past. Nothing out of the ordinary though, and besides, even if she tried to defend herself, her mother wouldn't listen. She wouldn't have wanted to know about how Max had fallen into the mud or how Toby had stolen her book and humiliated her by reading her secret story to the whole school. She could have been kidnapped by a pack of sumo wrestlers in front of a hundred witnesses and it still would have been Max's fault. No excuse was ever good enough for having dragged her mother away from work.

Max looked at her mother's new exclusive salon haircut and expensive designer suit as she stood there waiting for an answer. What she wanted to say was, 'Stop yelling at me in front of everyone. Don't you know how embarrassing it is? And what is *he* doing here? Only family members are supposed to come and pick kids up from school. You spend more time with him than me and if it wasn't for Ms Peasley calling you to school you wouldn't have spent more than ten minutes with me all week.'

But what she ended up saying was, 'I don't know.'

From the look on her mother's face, Max knew this wasn't the right answer and that she was in even more trouble than she was before.

'If you think for one minute that is any kind of reasonable explanation for your behaviour, young lady, then we'll see how the next week without television alters that opinion of yours. Now wait here while I see what Ms Peasley has to say about you.'

Max wanted to warn her to sneak away before old Peasers had a chance to sprout her hippie love babble all over her, but just then the door opened and Max's mother's already over-big eyes nearly rocketed out of her head when she saw a sore-looking and very bandaged Toby come out with Ms Peasley. Toby was gently sent on his way with Peasers cooing all over him before Max's mum and Aidan were invited inside.

Phew, thought Max, relieved to have a break from her mother's flip-out, but before the principal's door closed, her mother leant down and whispered, 'Make that two weeks without television!'

Toby was instantly surrounded by kids wanting to see his bandage and hear what Peasers had said. Others were role-playing the goggle-eyed frenzy of Max's mum and only just managing to stand up at how funny they were. The sounds swirled around Max as if she'd been dumped in a cement mixer on maximum speed.

After what felt like an hour, Max's mother came out. She took a hanky from her purse, dabbed her cheeks, and with barely a look towards Max said, 'Come with me.'

The words sounded innocent enough, but as Max peeled herself off the bench, she knew they meant big trouble.

The corridor that day seemed longer than it

ever had been as Max followed her enraged mother and a quiet Aidan outside. She thought about her punishment and the fact that she'd only have to wear it for a few days as the Easter holidays were coming up. This meant she was only days away from escaping the smirking faces of the kids she was passing, escaping her mud-splattered life and most of all, escaping her mother.

Max had been invited back to Ben and Eleanor's farm and the holidays couldn't come soon enough.

CHAPTER 5
BAD BEHAVIOUR
AND A
HOLIDAY FROM HELL

As Max and her mother drove away from Hollingdale, Max thought about what had happened in the last few hours. She'd been humiliated in front of the whole school, was covered in brown smelly muck and her Spy Force notebook was ruined as it lay at the bottom of her bag in two torn, mud-smudged pieces. Her life was so miserable at least things couldn't get any worse, Max thought. But when they got home, things got much worse.

Her mother was in one of her 'I'm-not-going-to-talk-to-you-until-you-learn-to-behave' moods. Which would have suited Max fine if she had been able to stick to it. These moods only ever lasted a few minutes regardless of how determined her mother was to keep quiet. Her need to talk was like an out of control train and no matter how much anyone tried, she could never be stopped.

'Max, you and I need to have a serious talk.'

Serious talk? Max knew trying to strangle Toby wasn't the smartest thing she'd ever done, but even prison would have been better than one of her mother's serious talks.

'I am very concerned about your behaviour lately and just for your information, so is Ms Peasley.'

Her mother paused to give Max time to say something. Max pushed a clump of muddied hair behind her ear and had nothing to say that she thought would help, so her mother continued.

'We've decided a few things need to change and that perhaps your complete lack of regard for other people, including that sweet boy you so viciously attacked, is perhaps connected to the lack of time you and I spend together.'

Sweet boy! Toby was a lot of things but anyone who thought he was a sweet boy was having serious problems with reality!

'So we thought you and I could change that by making plans to be together.'

What! Max thought. She'd just had one of the most traumatic days of her life and all that Peasley and her mother could come up with was a recipe for making it worse. She could just hear them now. Peasers blathering on about how all the world's problems could be solved with a 'pinch of love' and a 'dash of kindness'—Nos 43 and 45 on Peasers's Guide to a Better World—and her mum going on about how mothers and daughters really are best friends they just sometimes forget that—she would have dug that up from some women's magazine. And both of them finally agreeing to a whole lot of sickly, honey-coated stuff that would have been better off on the closest compost heap.

Max sighed as she waited to hear how this mother and daughter bonding time was going to be played out.

'So, instead of spending Easter on the farm, you and I are going to take a holiday together,' Max's mother said proudly, as if it was the best idea she had ever had.

'Sorry?' Max asked, feeling as if someone had sucked all the air out of her so she could only just whisper the question.

'You and I are going to Queensland!' she announced as if she was telling Max she had just won the lottery. 'We'll book a hotel, go to the beach, eat at fancy restaurants. Spend some real time getting to know each other again. Won't it be great?'

Peasers's talk had done more damage than Max had expected. Her heart sank as she saw her time with Linden, Ben, and Eleanor fading and her hopes of being in London for her Spy Force meeting disappearing in a cloud of New Age drivel.

Max would rather have had a ban on television, a stern talking-to, a thousand lines saying why she would never try to strangle Toby again—no matter how much he deserved it—but not a holiday with her mother!

'That sounds great,' she mumbled unenthusiastically.

'I thought you'd like the idea.' Her mother beamed unnaturally, as if some alien had taken over her face and was pushing up the edges into a smile.

Then there was this pause where neither of them knew what to say until Max said, 'I think I might go to bed.'

'OK, sweetie.' Her mother sounded relieved that the awkward silence was broken.

Max made her way to her room leaving a scattered trail of grass and dried mud behind her. Her shoulders drooped as if two heavy weights had been tied to them. She turned on the computer and had two messages. One from Linden telling her how excited he was about her visit and one from Spy Force confirming their meeting on 20 April. Steinberger said he would send more details in time and even added what an honour it would be to meet them. An honour!

This only made Max feel worse. She tried to write a reply to Linden, but didn't know what to say. How was she going to tell him she couldn't go to London with him? She had to think of a way out of this holiday with her mother. If she turned down this opportunity to visit Spy Force they might never want to meet her again. All her hopes of being a Superspy would be smashed for ever. She turned off her computer, picked up her pyjamas, and made her way to the bathroom knowing only two things: first, she needed to wash away the mud that had glued itself to her and, second, by tomorrow morning she needed a plan to save her from a trip that would be a holiday from hell.

CHAPTER 6
SPIT-FIRING MONSTERS
AND
HOLIDAY SALVATION

Alex Crane stood against the long, metal beam bound by titanium rope as the ragged jaws of chained crocodiles leapt towards her, missing her by centimetres.

But it wasn't the crocodiles that worried her most.

It was the spit-firing, giant Echidna that posed her greatest threat. The pink-haired, evil overlord, Sugarlips, had lured Alex to her dungeon hideout during a mission to save the world from another of her harebrained plans. This time Sugarlips had, Pied Piper-like, enticed the children of some of the world's richest people into her lair by means of a giant mountain of fairy floss that floated sweetly above the bedrooms of the children as they slept. Their dreams became filled with images of sweet mounds of sugared heaven which drew them, sleepwalking, towards the overlord's hideout. What the children didn't know was that once they were in her sugared palace, she would place them at the mercy of the spiny-backed Echidna, until their parents paid the hefty ransom she demanded of them.

Or else . . .

'Ms Crane, time is almost up. If those parents don't deliver that ransom soon, I'm afraid some pretty nasty things will happen,' Sugarlips said with a voice like melting ice cream on a hot day. 'And this lovely bell here will tell us when that time comes.'

Alex flinched at the sounds of Sugarlips's sickly words as she pointed to a large brass bell.

'It's no use struggling either,' she advised. 'I assure you the titanium rope that binds you is as strong as any substance the world knows and you're wasting your time if you think you can get free. Besides,' and at this her voice became syrupy and thick, 'if you could free yourself, you would be making my precious baby very happy.'

At this, the Echidna sent a soaring spitball through the air. When it landed against the opposite wall of the dungeon, it spawned a fiery explosion and once the smoke cleared, a gaping, terrible hole could be seen. If the spitfire had hit a human there was little guessing how much of them would be left.

Alex was trapped. Caught in a world where she didn't belong with one of the most sweetly vile people she had ever met, one of the most evil of pets, and a bell set to ring out the terrible fate of innocent children. Her choice was to stay and be mauled by hungry crocs or resist and become the main course for a freakish, oversized pincushion.

Would she manage to escape and save herself from certain doom? Would she be able to free the children who had been tricked into entering this grotesque world? How was she going to stop the bell from tolling certain doom?

Brinnnggggggggggg.

'Aahhhh!'

Max shot up in bed as if the mattress had been spring-loaded. One minute she was dreaming about a terrible overlord and her pet, the next she was . . . she was . . . it took her a few seconds to realize where she was. Then everything became clear. The phone was ringing downstairs. She was in her bedroom. It was the morning of another school day. Then she remembered the worst bit. She was still the girl who was doomed to spend her holidays with her mother.

Max sat there while the phone rang and watched her life fall into a tragic heap. There was nothing good about it. Nothing to look forward to. Everything was against her.

But then something happened.

'Max?'

It was her mother knocking at the door.

'Yeah?' answered Max, turning and falling into her pillow face first, hoping this would make the world go away.

It didn't, so her mother kept talking.

'Max?' She was now at close range sitting on her bed. 'I've had a call from work.'

She paused as if she was getting ready to say something difficult. 'There's a new show we are launching much earlier than expected and they want me to do it.'

Max closed her eyes even tighter waiting for what calamity it would mean for her. The world had better be careful, she thought. There's only so much bad news an eleven year old can handle before terrible things happen.

'Now I know this is going to be disappointing for you, sweetie, but I'm afraid we are going to have to postpone our trip to Queensland.'

Max opened her eyes. Did she hear right? Not going to Queensland? She was so happy she wanted to jump out of bed and swing from the light fitting.

Her mother watched as Max continued to lie face down in her pillow.

'I'm so sorry, darling. I know it was going to be so wonderful with just the two of us, but I will book another trip as soon as I can. I promise. For now, though, it will mean spending your holidays at the farm.'

Max thought for a minute. If she was clever, she could really play this to her advantage. She sat up next to her mother, ready to lay it on as thick as she could.

'That's OK, Mum. You couldn't help it. Sometimes your job must come first. There'll be lots of other times you and I can spend together later.'

Max's mother was impressed.

'You really are the sweetest kid a parent could ever hope for. Now, how about I make you some breakfast and we get you off to school.'

She kissed Max on the forehead and sprang out of the room.

It worked! Yesterday, Max was the pebble in the shoe of her mother's life, condemned to weeks of punishment, today she was the sweetest kid a parent could ever hope for. She leapt out of bed and got ready for school as if it was the best day of her life.

The Easter holidays were only four days away. Max woke every morning and struck the days off her calendar as if they were layers of wrapping paper hiding a present. Nothing could upset her. Even Toby's teasing about her mother's performance at school didn't bother her. All she could think of was seeing Linden again and going to London.

Finally the day arrived. The last day of school before the break. Max was waiting at the school gate for her mother to pick her up. Toby tried one parting shot before he left.

'Waiting for your mother, Max? After trying to strangle innocent children, I'm surprised she hasn't packed you off to reform school with all the other social misfits.'

Max wasn't biting and besides, she could see her mother's car driving towards her and with only seconds of Toby left in her life, she didn't even bother coming up with anything nasty to say to him.

'Bye, Toby. Have a great holiday,' she said brightly as she opened the car door.

Now this did two things for Max: first, it totally freaked Toby out and, second, it looked good in front of her mother that she was being nice to the boy she was trying to strangle only days before.

Max got in the car and kissed her mother hello. As they drove off, she watched Toby, his mouth gaping wide open in shock, get smaller and smaller in the rear-view mirror. She thought, today is a good day.

CHAPTER 7
RALPH ATTACK
AND A
DISMANTLED
DISASTER

As they drove through the rickety front gate that was only just managing to stand up (Ben and Eleanor were brilliant scientists, but they knew nothing about being handy around a farm), Max could see them all there: Ben, Eleanor, Francis, and Linden. Her heart slammed in one enormous leap against her chest. She'd missed them so much since the Christmas holidays, but it wasn't until she saw them again that she knew how much. The last few days blew away in a trail of dust behind her and Aidan, Peasers, Hollingdale, and Toby went with it.

When they pulled up, the following few minutes were pretty awkward and went something like this.

After the usual routine of Eleanor asking Max's mother to stay, her mother's eyes darted all over the place while she offered a few lame excuses why she couldn't. Ben stood by not saying much as a few more awkward pauses made their way into the conversation before Max interrupted them all by saying goodbye to her mother and everyone waved her off. After that the car window was quickly wound up (so none of the country could creep in and dirty the polished leather seats) and Max's mother breathed a sigh of relief as she headed back to the city.

They all watched the car disappear down the dirt drive and Max wondered why her mother always had to make a quick exit when it came to her own family. She didn't even say hello to Linden or Francis.

'Let me look at you,' said Eleanor, turning towards Max with a smile plastered all over her face.

She leant down and put her hands around Max's cheeks, the folds of her dress sweeping around them like sails and they were both on the high seas. 'You're even more beautiful than I remember from the last time.'

No one had ever said that to Max before and she'd never thought of herself as beautiful. Ben saw that Eleanor's words made her feel uncomfortable and stepped in to save her.

'Now, Eleanor, Max doesn't need you embarrassing her in the first few minutes she's here.' He put his arm around her and swooped her into the air.

'Yeah,' said Linden. 'There's plenty of time for Max to embarrass herself later.'

Linden! It was so good to hear his jokes again. Only Max would never let him know it.

'Good to see you haven't done anything about improving your sense of humour. Wouldn't want you to change just because I'm back.'

Linden smiled, glad to see Max could still be funny when she wanted to be.

There was one person left. Francis. When Max and Linden first met him in London a few months ago, he was scrawny and bent-looking, with hardly enough fat on his bones to count as anything. Now he looked fit and healthy, with his cheeks full of colour, his chest filled out and it seemed he stood a whole ruler length taller.

'Hi, Francis.' Max suddenly felt very shy.

'Hi,' he said quietly, looking down and not knowing what to do with any of his lanky body.

A silence sat between them like a giant clump of cow manure, until something happened to get rid of it. A great leaping sack of fur burst from the verandah, jumped down the steps and crash-landed on Max.

'Aahhh!' she yelled as her body flew through the air like a splattered pancake. This was followed by a lot of muffled cries as a mini dust storm rose around the confusion of fur and what were once Max's upright limbs.

Ralph!

It took a few moments for everyone to realize the affectionate mutt had escaped from his lead and was so excited by Max's return he'd forgotten all the rules of how to say a proper hello.

'Gerr 'im orff meee!' they thought they heard Max cry.

Ben and Linden charged towards the dusty muddle and pulled Ralph away, but not before he'd done a good job of covering her clothes in a solid coat of dirt and fur and her face in enough dog slobber to fill a bucket.

'I forgot about you,' she growled, as she wiped her sleeve across her mouth.

Ralph whined, suspecting perhaps he'd overdone his welcome.

'Sorry about that, Max,' said Eleanor. 'We tied him up but ever since he heard you were coming he's been falling over his own tail with excitement.'

It wasn't that Max didn't like animals, she just liked it better when they kept away from her. Ralph, unfortunately, never got the hint, no matter how hard she tried to let him know it.

'Linden, would you mind taking him out the back?' Eleanor asked. 'You can tie him to the peach tree. Make sure he has plenty of water. We'll go inside and welcome Max in a more pleasant way.'

Linden led the down-hearted Ralph away as Max followed Eleanor, Francis, and Ben inside.

Before she closed the door, Max stopped and looked around the farm. When she first arrived here last Christmas, she was determined to hate it, but now she was back it filled her with a warm, soft feeling in her stomach.

It was good to be back.

But as she turned to walk through the door, a squawking cackle of feathers exploded in front of her face like a feather pillow put through a shredder.

Max pulled her head back and only just avoided the soaring, screeching attack. The chicken! she thought angrily, realizing she'd only just avoided having her eyes plucked out.

'You think you're clever, don't you? Waiting until everyone has gone before you make your move,' she said to the clucking lunatic who was acting all pure and sweet and pecking seed from the ground as if it hadn't done anything.

'Don't think I'm not on to you,' Max warned.

The bird cackled quietly as if it was smugly mumbling to itself.

'Next time you pull a stunt like that there's going to be fried chicken all round.'

The chicken pecked and clucked louder, which made Max even more angry.

'And don't think I don't know what you're saying either,' she hissed.

'I didn't say anything.'

Max cringed as she turned around and saw Linden standing by the verandah.

'I wasn't talking to you,' she said frowning, annoyed that she'd been caught talking to a chicken.

'Well, who were you talking to?' he asked, acting as innocent as the chicken.

'No one.' Max hoped he'd accept that for an answer.

'You were talking to Geraldine, weren't you?'

Max laughed. 'As if I'd be talking to a chicken.' She tried to look convincing but even Geraldine stopped pecking and stared straight at her.

'You were talking to someone,' he said persistently.

Why didn't Linden ever know when it was time to let something go?

'Are you two coming inside?' asked Eleanor, popping her head out of the front door.

Saved! Max thought. 'Yep. Just having a look at the farm.'

'A pretty close look,' said Linden, as he picked a chicken feather from her hair.

'Let's go inside,' Max said quickly, wanting to

change the subject and suddenly remembering the other animal that had smudged itself all over her. 'I need to de-Ralph myself.'

Max headed straight for the bathroom and after a complete scrub-down she went to the kitchen to find a 'Welcome Back, Max, Feast'. Eleanor, Ben, Francis, and Linden, all wearing big hats, stood around a table so packed with food there was hardly any room for plates. There were streamers and balloons, and candles on a chocolate-covered cream-and-strawberry-filled cake, and above it a bright red banner strung across the length of the kitchen that read, 'We Missed You, Max'.

It was another of those times in Max's life when she was looking at one of the best things ever done for her and the only thing she could think to say was, 'Thanks.'

As if that was the signal to start, everyone sat down and dug in. Plates were passed over heads, gravy was poured over sausages, corned beef, and vegetables, spoons clanged against bowls as mashed potato was scooped out and piled high next to beans, peas, beetroot, broccoli, pumpkin, yellow squash, and honeyed carrots, making everything look as if giant tubes of paint had been squirted everywhere.

Eating was so quiet in Max's home. There was the correct amount of matching knives and forks, small portions of food carefully arranged on plates, and her mother always had on what she called her 'dinner' music. Something classical or something filled with tiny bells and the sound of dolphins or whales. She'd read that it helped digestion, which Max could have told her wasn't true because it always made her want to throw up.

At the farm, dinner was filled with clanging and laughing and excited talk that flew around the table. Max was burning to know the most important thing.

'Is the Time and Space Machine nearly finished?'

There was a brief silence as Francis and Ben looked at each other.

'We've been busy lately and haven't been able to spend as much time on it as we'd have liked,' said Ben, shovelling another spoonful of peas and mash into his mouth.

Everyone kept eating but Max had to know more.

'So it's only a little more ahead than when I was here last?'

'In some ways, yes,' stuttered Ben, shooting a quick look across at Francis.

More clanging and silence and eating. This was getting frustrating.

'In which ways?' Max was feeling a little nervous about how quiet everyone was being.

'Well, you see, Max . . .'

Max was instantly wary. When sentences started with 'well, you see, Max . . .' people were usually trying to avoid telling her something she wasn't going to like.

'. . . there's been a slight hitch,' Ben continued.

'What kind of hitch?' she asked slowly.

'When Francis got back to Australia it wasn't long before people found out he was here and were keen to get him working again,' explained Ben. 'We'd started work on the machine but had to stop because Francis kept getting called away for other projects.'

'So how far did you get?' asked Max, not sure if she wanted to hear the answer.

'Maybe it's best if we just show you.' Ben wiped his mouth and pushed back his chair.

When they got to the shed and Max stood in front of the machine, a few things happened. First, she felt numb and tried to focus on what she was seeing, then she felt confused, which was followed by a swift feeling of anger and finally panic.

And all of this in about one minute flat.

'What happened?' she asked when her mouth finally worked after the shock.

'In order to get the machine right, we decided that we had to start from scratch. Especially as we had the Time and Space Retractor Meter Francis brought back from London.' Ben was speaking calmly, like it was no big deal and he wasn't ruining every chance Max had of getting to London for her Spy Force meeting. 'And this is how far we got.'

In front of Max and spread from one end of the shed to the other, was the Time and Space Machine, but in so many pieces she wondered if they would ever go together again. It was like a huge asteroid belt of boulders and space junk, with bits of the machine strewn everywhere.

Linden was just as shocked.

'I knew they'd had a setback but I didn't know it was this far back.'

Ben looked at their disappointed faces and tried to cheer them up.

'In a few months, things'll calm down and the world will know the Time and Space Machine. Just not yet.'

Max and Linden sagged like two paper dolls left in the rain. All the colour and shape washed away.

Ben tried again to lift their spirits. 'We have made one discovery that is very important. Francis is great at desserts and has made an enormous sticky date pudding he needs help demolishing. So who wants to help us out?'

Max and Linden heard none of Ben's talking. All they could see were their hopes of going to London spelt out in the chaos of the Time and Space Machine ruins. Max had never felt so sad in her life and apart from a total reality flip or being transferred into someone else's life, she didn't know how she'd ever be happy again.

CHAPTER 8

VOMIT-INDUCING LOVE SONGS, ALIEN EYES, AND AN IMPORTANT MESSAGE

Max and Linden sat at Eleanor's computer and wondered what to write. They'd been staring at the screen for ten minutes and nothing had come to them.

'Maybe start with a joke,' Linden suggested. 'Make them feel relaxed.'

Max took her eyes away from the screen briefly just to show Linden how unwelcome his suggestion was. 'They're a major secret spy agency,' she said. 'I don't think feeling relaxed is a priority.'

She turned back to the screen as she thought of the Time and Space Machine spread out across Ben's laboratory floor like a scarecrow with all its stuffing pulled out. Her body slumped over the keyboard, feeling the same.

'We just have to tell them the truth,' she said sadly as she started to write.

From: Max Remy and Linden Franklin
To: rlsteinberger@spyforce.com
Subject: Spy Force meeting

Dear Mr Steinberger,
Please accept our sincerest apologies for not being able to attend the meeting at Spy Force on 20 April. Due to unforeseen circumstances (like our uncle dismantling

our mode of transport) we are unable to come to London at this time.

Regards,
Max and Linden

'What do you think?' she asked.

'I'm not sure. You don't think it sounds a little too casual?' he asked sarcastically.

'I want to show them we aren't kids.'

'But we are kids,' said Linden, not understanding why Max found it so hard to be herself sometimes.

'You know what I mean,' she snapped and pressed *send*. The message was gone.

They both sat staring at the empty screen.

'What do you think they wanted to meet us for?' asked Linden.

'I guess we'll never know.' As Max said this, she felt even sadder than she did before.

Outside, Ralph whined as if he was just as disappointed as they were.

'Coming, fella,' said Linden as he leaned towards the window and waved. 'Better go. It's my turn to have Ralph and he doesn't like getting home after dark.'

Linden stood up from the desk.

'Don't worry, Max. My mum used to say when one door closes another opens. You'll see, something will happen next that will be great.'

He waited for Max to say something but she didn't.

'See you tomorrow then,' he said and left the room.

Linden's words floated around Max's head like flying ants she wished would go away. When doors closed in Max's life, other ones locked ever tighter. When her dad went away, her mum became bossy and never seemed as relaxed as she used to be. When she left her last school and best friend, she ended up at Hollingdale where no one liked her. She wanted to believe Linden but she knew her life too well to know things worked any differently.

She shut down the computer and went to the kitchen to say goodnight but stopped when she was met with the three backsides of Ben, Eleanor, and Francis, whose heads were poking out of the kitchen window into the yard.

'What's going on?'

'It's Larry,' said Eleanor. 'He's been building a haystack out here for an hour.'

Larry was a pig who predicted the weather. Or

at least that's what Max had been told. She wasn't convinced this wasn't just Ben, Eleanor, and Linden nursing a mild dose of lunacy.

'What does that mean?' asked Max, curious despite her scepticism.

'Means there's going to be a windstorm,' said Ben, without a doubt in his voice. 'A big one judging by the size of that stack.'

Max stared at all three rear ends as they continued to poke their heads out of the window.

'Why a haystack?' asked Max, not sure why she even asked.

'He likes to see them tumble down when the wind comes up,' said Ben, chuckling. 'Gets a real kick out of it.'

That was all Max needed to know about Larry and his haystack for now. She suddenly felt tired and didn't want to talk any more.

'Night then.' She turned to leave them to their staring.

'Would you like me to come and tuck you in?' asked Eleanor, bringing her head in from outside.

'No, I'll be right,' said Max and dragged herself to bed.

When she woke up the next morning, Max didn't open her eyes straight away. The sound of Ben and Eleanor singing a soppy love song filtered into her room like the smell of rotting fish in the sun. Max loved Ben and Eleanor, but if they could sing in key it wouldn't have been quite as terrible. To add to that, the morning was hot and steamy with a warm breeze blowing directly onto her face, which nearly made her pass out with the smell of the farm it carried with it.

'Country life stinks sometimes,' she mumbled, referring to the smell and her memory of the broken Time and Space Machine. But when she opened her eyes she was met with something even more terrible. Two bulging, bloodshot eyes she was sure belonged to a weird, psychopathic alien.

Her heart pounded as she faced the fierce creature and remembered something.

She remembered to scream.

'Aahhh!'

The alien eyes became bigger and even more bloodshot before disappearing under the bed as Ben and Eleanor rushed into the room.

'What is it?' they asked, pushing their faces into hers.

'It was . . . I saw . . . I think . . .' said Max, not knowing what it was.

'Take your time, Max. Tell us what happened,' said Eleanor gently, just as a whimper was heard from beneath the bed.

Max's eyes narrowed. 'Ralph,' she whispered, as she saw images of the ragged mutt being packed off to the other side of the world on a very, *very*, slow boat.

Ben plunged under the bed as Eleanor winced. 'Sorry, Max. We told him to stay outside. Normally he's very obedient but he's taken such a liking to you he doesn't seem to listen to a word we say.'

'Come on, Ralph. That's your fun for the day over,' Ben wheezed as he pulled the reluctant canine out. 'It's the doghouse for you, sunshine.'

Ralph looked over his shoulder at a scowling Max as he crept outside after Ben.

'Why doesn't he get that I don't like him?'

'He can't help it. It's that magnetic personality of yours.' Linden was standing at the door munching on an apple.

Sometimes Linden did that. It was as if he never walked into a room but would somehow just appear.

'How about some breakfast and you can try out more of your eagerly awaited humour then?' said Eleanor, looking at Max and smiling.

Linden opened his mouth to say something else but before he could, the phone rang. 'Maybe I'll just get that.'

'You'd be doing the world a great favour,' said Max. 'Or at least this part of it.'

Eleanor sat down on the bed next to Max.

'I'm sorry about Ralph. He's usually so shy. Looks like you've brought out the wild side in him.'

'Great. I won't be chalking that up as one of my talents.'

'Max!' Linden called from the hall. 'Phone for you.'

Max froze. Maybe it was Spy Force ringing with a plan to get them to London. Or maybe they were going to bring the meeting here. Or maybe it was . . .

'It's your mum.'

My mum! she thought, as she got out of bed and walked to the phone. What does she want?

Linden put his hand over the receiver and almost in answer to her thought said, 'She wants to know how you're doing.'

'How I'm doing?' Max asked incredulously. Her mother never called to see how she was doing. 'She must have cooked up some other way to ruin my life.'

Linden handed her the receiver.

'Hello,' she said, warily.

Pause.

'Yep, I'm fine,' she said, not sounding fine at all.

Another pause. Longer this time.

'Sounds great.' But the way Max said it, whatever her mother said didn't seem great at all.

An even longer pause and then, 'OK, bye.'

Max hung up and stared at the phone. 'Peasers! That speech of hers really worked its way into Mum's head and I'm the one who's going to have to pay for it.'

'What did she say?' asked Linden.

'She wants to spend a lot more time with me when I get back. Wants to sit with me while I do my homework. Make quality time every afternoon to talk about our days and share our feelings.'

'Are you sure it was your mother?' asked Linden.

'Sounded like her. And she wants us to share time with Aidan.'

Linden had heard all about Aidan from Max's email.

'So the forecast is bad?'

'Couldn't be worse.' Max turned and made her way to the kitchen.

But after breakfast, something happened to

change everything. Max and Linden were sitting at Eleanor's computer when an email from R. L. Steinberger arrived. It had one simple message:

Don't worry about transport problems. All will be taken care of. Be in the back paddock at eight o'clock tonight.

And that was it.

'What does it mean?' asked Linden.

'Not sure, but I guess we better be in the paddock at eight o'clock to find out,' Max said slowly, letting the message sink in. 'And that we're going to be at that Spy Force meeting after all.'

Max and Linden stared at the screen before turning and smiling at each other.

'Aaaahhhh!' they both screamed excitedly.

Eleanor rushed in to see what was wrong.

'What happened?' she asked, worried it was another animal attack.

Max and Linden looked at each other. They couldn't let Eleanor know what they were planning. She'd think it was too dangerous and try to stop them. Max had wanted to be a spy all her life and she couldn't risk anything spoiling it now.

'Nothing,' she said, trying to think of a cover. 'Linden just told another one of his jokes.' She smiled, pleased she could have a dig at his humour.

'Maybe you could hold over on being funny for the rest of the day, Linden. I think my heart has had about as much as it can take of it for one morning.' Eleanor gave a half smile, half frown as she left the room.

Max was chuffed. 'Sorry. Just had to get that in.'

'It's OK. It's your way of coping with being in the presence of great comedy.'

'So that's what they're calling it these days, are they?' she asked.

'You better believe it.' Linden smiled. Max did have a sense of humour when she wanted to.

They both turned to the screen. After all Max had been through in the last few days it felt as if the world was finally going her way. She'd have given anything to go to London. Even spending more time with fashion-tragic Aidan didn't seem so bad now.

A smile trickled on to her lips as she knew her life was about to change for ever.

CHAPTER 9
A GIANT WINDSTORM AND A MYSTERIOUS LANDING

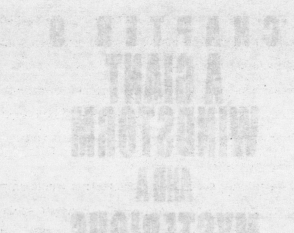

Alex Crane looked out from her precarious position balanced on the tip of the mast of the sailing ship *Inferno* and knew that now help had arrived, her life, which was teetering on the edge of oblivion, would be saved.

'Max! Thank heavens you're here,' she called through the panicked squall of wind and rain that lashed against them.

Max was new to the business, but even with little solid experience, she was proving to be one of the best spies Alex Crane had ever come across.

Brilliant. Clever. A natural.

'We've only got minutes before this whole ship is blown into the sky and us with it.' Alex spoke into her lapel transceiver in her usual direct and unflappable manner.

Max knew she had to think, and fast. The wind buffeted against her like an overzealous bully as she dangled by a rope from the battered helicopter overhead. The aircraft swayed above them like a cancan dancer, its blades kicking out against the blue-black sky, lit by the angry flare of lightning.

She operated the helicopter by remote control, trying to manoeuvre herself closer to the mast and Alex before the lit fuse inside the vessel ignited the cargo of deadly explosives.

All she had to do was expertly guide the helicopter closer, making sure a sudden updraught didn't spin it out of control and send it spiralling into the sea. Just a little closer towards Alex and she would—

'Max?'

The voice behind her made her jump, sending her pen sliding across the page and her backside bouncing off the log she was perched on so she landed unglamorously on the ground. Legs splayed, head hurting and her fingers softly nestled in a warm cushion of chicken poo.

'Sorry,' Eleanor apologized. 'I didn't mean to scare you.'

'That's OK.' Max glared at Geraldine who clucked loudly and pranced away as if she'd just laid a golden egg.

'I didn't hear you coming.' Max pulled herself back onto the log and looked for something to wipe her hand on. She never understood why she ended up on the ground more times than the average eleven year old did.

'I just wanted to tell you that we're so happy to have you back.'

Max looked through her book to find a blank page to clean her fingers with. Also to avoid further embarrassment because she could feel herself blushing at what Eleanor had said.

'The place didn't feel the same when you left.'

Max looked up. Eleanor had this smile that was like a big, warm duvet that made her want to crawl in and curl up inside.

'How's Sydney?' Eleanor asked.

'Good,' said Max. She'd been concentrating so much on Alex Crane that she'd totally forgotten about everything in Sydney. The farm had a way of doing that.

'And your mum?' Eleanor was twisting a ring on her finger. Max's mum had one exactly the same that she kept locked away in a silver box. Max knew that because she'd take it out and wear it when her mother wasn't at home. It had a red stone and was set in a gold bed of interlinked roses.

'She's good.'

'That's good.' But the way Eleanor looked away when she said this made Max think something wasn't quite right.

'Where did you get the ring?'

Eleanor noticed she'd been playing with it and stopped.

'Just before your gran died she gave identical ones to me and your mother, asking us always to look out for each other.'

Eleanor sat quietly staring at the ring.

'Why don't you and Mum get along?' Max asked.

'Now there's a question.' Eleanor clasped her hands and looked at the horizon. 'Even when we were little girls we weren't very close. It's just always been that way. I think that's why Gran gave us the rings. She hoped it would bring us closer together.'

She drew the colourful layers of her skirt around her knees so she looked like the inside of a kaleidoscope. Her face creased into a sad frown.

'She has a boyfriend now,' Max informed her.

'Really?' Eleanor was curious to know more and Max was happy to tell her, but she wasn't going to sugarcoat anything. She was going to tell it exactly like it was.

'But he's a real jerk who spends a lot of money dressing like he hasn't got any, stays in the bathroom so long he might as well move in there and wears so much aftershave there should be a pollution warning put out whenever he leaves the house.'

'So you're not a fan?' Eleanor asked in a serious tone, making Max think she may have overdone it a little.

'Not much.' She looked at her fingers and wiped off the rest of the chicken poo. Max was disappointed. She was hoping Eleanor would be on her side.

They sat in silence for a few seconds.

'Even though he does sound like a real jerk.' Eleanor smirked and tried to stop herself from laughing.

Max looked up from her fingers and smiled too. Then Eleanor started to laugh. So did Max. They laughed even harder until they were holding their stomachs and giggling so loudly that crows in the trees nearby swooped away in fright. They rocked back and forth with laughter until they toppled backwards and fell off the log straight into another fresh batch of chicken poo.

This time Max didn't care and didn't see Geraldine as she scratched in the dirt as if she was doing a victory dance. They just kept laughing and lying on the ground.

'Were you thinking about something funny I said earlier?' An upside-down Linden was staring at them from overhead.

'Yep, that's exactly what happened,' Eleanor chuckled, catching her breath and sitting up before helping Max to her feet. 'And now that we've got that out of our systems, I better go and give Ben a hand with dinner.'

She laughed to herself as she walked away, the layers of her skirt creating a trail of dust behind her with each cheeky giggle.

'What was that all about?' asked Linden.

'I told Eleanor a joke and she thought it was the funniest one she'd ever heard.'

'She doesn't get out much,' explained Linden.

Max smiled. Linden was good.

'Let's go and eat. We've got an appointment to keep.'

After dinner, Max and Linden excused themselves and walked towards the paddock. It had been arranged that they'd stay at Linden's house for the night and would make their way back the next day, which gave them lots of time for their meeting. Except that when Ben and Eleanor said goodbye, there was something about the way they said it that felt a little more important than usual. Like they knew something. Max thought she was probably being paranoid and they headed off into the dusk.

'Have you done your hair?' Wild strands of Linden's hair were ballooning into the air like towers on miniature jumping castles. 'We *are* about to go to a very important meeting after all.'

'I even put on some of Dad's hair grease.' But the look on Max's face told him it didn't do much good. 'Mum used to say I've got hair with a lot of personality, what can I do? And besides, you can't keep a good strand down.'

He giggled at his own joke. Max tried to ignore the joke and his hair and walked on.

'Where should we wait?' asked Linden.

'Not sure. I guess we should just go somewhere in the middle,' Max answered, starting to feel nervous about the whole thing and hoping she didn't mess up.

They walked a little further as Linden started to guess how they might get to London.

'Maybe they're going to send some little green men in a super-advanced spaceship to take us away?' he suggested.

Max's nerves got worse. She pictured herself walking into Spy Force's plush secret headquarters and, at the earliest possible chance, falling down in front of everyone.

'Or maybe they're going to use a high-density matter scrambler to dismantle the atoms from our bodies, fling them through space at the speed of light and reassemble them in London.'

Linden was getting more excited at the possibility of what might happen. Max, on the other hand, wasn't. Her head jammed with images of disaster, like the one where she was being introduced to the head of Spy Force and accidentally knocked hot coffee from the table all over him. Or the one where she attempted to clip on her fingerprint-sensitive identity pass and accidentally flicked it across the room, breaking the invisible laser beam that set off a high security alert. She could see the chaos as she tried to apologize among the running feet and barked orders of Spy Force's top security agents.

Linden, oblivious of her panic, talked on.

'Or maybe we'll be sucked into space at a million miles an hour in a giant straw-like transporter tunnel and spat out at Spy Force headquarters.'

Max had had enough of Linden's speculating.

'Or maybe you should just keep quiet so they don't hear how much you talk and decide not to meet us at all.'

Linden stopped abruptly as if an enormous cement wall had suddenly dropped in front of him. He thought it was fun trying to work out what might happen.

Max walked on until she found a place that looked like all the others and decided to stop.

'I think here is a good spot,' she announced, and sat down and checked through her pack to see if she had everything.

Linden followed her wondering what it was about Max that made her so hard to understand. One minute she was fine, the next she wasn't. He sat down beside her, deciding it was best not to think too much about it.

'What's that?'

Max flinched as a muffled ringing sound was heard from somewhere close by.

'I brought the CTR just in case we need it,' Linden explained as he rummaged through his pocket.

'Great,' said Max, not sounding at all as if she thought it was great.

'Hello?' Linden asked, followed by a quick and surprised, 'Ella!' as if it could have been anybody else. 'How are you?'

The CTR was a Communication Tracking and Recording device that Ella had given Linden on their last mission in London. Max knew it could come in handy, but refused to like anything about Ella so she wasn't about to admit it. She sat slightly away from him as he blahed on and on with a lot of *really's* and *no way's* and *that's great's*.

After a few minutes, Max couldn't stand it any more. She snatched the device from Linden's hand, spied a large rock nearby and threw the CTR so hard it fireworked into the sky in a million pieces. She watched as it all happened in slow motion. First the throw, then the flying curve through the air and finally the impact, sending sparks and CTR bits everywhere in an impressive, airlifted shower.

'Thanks for calling. I'll speak to you later.'

Max never snatched away the CTR and Linden finished his conversation oblivious of her imagined outburst.

'That was Ella.'

Max didn't respond but looked towards the darkening horizon.

'She said Blue has this new range of kids' foods that she and her mum are convinced can't be good.'

Max tried not to listen but couldn't help spark up at the mention of Blue's name. 'They reckon if Blue is behind it there has to be something bad about it. Trouble is, the stuff tastes so good that once you've had some you can't get enough. You know, like those hamburger chains that sell you burgers that make you feel queasy afterwards but you keep going back and buying more.'

Max was dying to ask about Blue's foods but refused to act interested.

'Maybe that's why Spy Force want to see us,' Linden persisted.

'Maybe.' Max shrugged, thinking he was probably right.

'Oh, and she said to say hi.'

Max looked down at her watch and really pretended not to hear this one.

'It's almost eight o'clock. I guess we just wait now.'

Linden sighed and put the CTR safely back in his pocket. He didn't understand why Max didn't like Ella, but knew she'd have to come round one day.

They sat in silence for ages. Nothing much happened apart from a few owl hootings and the odd rustling of grass nearby, which Max told herself was the innocent scrambling of lizards and not the sneaky slithering of deadly brown snakes.

There were certain things in the country Max still couldn't get used to.

'What was that?' She jumped up in a panic as something fluttered quickly past her face.

'Moth, most likely,' said Linden calmly, watching her hands swish frantically around her like a human fan on high speed. 'They can get as big as small birds out here. Can't hurt you, though. Any sign?'

Max stopped waving her hands, put them on her hips and looked around, trying to pretend she wasn't spooked.

'Not yet.' She sat down and started to feel calmer. Linden had a way of doing that. When she felt nervous he would say things that made her feel OK again. Max relaxed for the first time in ages. 'Little green men?' she asked.

'OK, so it's more likely we'll be collected in the transporter tunnel,' Linden said authoritatively.

They both smiled and sat there again, waiting for what would happen next.

'We should say our pact,' Linden suggested.

Max cringed. She was hoping to get through this part of their mission without having to go through any soppy stuff. 'I think it's better we stay quiet in case we miss anything.'

'You know I'm not going until we do it. I think it's important.'

Why did Linden do this? thought Max. Mostly he was pretty easygoing but there were times he had this look on his face that told her he was going to get what he wanted.

'OK.' She sighed. 'How does it go again?'

Linden held out his hands and closed his eyes.

'Oh, that's right.' Max wilted. 'The holding hands bit. My favourite part.'

'If Max should come to harm or get lost or be in danger in any way, I, Linden M. Franklin, will do everything I can to help her and bring her to safety.'

Max squinted through half-closed eyes for something that would interrupt this overly sentimental moment. Nothing happened so she tried to remember the pact.

'If Linden should get into trouble . . .'

'. . . come to harm,' he corrected.

'. . . come to harm,' Max struggled to remember, 'or get lost or be in danger in any way, I, Max Remy, will . . . um . . . will . . . um . . . help him out . . .'

'. . . do everything I can . . .'

'. . . do everything I can to help him and bring him to safety.'

'Now that wasn't too hard, was it?' Linden smiled and let go of Max's hands.

Pleased now that it was over, Max looked at her watch again for what felt like the hundredth time.

'It's almost nine o'clock,' she said frowning.

'Maybe they've forgotten about us.'

'I don't think that's possible. You're a pretty hard person to forget.'

'Is that right?' Max replied. She was about to let fly with something witty when they felt the ground beneath them start to vibrate.

'Can you feel that?' she asked.

'Either I've developed a bad twitch or we're about to find out what the email from Spy Force meant.' Linden put his hands on the ground and looked around.

The vibrating became more intense, as if a gigantic steamroller was coming towards them.

'What do you think it is?' Max strained her eyes to see through the dark.

'Not sure, but it's something big.'

'What should we do?'

'I don't think we've got much choice but sit here and shake.'

Just as Linden finished saying this, a mighty thump shook the ground. They closed their eyes as a powerful gust of wind swept around them, encircling them in dust and almost lifting them into the air.

'Aaahhh!' Max and Linden held on to each other.

After a few minutes, the vibrations decreased and the wind dropped down as if someone had switched off a huge propeller.

And then, nothing.

Max and Linden looked around them. Their hair was plastered upwards and their teeth were gleaming white against their dirt-covered skin. Apart from that, everything seemed as it was before until they realized one horrible thing.

They had their arms around each other.

'Errrrrrrr!' they screamed and pulled away, quickly wiping their hands against their clothes to brush away the hug as much as the dirt that had caked itself to them.

'What happened?' Linden wiped his eyes so that he left two dirtless stripes as if he was wearing a bank robber's mask.

'I can't see anything.' Then Max remembered. 'Maybe it was that windstorm Larry predicted.'

'He's got a good nose for weather that pig.' Linden smiled proudly.

Max was getting annoyed. 'Where are they? They said they'd be here,' she said huffily. 'We've been waiting over an hour and—'

Before she could say any more, a mechanical hum began to whirr in front of them from the inky night blackness. Max and Linden squinted hard to see what it was and couldn't keep their mouths from falling open when they saw what happened next. A large metal hatch was being slowly lowered to the ground. Nothing else. Just a large metal hatch.

'Maybe it's the alien theory after all.' Linden gasped, not sure he was ready to have his first extra-terrestrial encounter.

A silhouetted figure stepped carefully forward as if between two walls of light, leaving behind a solid glow that poured out of the hatch in a blinding flood.

Max and Linden sat wide-eyed and frozen like two rabbits caught in headlights as the mysterious figure loomed before them.

'I guess it's too late to make a run for it?' joked Linden, hoping to ease the tension.

It didn't. Before Max could answer, the figure removed a long, solid object from its pocket, stepped down from the hatch and headed straight towards them. They nervously imagined what the object could be. A gun. A knife. A Spectral Atom Pulverizer (this was Linden's thought, not Max's).

Whatever it was, Max and Linden watched the figure getting closer and closer, knowing they could be facing the final, terrible moments of their lives.

CHAPTER 10
A WILD RIDE

'Max?'

'Yeah.'

'If you survive and I don't, could you make sure my goldfish Henry gets fed?'

'You'll survive,' said Max, trying to work out what their next move should be.

'And could you let my dad know he's the best?'

'Linden, nothing is going to happen to you,' she shot back, his questions pestering her like a small yapping dog.

The figure got closer. The long object in his hand dangled like a slow pendulum with each step, as if it was counting down the last minutes of their lives.

'I've also got a subscription to *Spy Monthly* that will need to be cancelled. And I have—'

Max had had enough. 'Linden, if you keep going, the only person you'll have to be worried about is me.'

He took her point and was quiet.

The silhouette stopped a few metres before them. The light from the hatch formed an angelic halo all around him. Max and Linden huddled together, desperately thinking what to do. Then slowly, menacingly, the figure raised the long, slender object so that it was pointing straight at them.

'What are we going to do?' Max whispered as her brief life flashed before her eyes like a video clip on fast forward.

Then something happened to answer her. The figure moved the object even closer towards them and muttered one, short word.

'Mint?'

Both of them frowned.

'Did you say "mint"?' asked Linden, double checking that he'd heard right.

'Yep. They're the chewy kind. My favourite,' said the figure.

There seemed nothing much else to do but accept.

'Thanks,' said Linden, relieved to be alive as the figure dropped mints into their hands.

'No matter how many times I do it I can never quite get used to the effect this whole travel thing has on me. Leaves me sort of light-headed. Takes me a good few minutes to get my mouth working again. I guess it has something to do with the speed. Not quite as fast as light yet but they're working on that. Even though some scientists think it's impossible, what with the infinite amount of energy needed to push an object through space at that speed. But I guess people thought we'd never walk on the moon until Armstrong put on a spacesuit one day and up and did it.'

The strange man, who was getting stranger by the second, paused long enough to realize he hadn't told them his name.

'Oh! How rude of me. I haven't introduced myself. I'm Steinberger. R. L. Steinberger. Administration Manager of Spy Force. And you are Max Remy and Linden Franklin. Pleased to meet you both.'

He held out his hand.

It was hard to believe the person who had sent Max such brief and formal emails could turn out to be this man with a mouth like a running tap.

Max and Linden held out their hands but before they could make contact, they heard a beeping sound.

'Oh.' Steinberger looked down at a pager, disappointed to have to end the conversation so quickly. 'Looks like the jet's ready for take-off.'

This was too much.

'The jet? What jet?' Max wondered if perhaps this Steinberger person had lost a few rungs on the ladder when it came to the brain department.

'Oh, I haven't mentioned that yet?' He

laughed. 'Silly me. The superfast, deluxe TXR-5 Invisible Jet that's behind us.'

He flung his arms out as if he was a game show host introducing the grand prize.

'An invisible jet?' asked Linden, looking at nothing but a well-lit hatch.

'Yep. Only one of its kind. Except for the TXJ-7, but we don't like to mention that one because it tends to get Frond upset over the issue of fuel consumption. A little guzzler it was, but we soon fixed that so that now this one runs on a purely plant-based formula that creates no pollution whatsoever. In fact—'

Beep, beep, beep, beep!

Steinberger was again interrupted by the pager.

'It's Sleek. He tends to get upset if we don't keep to schedule and after that unfortunate incident with the weather balloon on the way here, we're already a bit behind. Shall we?' He took a notepad out of his pocket and moved towards the hatch.

Max and Linden stood up and cautiously followed him, wondering if taking this strange man's lead was a very wise thing to do, while a million questions crash-landed in their heads. Who was Frond? What was a 'Sleek'? How is it possible to have an invisible jet? And why did this guy talk so much?

As they approached the hatch, Steinberger stood aside and invited them in.

'Welcome to your superfast ride to London in the world's most luxurious, high-tech mode of transport to ever—'

'Steinberger! We've got a schedule to try and keep,' said an agitated voice from nowhere.

'Right you are, Sleek,' he replied, and ushered them quickly in.

The entrance to the hatch was blocked by two glowing balloon-like walls. Max and Linden looked at each other and shrugged before pushing their way in. Once inside, they found themselves in a small, white, rubber room. They could hear ticking.

'What's going on?' But just as Linden asked this, an alarm bell sounded and a blast of vacuum-like air lifted them off their feet. It sucked at their hair and clothes, whisking them round in circles and bouncing them off the soft walls.

'Aaahhh!' they screamed.

Max felt dizzy and hoped she wasn't getting her brain sucked out.

They were bounced and twirled and jostled in a fierce vacuum frenzy. Then suddenly the suction stopped and they were spat out of the balloon chamber and left toppling about, trying to find their balance.

Max was starting to get annoyed at how they were being treated but before she let Steinberger have it, she took a good look around at where they'd landed.

They really were inside a jet! And it was enormous. There were fluffy, lined seats and carpets, digital screens that folded out from the armrests, giant beanbags, a glass cabinet filled with every drink imaginable, a spa and even a small pool.

Steinberger looked very apologetic.

'I'm sorry about that. I should have warned you about our Automatic People Sanitizer. When a passenger steps into the jet, the sanitizer detects if there is any material on them that might interfere with the smooth running of the machine—dirt and dust, for example—and it turns itself on if it thinks a good clean is needed. Very efficient for getting rid of any pesky bugs or cleaning up after a particularly messy mission, and I can tell you there have been plenty of—'

'This is your captain speaking,' interrupted a stern message on the intercom. 'Would all cabin crew and passengers get ready for take-off. Make sure your tray tables are stowed correctly and your seatbelts are firmly fastened. Take-off will be in approximately thirty seconds.'

Max and Linden were shown to their fluffy seats by a tall, unsmiling, uniformed man who asked if they were comfortable and without waiting for a reply, went to the back of the jet and strapped himself into a seat.

'We're a little pushed for time.' Steinberger explained the apparent rudeness as he took a seat opposite them.

The jet silently rose a few metres into the air, rotated so that it faced the opposite direction and took off into the night at a powerful speed. Max and Linden were pressed into their seats by the force of the take-off and could only just manage to look out of the windows as the jet flew high above the ground.

'Well, here we are,' Steinberger announced, smoothing down his notepad that had been mangled in the sanitizer. 'If there are any questions you'd like to ask about the plane or Spy Force, fire away. I'm here to be your personal guide. In fact, you might even want to know a little about me. I'd be flattered to help you out there, it's a fascinating—'

'What are these things for?' Linden interrupted, fearing another long-winded yabberfest and pointing to the digital screens that materialized in front of them.

'Those are some of technology's finest,' Steinberger declared proudly. 'They are Digital Think Amajigs with Triple Megapixel Microdrive and integrated audio with Hyper Blaster Sound compatibility. You can do all sorts of things with these, including ordering food, which you might like to do now. Just tell the computer what you'd like and Roger, our friendly cabin assistant, will bring it to you.'

Max and Linden typed in their requests on the touch screens. Chocolate ice cream with caramel sauce and hundreds and thousands for Linden and a banana smoothie with yoghurt and honey for Max.

'Your request will be here directly,' announced the computers.

'I knew there was something missing in my home.' Linden pictured himself with a brand new computer in his room. Then he remembered there was something else he wanted to know as well. 'How can you make a jet invisible?'

'Ah, terrific question,' beamed Steinberger, leaning forward and almost falling off his seat. 'A few years ago Irene was in the middle of one of her experiments, mixing all sorts of concoctions together, when she added a special liquid that was to be the finishing touch and all of a sudden what she was working on just disappeared. At first she thought it was her eyes playing tricks on her—she's not as young as she used to be, as she'll probably tell you when you meet her—but when she realized she could see everything else perfectly, she knew she had hit upon something remarkable. After a few more adjustments in the lab, Spy Force perfected and patented it. All rights belong to us and, I'm sure I don't have to tell you, the formula is top secret.'

Max and Linden were impressed.

'Is Irene one of your scientists?' asked Max.

'No. She works in the kitchen. Does a mean sponge cake.'

Steinberger's eyes went droopy just thinking about it.

The jet sped silently and smoothly through the night sky like a stingray gliding through the ocean.

'What can you tell us about the meeting?' asked Max, eager to know more about what they could expect.

'Ah, that is the one thing I've been asked to keep quiet about until your arrival in London. I *can* say it's for something very important, but until we get to Spy Force, I'm afraid I can't say any more.'

Steinberger turned his fingers in front of his mouth as if he was locking his lips shut.

'What can you tell us about Spy Force?' Max probed further.

'There's lots to tell there.' Steinberger folded his hands in front of him and sat back in his pink fluffy chair. 'It was created in the early 1960s by Harrison Junior, the father of the current Chief of Spy Force who is also called Harrison. Harrison Junior and his father, Harrison Senior, were top chefs at one of the finest restaurants in London, which was called Harrison's, naturally enough. Anyway, one day, the two decided they needed a career change and, putting their heads together, came up with an international agency for fighting crime everywhere, which they called Spy Force, or the Security Protection Unit For Ousting Rotten Crime Everywhere. That spells Spy Force when you work it out.'

Max and Linden ran it through their heads.

'No it doesn't. It spells Spu-force,' Linden advised quietly.

Steinberger shifted uneasily in his chair.

'Well, the . . . err . . . Marketing Department thought having an international spy agency called Spu-force might be bad for business. You know.

Sounds like spew-force. People might joke and call it Vomit Force. So they decided just to fudge it a little.'

Just then, the steward arrived with their orders. Linden's tastebuds turned over themselves as he tucked into the best, creamiest ice cream he'd ever had in his life.

'Homemade. You can't take the chef out of the chief,' Steinberger mused dreamily.

'How long does the jet take to get to London?' queried Max, slowly sipping her smoothie to savour each taste-tickling mouthful.

Steinberger looked at his watch.

'Should be there . . . about . . . now,' he declared.

In a flash, the steward reappeared, grabbed their plates and glasses mid slurp and disappeared towards the back of the jet.

'This is your captain speaking,' said the voice on the intercom.

'He loves saying that,' whispered Steinberger excitedly, putting his notepad in his pocket.

'We will shortly be arriving in London. Remember what I said about the tray tables and seatbelts and get ready for a smooth landing.'

Max and Linden tightened their belts and looked out at the city of London below. The jet's windows were jammed with the bumpy spread of old buildings, towers, palaces, churches, and cathedrals. Roads wound through like ant trails swarming with cars, trucks, motorbikes, pedestrians, and lurching black cabs, while the River Thames snaked its way under bridges that crisscrossed over it like antique matchsticks.

Max looked down at the city and took a deep gulp of air as she tried to take in what was about to happen. In just a little while, she and Linden would be face to face with the world's top spies.

CHAPTER 11
VARTS, VIBRATRONS, AND SPY FORCE!

It was the largest gathering of secret agents the world had never known. A top secret affair with security at its highest level. And with good reason. It wasn't every day the world's top spies assembled together under the same roof. In fact, it was only once a year, during the annual Spy Awards Night, a prestigious event that recognized the talents, skills, and contributions of spies from all over the world. Spy Force often topped the bill for the night, taking home many of the awards, including the coveted and highly respected Spy Agency of the Year award.

The rest of the world never knew about these events. If they ever did know, the existence of these intelligence networks would be in grave jeopardy, many would even cease to exist as soon as news got out.

The location of the ceremony was announced only the day before and even then, just the chiefs of the organizations were informed. As technology could sometimes be tampered with, they were told by specially trained mynah birds, the perfect messengers, as they worked in pairs and always delivered. A secret rendezvous point would be arranged where the chiefs and mynah birds would meet and the message would be tweeted out in a few short cheeps before the birds would fly innocently away. Very discreet, very professional and very top secret.

This year was a highly unusual type of award night. This year a new spy had been recruited by Spy Force who was causing a stir throughout the ranks of spies everywhere. She was changing the face of intelligence work with feats of daring and skill the spy world had never seen before.

This spy's name was Max Remy.

But many knew her as Max Remy, Superspy.

As clusters of intelligence agents hushed over dimly lit tables, spoke in secret whispers and quietly clapped each award winner, most were anxiously awaiting the announcement of who would be Spy of the Year.

As the head of the Academy of World Spies approached the podium, the room fell silent. In just a few moments, she would announce the Spy of the Year. An honour bestowed on the bravest, most intelligent spy who had, in all their work, made the world a safer, better place.

'And the winner is,' the head of the academy began as she prised open the specially sealed gold envelope, 'Max Remy!'

Max's hands sprang to her mouth in shock. She was not only brave and intelligent, she was also a very humble person, not used to such attention. Alex Crane leant over from her seat and gave Max a hug.

'You deserve this,' she whispered proudly to her one-time apprentice.

Max stood up, her legs becoming jelly-like beneath her, and made her way to the podium. She accepted the statue of the Golden Spy Binoculars, held it against her chest and began her speech.

'I would like to thank the academy for this very generous and unexpected award. Ever since I was a little girl, I've wanted to be a spy and do all I can to make this world safer for people everywhere. I dedicate this award to spies all over the world who risk their lives every day for the same cause. I would like to thank Spy Force for believing in me, and Alex Crane, for being my mentor, my guide, and my inspiration.'

The room exploded with the emotional clapping of agents as they applauded in admiration the spy they could only ever hope to be. Max looked around the room at the awe-struck faces and gave a small bow. Soon there was a hushed call of 'Max' from the audience. Then another. Then another. Until soon, the whole room echoed with the quiet chanting of 'Max, Max, Max'.

Max held her award high above her head.

The applause continued on . . .

'Max!' cried Linden.

Max snapped out of her daydream.

'Are you coming or not?' Linden was standing at the exit of the jet wondering when Max was going to get off.

She looked around her. They'd landed. She wasn't sure where, but she quickly undid her seatbelt to find out.

'Sure,' she said, rushing to the hatch and feeling as if she'd slept in for an important exam.

'I'm glad to see you've finally decided to join us, Ms Remy,' Linden remarked in a teacherly voice. 'This tardy attitude of yours is going to do you no favours, young lady. And another thing—'

'Linden,' Max warned. 'It's not too late to hand your body over for medical research, you know.'

Linden's mouth collapsed open in an attempt at looking offended.

'And what would you do for entertainment then?'

'I'd watch grass grow or paint dry, something as funny as you.'

'It's time to go,' interrupted Steinberger, poking his head into the jet.

Max and Linden stepped out on to a boardwalk-style metal deck. They were inside a cavernous, shiny aircraft hangar. Everything was quiet except for a low motorized hum and the echoing noises made by their footsteps. Dim lights hung from the towering roof above them like stars in a miniature universe, just barely revealing a pristine, orderly metal cavern filled with all kinds of contraptions and vehicles. There were all-terrain trucks, submarines, planes, helicopters, one-seater mini-choppers, hovercrafts, gliders, and a stretch of other machines they'd never seen before.

A man dressed in overalls lay on his back on the floor below the metal deck.

'What's he doing?' asked Linden, wondering why the man's hands were clutching tools and working away in thin air.

'He's giving the jet a service now that we've returned,' Steinberger explained. 'He's also the pilot. Let me introduce you.'

He moved closer to the edge of the deck.

'Sleek, these are our esteemed passengers, Linden Franklin and Max Remy.'

The overalled man kept working on the invisible jet and gasped a mysterious reply that sounded something like, 'eeooorr ooo ahhh inmyanr'.

'Sleek gets very focused when he's busy,' Steinberger informed them in a hushed voice. 'This is our Vehicular All-Response Tower, or VART for short, and Sleek is crucial to this part of Spy Force. Not only does he fly and know everything there is to know about all these aeronautical thinga-majiggies, he's our extreme member of the team. No mountain is too high, no high-speed chase too fast and no vat of worms too icky for him. You name anything extreme that has happened in Spy Force and Sleek has been there.'

Just then, a black cat jumped from behind them down to the ground where Sleek lay working. In a single reflex action, Sleek moved his head sideways and noticed the cat staring straight at him.

'Aaaahh!' he yelled and performed a manoeuvre that astounded Max and Linden so much, their eyes only just managed to stay in their sockets. He leapt from the floor, completed a double backflip, and landed on the deck, which was a whole three metres above him, in one swift move. He stood next to Max, open-mouthed and goggle-eyed as if someone had stretched his head longways and forgotten to put it back to normal. The black cat caught her eye and then walked away with what Max thought were arrogant and calculated steps. A steely tremor ran through her as she was caught by the cat's gaze.

Sleek, meanwhile, noticing the others were staring at him, closed his mouth, ungoggled his eyes and tried to pretend everything was fine.

'I think that's all for today,' he said wiping his hands on an oilcloth he pulled from his pocket. 'Jet's in good condition. Enjoy your visit.' And with that he walked off trying hard to look relaxed, but all he managed to do was look terribly awkward.

'One of the bravest men I know.' Steinberger looked after him admiringly. 'The cat belongs to Dretch, our maintenance operator. Her name's Delilah and she's taken quite a liking to Sleek, but he's not too good with black cats or other superstitious things. Apart from that, though, he's one of our best. Now,' he clapped his hands together, 'let's go and meet everyone else.'

He walked off with clipped, excited steps, mumbling to himself and consulting his notepad.

Max felt uneasy.

'There's something about that cat I don't like,' she whispered to Linden.

Linden stopped walking. His eyebrows reached new heights of incredulity as they arched up his forehead.

'Max, you're a person with a lot of talents but I think it's only fair to tell you an affinity with animals isn't one of them.'

'I'm fine with animals,' she protested.

'Which ones?'

Max was stumped.

'That's not the point. That cat looked at me and gave me a strange feeling.'

'I wouldn't take it personally. Cats are really perceptive and she just needs more time to realize that deep down you really are an animal lover.'

Linden's grin spread over his face before he hurried to catch up with Steinberger. Max turned around and saw Delilah sitting in a corner licking her fur and acting no more suspiciously than any other housecat. Maybe Linden was right, she thought, but she'd keep her eye out if Delilah crossed her path again.

Max was doing her best to take everything in, including the fact that what she thought was a fictitious spy agency was now all around her. She was at Spy Force, the international intelligence agency, bursting at its high-tech seams with spies, missions, intrigue, and top secret secrets to save the world. Important stuff that no part of her regular life had. She heard nothing of what Steinberger was saying to Linden as the three of them walked along the gleaming deck. She looked up at the VART's roof with its twinkling low-level lights and sighed, knowing her life would never be the same again. Would be filled from now on with—

Booof!

Silence. Except for the quiet motorized humming.

'Max, are you all right?'

The room blurred in front of her eyes like a thick, swirling fog.

'Can you hear us, Max? How many fingers am I holding up?'

Max could see little snippets of Linden and Steinberger through a churning, confused mist. Molecules of man and boy floated past her, urging her to understand what they meant.

Then . . .

'Urgh! What is that?'

She sat upright holding her nose.

'A little something they came up with in the lab. Instantly revives you if you've had a temporary collapse,' explained Steinberger, removing a small brown bottle from beneath her nose.

'Or in your case, if you've run into an enormous and pretty unmissable giant metal cylinder.' Linden smiled.

Max rubbed the spot on her forehead that was starting to blush into a deep, red welt. The type of welt that comes up just before a bruise and a big, ugly-looking lump.

'Maybe they should bottle your jokes instead, because they sure smell enough to bring back the dead,' Max shot back.

'She's fine,' diagnosed Linden. 'Only an in-form Max could have a comeback like that.'

'What's in that stuff?' she grizzled, wincing and breathing out hard to get the stinky potion out of her nostrils.

'All natural ingredients.' Steinberger smiled, relieved that his young guest seemed to be in one piece. 'Nature can be just as smelly as chemicals when she wants to be.'

Holding his notepad in front of him,

Steinberger checked over his list.

'And now we must go. There's so little to see and so much time to do it in.' He looked up and frowned. 'Why do I feel like I've just quoted a line from a famous book?'

He rubbed his hand across his chin trying to work it out.

Max stared at him with her head throbbing, wishing he'd get on with it.

'Oh well, not to worry. Let's continue with our expedition, shall we?'

Steinberger pivoted on his overzealous feet and cracked a quick pace along the deck and out of the VART. The sound of his clicking heels echoed around the hangar like a cicada-filled summer day as Linden put on a quick double-step to keep up. If the hangar for the aircraft was this big then the rest of Spy Force must be enormous, he thought, enjoying every minute of their tour.

Max lagged behind, annoyed at finding herself on the ground once again and especially annoyed at the lack of sympathy she'd received over her aching head.

Steinberger and Linden stopped before a darkened exit. Max eventually joined them.

'Before we go any further, you need to step on

to the Vibratron 5000 and have your vibrations recorded.'

'Vibra-what?' asked Max, thinking some of Steinberger's brain cells must have come loose during their high-speed flight.

'The Vibratron 5000. There is one at every possible entry point into Spy Force. All you need to do is step on to these specially sensitized tiles which will read the vibrations of your body.'

'And why would I want to do that?' blurted Max, thinking she was going to be pushed around again just like in the Automatic People Sanitizer.

'It's one way we identify people who enter the agency,' Steinberger continued, not seeming to notice Max's bad mood at all. 'The floors throughout Spy Force are made out of a specially constructed material that is very absorbent, very quiet, and can identify the person walking on them merely by reading their vibrations.'

'That's excellent!' Linden exclaimed. But Max was doubtful as she looked down at the arrangement of dark tiles at her feet.

'Would you like to go first?' Steinberger asked her as if he was granting her some great wish.

Thinking she'd probably regret it, Max stepped carefully on to the tiles. As soon as she did, they lit up in a rich, pulsing red colour like burning hot coals. She became nervous, but when she tried to jump off, her shoes felt as if they were glued to the floor. She was about to scream when a gentle buzz trembled inside her like a million soft drink bubbles making their way up her body.

Then . . . Ping! The red pulsing light faded and the process was finished.

'Now anywhere you go in Spy Force you can be positively identified. Linden?'

Linden jumped on quickly as soon as Max got out of the way, ready to experience the full force of the Vibratron 5000.

The tiles lit up again and Linden's face broke into a wide smile as the bubble effect tingled throughout his body.

'Good, isn't it?' asked Steinberger, remembering his first experience of the device. 'It's never quite the same after the first time. Now, on with the rest of the tour.'

Steinberger turned down a corridor that seemed to go on for ever. Small lights on either side of the floor and ceiling disappeared far away, so that it looked as if they were walking in space. He marched quickly ahead, blathering away and pointing out other special characteristics of the building.

Suddenly a small, bent man appeared in front of Max and Linden stopping them dead in their tracks. His eyes burrowed into them from behind half-closed lids and a long grey fringe that sagged in front of his face like stringy old washing. A ragged scar ran the length of his cheek and down past his grey stubbled chin before it disappeared into the collar of his shirt. His hands were buried in a deep maroon coat that hung limply over two spindly, insect-thin legs and long white socks like chalk sticks that crept up to his buckled knees.

'What are you doing here?' he snarled at them as Delilah appeared from nowhere and jumped into his arms.

Max and Linden felt the temperature around them drop as Steinberger walked on prattling merrily to himself, oblivious of the mysterious stranger's sudden and unexpected appearance.

Max tried to explain.

'We're—'

'I know who you are,' the old man snapped, running his bony fingers along the length of the purring feline. 'I know everything that goes on around here. Just don't think you're anyone important because you've been given some kind of special invitation to this place. Others like you have come before and have never been seen again. So be warned. Stay out of my way and you'll stand a chance of getting out of here in one piece . . . if you get out at all.'

'Ah, Dretch,' Steinberger called from down the corridor, turning to see where Max and Linden were. 'I see you've met our two guests.'

Steinberger clopped gaily towards them as Dretch leant down and whispered an icy caution.

'I've got no intention of playing nursemaid to you two, so don't come looking to me for help when you get into trouble,' he spat, as if he'd had more than his fair share of meanness handed out to him at birth.

By this time Steinberger was standing next to them.

'Let me introduce you properly,' he said. 'My guess is Dretch has been too modest about himself and has neglected to tell you that he is one of the best agents Spy Force has ever known. He now works exclusively on-site as our maintenance expert at the agency and I can tell you, if it wasn't for him, this place would have fallen apart a long time ago.'

Dretch looked away. Whether because it wasn't true or because he had something to hide, Max couldn't tell.

'And of course you already know Delilah. Here, kitty,' cooed Steinberger, but as he tried to pat her she offered a disgruntled hiss and turned her head away. 'Well, ah, we must keep moving. There are a few more things we need to do before we meet Harrison,' he said, ticking something off on his notepad.

Max thought she saw Dretch flinch when he heard the name Harrison, but after what he'd said to them, she thought it also could have been because of his instant dislike of them.

Steinberger walked down the corridor. Before Max and Linden could follow him, Dretch left them with one final word of warning.

'Watch your backs, kiddies. Because if you don't, something bad might happen and it would be a terrible shame to lose our new guests so early on in their visit.'

He stepped aside for them to catch up with Steinberger.

Max's and Linden's heads swam with a mixture of fear and curiosity as they moved past the crooked old man. Who was he and why was he so mean? And what did he mean when he said others had come before and had never been seen again? And what happened to change him from a top agent to a maintenance man?

Max and Linden stuck close to Steinberger, deciding to avoid Dretch as much as they could, but something about what he said echoed in Max's mind like a beacon warning ships of treacherous rocks ahead.

CHAPTER 12
SLIMY TOADSTOOLS AND A WALL OF GOODNESS

'Go on, try it.'

Max and Linden sat in the glare of the Spy Force canteen lights. Black-suited adults moved around them ordering multicoloured muffins, crunching on striped toast, and sipping hot pink coffee. It was morning tea time and the canteen was busy. They sat beside Steinberger and looked at the lumpy green concoction in front of them and tried to think of a way of getting out of having any.

'It looks really lovely,' Max fibbed. 'But I'm still full from the banana smoothie I had on the jet.'

'Yeah,' added Linden, rummaging through his brain for his own excuse. 'That ice cream really filled me up too.'

Steinberger tucked into the cake as if it was made with the best-tasting ingredients in the world.

'I don't know what it is, but I just can't get enough of Irene's sponge cakes. Take my word for it, you won't regret it.' He pushed the bulging, baked mess on the platter closer to both of them. 'Go on. Just try a bit. If that's not the best piece of cake you've ever had, you can stand me on my head and call me Charlie.'

Steinberger was getting stranger and stranger by the minute, and pouring another helping of fluorescent blue, gooey stuff over the slime green muck on his plate only proved it further. Max and Linden didn't want to offend him, especially as they might need his help if they ran into Dretch again. They reached for a spoon and squelched out two minuscule portions.

The spoon made a kind of sucking sound as it made its way out of the gloopy frog-coloured mess. Maybe that's what gave it its colour, mashed frogs, Linden thought as he stared at the Kermit-tinted spoon in front of him. Max looked at hers and held her breath, thinking that at least if she blocked her nose she wouldn't taste very much of it. They took one last look at each other and in a silent countdown to three, closed their eyes and prepared to sample the chunderful paste. As soon as the spoon touched their mouths, however, something wonderful happened. It was as if their tongues were being zapped by the yummiest tastes ever.

'Wow, these spies really know their food,' Linden squished through another mouthful of cake. 'Even if the colour scheme's a little bizarre.'

'What's even more bizarre is a life that's got no colour in it at all,' boomed a voice behind them, velvety and smooth like a rich chocolate sauce.

'Ah, Irene,' said Steinberger, wiping away two splodges of fluorescent blue gunk lighting up the corners of his mouth. 'Max, Linden, and I were just admiring your latest work of art.'

'So these are our two little visitors, eh? Welcome to Spy Force and to my newest creation—the Slimy Toadstool.'

So this was Irene. The inventor of the invisible jet formula. She was a rounded woman wearing almost every colour imaginable so that she looked like a human carousel. She had bright orange hair, red glasses, pink earrings, and a bright dress that raced around her curves like the blurred colours of a Formula One track. Her apron was decorated like a tropical greenhouse and her shoes were made in the shape of green tree-frogs. Irene obviously wasn't asked to do any undercover work.

'Everything our Irene touches is always original and always tasty,' declared Steinberger. 'Why, she used to be one of London's finest chefs before coming here.'

'Yeah, but I got sick of making tasty meals for skinny girls worried about being fat when they should have been more worried about being blown over in the wind,' complained Irene, waving her hands all over the place and just missing a spy carrying a plate of blue sausages balanced on a pillow of red mash. 'And men whose clothes cost more than a small country makes in a year with no interest in anyone's conversations but their own. Oh, the fame was good. Lots of perks and all. Even got invited to afternoon tea with the Queen once. But I'm not as young as I used to be and didn't want to waste any more time with people like that, so I joined Spy Force. Haven't looked back since. Anyway, got to get on. Harrison's got a do with some important people from Brazil later and needs something special whipped up.'

And with that Irene was off along the steaming bain-maries crammed with their unusual creations before swooping through the swinging kitchen doors like a toucan nose-diving for her next meal.

Steinberger finished off his last piece of Toadstool and wiped his mouth.

'Ah,' he sighed. 'That hit the spot. Now we're ready to meet the rest of the team. Come with me.'

Max and Linden hurriedly scraped their plates clean of green-blue cake, not wanting to waste a morsel, but as Max stood up her head thumped into something hard above her, sending plates, cutlery, and a wobbling, orange concoction flying through the air. Now normally everything would have landed all over her, covering her with some kind of muck, so she flung her hands over her head ready to be slimed. But when the crashing stopped and she realized she was fine, she opened her eyes and turned to see what damage had been done.

Crouching on the floor near her was a small man with his hands pressed against his ears. The wobbling orange concoction slithered down his hair and what was once a crisp, white lab-coat.

'Everything's fine, Plomb. Just a simple accident.'

Steinberger was kneeling next to the man, looking into his eyes and talking slowly and weirdly as if he had peanut butter stuck to his teeth and he was trying to get it off.

'These are our two guests I was telling you about. Max and Linden.'

The man looked round but didn't take his hands away from his ears.

'Pleased to meet you,' he said in a voice so soft Max and Linden could hardly hear him. He then gave a small smile before quickly standing, stepping over the broken pile of fallen plates and hurrying out of the place.

'Who was that?' asked Linden.

'That was Professor Plomb, our bomb expert.' Steinberger stood up and wiped some orange goop from his shoulder.

'Why did he look so scared?' asked Max, feeling bad because she'd made him run off so suddenly.

'He doesn't like loud noises.'

'Isn't that a bit of a disadvantage for a bomb expert?' Linden frowned.

'It actually works out quite well,' Steinberger pointed out as he made his way towards the canteen exit. 'His father was a bomb expert and his father before him. Plomb had always wanted to be a world class surfer until he realized he had an extreme case of hydrophobia, which left him with an unfortunate inability to go in the water. No good for a world champion surfer, of course, so he said goodbye to his watery ambitions and followed his father's footsteps making bombs. But he did it making his own special mark. All the bombs he makes are silent.'

'Silent bombs?' Max and Linden asked together.

'Yep. He's brilliant at them. Great for enabling Spy Force to infiltrate places without being heard. He makes all kinds too: stink bombs, tear bombs, coloured fart-gas bombs. He normally doesn't come out of his foam-walled lab but it looks like Irene has her orange and pumpkin mousse on today. He can never say no to that.'

Black-suited agents slid past them in the corridor like silent shadows, speaking in quiet mutterings into small palm-sized gadgets, whispering to each other in darkened corners or quietly hurrying by as if they were on their way to an important mission.

Steinberger pulled out his notepad and, looking down his list, gradually came to a slow stop.

'Ah,' he said with a withering look. 'Frond is next.'

His pen slowly circled the name as his expression became all glazed and dreamy-eyed.

Max and Linden gave each other a quick look. Max had seen this kind of behaviour before. She sighed and screwed up her face into an annoyed grimace.

'Um, Mr Steinberger?' she said, trying to snap him out of it so they could get on with the tour.

Steinberger didn't budge. He was now drawing flowers and hearts around Frond's name and humming some kind of off-key love tune.

'Mr Steinberger?' she said a little louder.

Still nothing.

Max pursed her lips. She'd had enough of this schmaltzy drivel.

'Quick! Fire!' she yelled as loudly as she could.

'Where? What? Who?' stammered Steinberger as he spun around and tried to work out what the emergency was.

Agents near them stopped in their tracks. They stared at the two young strangers and rested their steady fingers against their jackets ready to reach for the secret weapons concealed inside.

Steinberger stopped spinning and seeing everything was fine realized he'd possibly been a little preoccupied.

'Sorry about that.' He blushed. 'All seems under control now, everyone,' he said to the agents who lowered their hands and cautiously continued on their way.

Linden made a bad attempt at hiding a smile as Steinberger pushed his hair back into place and tried to look a little more normal.

'Let's get on with it, shall we?' He was doing his best to sound professional. 'Otherwise we'll be late for our meeting with the boss himself.'

Harrison! Max and Linden's faces wiped clear of grimaces and smiles as they followed Steinberger down the hall and remembered their meeting. What would the head of a major spy organization be like? And what did he want with them when he had the responsibility of the whole world to look after? Whatever the answer, if he flew them halfway across the world, it must be important.

At the end of the corridor they stopped and faced what Max and Linden quickly worked out was the end of the corridor.

No doors. No windows. Nothing.

With her hands firmly placed on her hips, Max swung around to face Steinberger.

'And now?' she asked in a voice that couldn't be described as her most polite.

'Now for the best part.' Steinberger was unable to contain his excitement and missed the Max attitude altogether. 'This is called the Wall of Goodness. There isn't another wall like it in the entire world,' he said importantly.

'The Wall of Goodness? What happens here?' Linden was drawn into Steinberger's enthusiasm and was keen to have another Vibratron 5000 experience.

'This is the entrance to the part of Spy Force that is restricted access and requires a further level of identification. As you will know, the location and layout of Spy Force is a heavily guarded secret from most of the outside world. Other areas of our agency such as the canteen, the sleeping quarters, and the Finance Department, are low-security areas, but where we are about to enter is the inner sanctum of the Force,' he said grandly, as if he was in the middle of an important scene from *Star Wars*.

'What about the Vibratron 5000? Isn't that enough to identify who we are?' Max was getting a little impatient and wasn't sure all this drama was necessary.

'To a certain extent, yes,' Steinberger's *Star Wars* voice continued. 'But the Wall of Goodness acts as an advanced form of the old-fashioned lie detector. It has been made with a super-malleable substance that has been programmed to read bodily reactions to establish a person's current state of goodness. Only if it recognizes you as a good person will it permit you entry.'

'Has it ever recognized anyone as being bad?' Linden was intrigued.

Steinberger's face fell into a hurt scowl as though he was remembering something painful.

'Only once.'

'Who was it?' Linden breathed, hanging on every word of the story.

'An agent who was expelled from the Force in "unhappy" circumstances.'

'A Spy Force agent?' gasped Linden.

'Yes. He'd stolen someone's vibrations, got past the Vibratron and was headed for the nerve centre of the Force when the Wall of Goodness raised the alarm and one of the most dangerous infiltrations of Spy Force was narrowly averted.'

Linden was stupefied. This was better than any spy story he'd ever read.

A few seconds of silence passed as Max stared at the two star-struck goons she was standing with.

'I really hate to break up this beautiful moment but do you think we could get on with it before I reach my next birthday?'

'You're right.' Steinberger collected himself and looked at his watch. 'Time is running a bit thin. This next step we can all do together to save time. Just stare directly at the Wall of Goodness and stand as still as you can. You will notice it start to move like jelly. That's the wall's atoms reconfiguring at the approach of a human being and going into identification mode. It will then reach out and envelop you. Nothing more spectacular than *Terminator* I'm afraid, but it's still pretty good when you see it up close. After a few moments it will take a reading of your vital signs and your level of goodness before totally surrounding you and absorbing you into the heart of Spy Force.'

Great, thought Max. Why does everything in this place have to be so complicated?

Max, Linden, and Steinberger stared at the wall in front of them. After a few seconds, everything happened just as they were told, except that when the wall oozed out and wrapped itself around them, it felt like warm, sticky custard. It squelched all over them and within a few seconds, Steinberger was sucked into the squishy structure in one quick slurp.

Linden's eyes widened as if they'd suddenly doubled in size.

'Wow! Did you see that?' he gasped, finding it hard to speak while the wall kneaded him like a ball of human dough.

'Despite the fact that I'm being mauled by a half-crazed wall, I can still see, you know,' Max retorted.

And then, just as the words were out of her mouth, Linden also disappeared in a guzzling splurt.

As the gooey body search continued, Max was definitely running out of the tiny scrap of patience she had left.

'Look, Wall. Let me save you the trouble. I'm good, OK? So can I just go in now?'

The Wall of Goodness seemed to be having

trouble deciding whether to let Max pass. It made choking, gurgling noises and jostled her around even more so that the massage became more like the spin cycle of a washing machine.

Max started to worry that she wasn't going to get through.

'Come ... on ... Wall. Pl ... ease?' she wobbled.

After one final heaving lurch, the wall enveloped her and she was gone. Then it reformed its atoms, leaving nothing more than a solid stone structure that looked impenetrable.

CHAPTER 13
SLOPPP!

'Whaaa!' exclaimed Max as she was thrust head first out of the other side of the Wall of Goodness into a gaping tangle of lush fern leaves.

'Congratulations!' Steinberger exclaimed to her awkwardly positioned backside sticking out of the fern. 'You made it. It's one of the toughest tests within Spy Force. You don't have to be truly evil to be denied entry. The wall will even stop people simply for not having the best interests of the agency at heart. Anyway, how was it?'

Max weeded herself out of the clinging fronds to see Linden's and Steinberger's eyes lit up like fireworks on New Year's Eve.

Only she hadn't been invited to the party.

She was furious.

'How was it?' The way she asked the question, Linden knew her answer wasn't going to be pretty. 'I was just mauled by an arrogant wall that slobbered all over me like elephant's drool and treated me as though I was a leftover piece of modelling clay. And when it'd finally had enough of me it vomited me out face first into this pile of nature clutter.'

Steinberger was disappointed that Max didn't seem to have enjoyed her experience.

'You did unfortunately have a rather bumpy

landing,' he apologized. 'Most people come out of it a little more gently than you did. In fact, that's the first time I've seen anyone have such a rough landing.'

Max plucked greenery from her hair and dropped it to the floor.

'Max has many talents, Mr Steinberger, but gentle landings isn't one of them.' Linden's explanation failed to amuse Max and earned him one of her well-measured glares.

'Thanks, Mr Hilarious. The world has just become a better place now that it can add that joke to its list.'

'I assure you both, that is the last of our identification procedures,' Steinberger promised. 'If you'd like to make your way through the green aisle in front of us we will meet our next important Spy Force agent.'

They were in a multi-level greenhouse where there seemed to be almost every different kind of plant in the world. There were weeping willows, oaks, eucalypts, jacarandas, fruit trees, flowers of all kinds, multicoloured algae, mosses and funguses splattered on rocks and cliffs, cactuses in special desert areas, palms, shrubs, bulbs, grasses, vines and waterlilies.

Max strode ahead at Steinberger's invitation,

careful not to trip over any vines or roots that might be lying in front of her.

'Don't worry about her.' Linden leant into Steinberger. 'She really is a nice person. It just doesn't come as naturally to her as it does to other people.'

Linden smiled a sweeping grin before he and Steinberger made their way down the palm-strewn pathway.

Among all the greenery were white-coated people beavering away like termites building a vast natural city. They were spraying, weeding, pruning, clipping, and watering. They were leaning over boiling pots, crushing roots, extracting oils, and dissecting delicate flower stems. Some were even standing on small white platforms hovering like dragonflies at the tops of the tallest trees.

In the middle of the greenhouse was a woman in a long red coat with her hair dressed up on her head like a overloaded beehive. Small flying bugs could be seen zooming in and out of the swaying mass of hair as if they'd made their home there. She had little round glasses shaped like roses and a chain hanging from them that looked like red and yellow ladybugs.

When Max and Linden reached the woman, Steinberger was nowhere in sight.

'You must be our two guests.' She smiled widely. 'My name is Dr Frond. I'm in charge of the Plantorium here at Spy Force. Have you come here alone?'

Almost in answer to her question, a splash was heard somewhere behind them.

'Steinberger's here, isn't he?' asked Frond. 'Quick, grab that rope will you?'

Linden reached behind him and took a rope that was hanging beneath Frond's workbench. Both he and Max followed her as she wove effortlessly through an intricate maze of plants, her red coat swishing behind her like a red light on a rescue truck.

'The Japanese pond. I thought so,' said Frond as they stood in front of a rich turquoise pool teaming with giant goldfish. She took the rope from Linden and threw it to a waterlogged Steinberger.

'Ah . . . Frond,' he managed soggily, once he'd been hauled out of the water. 'How lovely to . . . ah . . . see you. Um . . . nice day outside.'

He had a lily pad perched on his head, a string of reeds dangling from his left ear, and a flustered and peeved-looking goldfish poking out of his top pocket.

Max and Linden wondered when it was that the normally calm and collected Steinberger had been replaced with the bungling, stammering idiot standing in front of them.

'I think you'll find it's been raining,' Frond replied to Steinberger's misguided weather report. She gently rescued the fish from his pocket and returned it to the pond. It gave what Max thought was a scowl before it flipped around and swam away.

Then something happened that twisted the puzzled expressions on Max's and Linden's faces even further.

Steinberger was lost for words.

He had nothing to say.

They could see the normally free-flowing words getting stuck somewhere between his throat and his blushing red face, which screwed up as if he'd been given some horrible stew he was being forced to eat and was threatening to go down the wrong way.

Linden thought he'd save the situation from becoming even more awkward than it already was.

'What happens in the Plantorium?'

There was an almost audible sigh of relief from everyone, especially Max, who thought if she had to deal with any more of Steinberger's gooey-eyed mush, her brain would come screaming out of her head in protest.

'This is where we make the serums, potions, powders, creams, lotions, pills and ointments that are used in Spy Force operations. We use only natural and plant-based ingredients to make our products, and, of course, we never test them on animals. We here at Spy Force believe that animals are human too and plants can do as much as chemicals when it comes to fighting crime. And let's face it, we're not in the twentieth century any more. If you don't have a green beating heart, you're behind the times.'

'What kinds of products do you make?' queried Max, thinking the Plantorium sounded more like a cosmetic factory than the important arm of a major spy agency.

'Come and I'll show you. Do we have time, Steinberger?'

Silence.

Max and Linden turned around to see him staring at Frond as if someone had sucked the insides out of his head and turned him into a zombie.

'Well?' Max's patience was really being given a good workout. 'Do we have time?'

'Time?'

Glazed eyes. Lilting mouth. Steinberger had it bad.

'Time to see what Dr Frond has to show us?'

'There's always time for Dr Frond,' he spouted, and a great slooshing smile swung on to his cheeks.

Max and Linden continued to stare at him.

Steinberger noticed their staring and looked sharply down at his watch.

'I mean, yes, there is a little time before we have to move on,' he said more seriously.

'Good. Follow me.' Frond swished her red coat around her and eagerly scurried through the trees.

At one corner of the Plantorium, across a thick patch of woolly butt grass (it's actually called that) and through a heavily flowered wall of mimosa bush, was a frosted glass door. Frond opened the mossy hatch on a small algae-covered panel and pressed in a secret code. The door clicked open and allowed them all inside what looked like a giant pharmacy. There were long gleaming white shelves that ran so high it was hard to see where they ended and the ceiling began. They stretched far back into the room like rows of schoolkids during an assembly, and nestled on each one were all sizes and shapes of bottles, tubes, jars, containers, boxes, and tins.

'We call this room the Secret Library for Ointments, Powders, and Plant Products, or SLOPPP for short.'

Frond stepped up to one of the shelves and took down a small glass jar.

'This is invisible cream,' she announced as if she was holding a precious stone. 'With just a thin layer of this cream applied to the skin, a person will become completely invisible. Some scientific theory dates the origin of the cream back to the thinkings of the ancient Egyptians. Why, there is a group of historians who believe invisibility creams had been in use in the ancient world for hundreds of years.'

Max and Linden were impressed.

'Try some,' she offered, but seeing their hesitation, Frond asked Steinberger if he wouldn't mind volunteering.

He managed to take a small step forward but failed miserably in trying to get his mouth to work. He flinched slightly as she took his hand and winced when a low giggle escaped from his lips.

'This is very powerful stuff.' She took a small swipe of the dark green cream and rubbed it into Steinberger's hand. 'It can even be watered down and applied as a rinse if you need to become invisible in a hurry. All you need is the smallest amount, and there you have it.'

It was hard to tell if Steinberger was enjoying the experience or was about to pass out at any second, but what was easy to see, or rather not to see, was his disappearing hand.

The invisibility cream worked!

'And here . . .' gasped Frond as she stretched for a jar almost out of her reach, '. . . is the antidote. Just a little of this and all will return to normal.'

Steinberger quivered as Frond's fingers dipped into the blue-black antidote and were coming straight for him. Little beads of sweat appeared on his forehead like balls of fluff on woollen socks.

'Done.' She finished applying the cream and, like a wave pulling away from the beach, Steinberger's hand reappeared. 'And that's just one of the many products we've developed here at the Plantorium. There are many more but I'm sure you have to be on your way. Harrison doesn't like to be kept waiting.'

'Dr Frond?' asked Max, picking up a bottle of purple liquid near her labelled 'Stun Perfume No 5'. 'What is the story with the labels?'

Pasted across the front of all the items on SLOPPP's shelves were green and gold labels that read 'Plantorium Health Co.', and beneath that was the slogan 'Your health is our business. (A Kind to Trees initiative.)'

'This is one of the commercial sides of the Force,' explained Frond. 'While experimenting with plants we have come up with an array of natural products that have many benefits in everyday life. Wrinkle creams, anti-sag ointments, buttocks-firming lotions. That last one in particular is very popular and is one of Spy Force's biggest sellers. As long as there are sagging bottoms and wrinkled brows, we'll be in business for a long time. It costs a lot of money to run a spy agency and in these days of budget cuts and strict cost-cutting measures, we have to do all we can to stay in business.'

Max was perplexed.

'So it's not good enough just to try and find bad guys and make the world a better place?'

'In the old days. And in the movies, of course. But saving the world is an expensive business and we've got to earn our keep. This is our way of doing just that.'

Beep, beep, beep, beep!

Everyone looked down at Steinberger's pocket, which seemed to be beeping. Everyone except Steinberger, of course, who was busy trying to remember how to breathe and listen to Frond at the same time.

Frond offered a crooked smile. 'That'll be Harrison, I expect.'

At the mention of Harrison, Steinberger's eyes snapped wide open. He reached into his pocket and pulled out his beeper, and after removing some green slime he'd picked up from the pond from the screen, read the message.

'So it is. Well, must be off. It's time to find out the real reason you've been asked to Spy Force.'

Steinberger stood in front of Frond and fretted over how to say goodbye. Suddenly he felt as if every inch of him was on show and that any part of him could embarrass him terribly at any moment. He smiled painfully, then found he had the hiccups. He wiped sweat beads from his brow that were forming so fast they were like ants that'd found a picnic. Finally, he held out his hand, but as he did so Frond lifted hers to wave goodbye. They both laughed awkwardly. Then as Frond lowered her hand Steinberger raised his. They laughed again and lowered both their hands, at which point Steinberger dropped his pencil. As he bent down to pick it up, so did Frond, and their heads collided in a thudding bump.

Max was hoping this was going to be over soon before someone got really hurt.

'Bye,' Steinberger muttered to Frond. Rubbing his brow, he turned sharply and collided with one of the shelves sending Plantorium products cascading domino-style into a pile of all-natural mess.

He apologized to Frond and offered to clean up but Frond refused, saying it would be better if they were off.

Steinberger managed a muffled 'thank you' and turned to leave the SLOPPP followed by Linden and Max.

'Good thing love doesn't make everyone this clumsy or hospitals would be filled with bleeding hearts and love-sick fracture cases,' said Linden.

'Better off without it at all,' complained Max, watching Steinberger trap his finger in the door and wondering how he'd got this far in life. 'For now, though, we've got to worry about what Harrison wants.'

Steinberger's injuries quickly faded from Max's and Linden's minds as their thoughts focused on the next few moments in front of them, which were going to put them directly in the middle of possibly the most important meeting of their lives.

Max steeled herself.

I'm ready, she thought. Spy Force, here I come.

C H A P T E R 1 4

MEETING THE CHIEF AND AN URGENT PHONE CALL

CHAPTER 14

MEETING THE CHIEF AND AN URGENT PHONE CALL

Max and Linden followed a squelching Steinberger into the secret elevator that would plunge them through many levels to Harrison's hidden office buried deep within the subterranean bowels of Spy Force. It was a secret elevator because not many people knew about it in the Force, and therefore the world, but also because it was concealed in a series of terracotta pots as big as phone boxes. Harrison had a real passion for terracotta pots, Steinberger had told them. Not all elevators were pots and not all pots were elevators, though, he went on to say, but a simple tap to the side of a pot to test if it was hollow would soon let you know.

Their terracotta elevator descended through the many secret levels of Spy Force as a back-to-normal Steinberger chatted on as he would have done in pre-Frond times.

When it came to a stop, a female voice melodiously hoped that they'd had an enjoyable journey and wished them a pleasant stay. Ducking their heads, they made their way out of the potplanted conveyor to Harrison's floor, leaving the elevator to slip off behind them. Max flicked a clump of dirt from her shoulder and Linden picked a worm from his jumper and returned it to the soil as they took in their surroundings. They were in a plush and opulent foyer full of dark wooden tables and chairs that stood against the walls, reminding Max of starched waiters waiting for instructions. Lining the walls like a stiff-chinned guard of honour was a line of darkened paintings of suited men and women. They were like old portraits of queens, nobles, and rich merchant's daughters, except that all these people had their faces blurred by a coloured, misty fog, like when someone's on the news they don't want you to see so they smudge their faces. And at the bottom of each painting were gold plaques with a series of numbers and letters.

'These are paintings of the most accomplished agents who have ever been at Spy Force,' Steinberger intoned as if he was leading a tour of Buckingham Palace. 'It's our very own Hall of Fame. Of course we can't show their faces. If any of these agents were to be seen by the wrong eyes, there would be ghastly consequences.'

Max looked at the blurred faces as she followed Steinberger who was recounting tales of brave agents and their missions. She stopped in front of one of the paintings.

'Linden?' she said softly. 'Does this remind you of anybody?'

'Yeah,' he replied seriously. 'But I was in a

snowstorm at the time so I can't be too sure it's them.'

He smiled broadly.

'Look at the ring.' Max ignored his joke as Linden leant in and saw a small ruby ring on the agent's hand.

'Eleanor has a ring like that. So does my mum. My grandma gave identical ones to both of them before she died.'

'Maybe it's your mum,' he quipped, knowing from all he'd heard about Max's mum there was more chance of a herd of elephants performing a ballet.

'Sure, brainboy. If it is Eleanor, why hasn't she ever told us?'

'Maybe because it's someone else.' Linden was finding it hard to picture Eleanor as a spy.

'Maybe.' But Max wasn't convinced. It was a pretty unusual ring.

'Coming?' Steinberger stood a little way ahead and stopped to let them catch up.

Their shoes sank into richly textured Turkish carpets—except Steinberger's which hadn't dried out yet so were still squishing—and took them past glass cabinets crammed with trophies, awards, medals, relics, letters of gratitude, and keys to various cities around the world.

Max came across a prominently positioned cabinet that held a blue silken cloth. Cradled in the cloth was an ornate, well-thumbed, and important-looking book.

'What's in this one?' she asked.

'Aah.' Steinberger placed his hands in front of his face as if he was about to pray. 'That is the original Spy Force manual. Written by Harrison's father and grandfather themselves. It contains the very essence of the Force itself.'

Steinberger lost himself somewhere Max and Linden couldn't see.

'But we must get on. So much time and so little . . . No, wait, I've done that. Let's just go.'

A few steps later, they came to a large wooden door with intricate images of eagles and anteaters carved into it. The eagles made sense, but anteaters? Max was starting to think that sometimes it was better not to ask too many questions.

Steinberger pushed a clump of dampened hair across his forehead and patted down his soggy blue suit in a futile attempt at dewrinkling it. Neither worked to improve his appearance which had been thoroughly restyled by the Japanese pond.

He stared at his watch. The second hand ticked its way towards twelve.

Slowly.

Max and Linden wondered what they were waiting for.

'Usually when people want to enter these things, they just knock,' Max offered.

'Yes, of course.' Steinberger nodded, his eyes fixed firmly on the dawdling second hand. 'We're almost there.'

'Aah,' he aahed as the hand pointed to the twelve. 'It's time.'

He knocked on the door. First two short knocks, then three longer ones, followed by two more quick ones.

'Harrison will see you now. May the Force be with you.'

At that he erupted into a throaty, deep-from-the-belly kind of laugh that jounced his tall, lanky body as if he was being dangled at the end of a piece of elastic. A few seconds later, he calmed down and realized Max and Linden weren't amused.

'It's a bit of a joke here at Spy Force,' he tried to explain but saw that his young companions were unmoved. 'Need to attend to my next task. Good luck,' he offered seriously and squelched off to his terracotta ride.

'I guess we better go in,' said Max as she reached for the golden doorknob.

The door opened easily and quietly onto a darkened room with a high ceiling and long stained-glass windows. They could just barely make out the sunken leather sofas crowded with cushions, the plush, red velvet curtains, and the fireplace with its twisted marble sides like bleached candy canes. Covering every measure of wall space were more portraits—their faces still obscured— certificates, awards, accolades, diplomas, the odd tennis racket and fishing rod, and shelves of books that looked as if they were clinging to each other to stop from tumbling to the floor. Peppered throughout it all like out-of-place garden gnomes were all sizes and shapes of terracotta pots.

Max and Linden squinted through the dim light and spied a heavy oak desk in the centre of the room. They stepped over a collection of smaller-sized pots and came across a sign on the desk that said, 'The boss'.

'Looks like we've got the right place, but where's Harrison?' Linden squinted even harder.

He picked up a copy of Drusilla Knucklehead's

crime thriller *Dr Mullet and the Case of the Missing Toilet*. 'I've read this one. Not one of her best. Wussed out on the ending.'

Max wasn't thinking about toilets, she was wondering where Harrison might be.

'Maybe he was called away at the last minute on some really important business.'

Linden's head filled with other ideas. 'Maybe he's foiling the plans of top criminals even as we speak!'

'Maybe he's—' Max's theory was interrupted by a dull thud and a muffled grunt that came from under the desk. She put a finger against her lips in a shhh-like gesture and then, pressing her hands into the green leather top, she leant over the desk as far as she could.

There was a pause as her puzzled mind tried to catch the words in her head to describe what she was looking at.

'Or maybe he's under the desk with a flowerpot stuck on his head.'

A stifled snort wriggled out of Linden's mouth.

'Right. I can see it now. The head of Spy Force under the desk with his head—'

His sentence was cut short by the appearance of a flowerpot rising from underneath the desk.

Attached to the flowerpot were the shoulders and body of a man.

'Effuff eee or eye aynge affearance uh ah ab im a mit of fubble,' said the flowerpot.

Max's and Linden's faces screwed into puzzled stares. Was this some sort of code they were supposed to know? Were they also supposed to take a pot and put it on their heads as a sort of cone of silence to keep their meetings top secret? The arms beneath the pot pointed at the place where a head should be.

'Oou oo eow ee?'

Linden decoded the muffled plant-speak.

'I think he's asking for our help.'

The pot nodded enthusiastically.

Max and Linden made their way around to the other side of the desk and, grabbing hold of either side, tugged at the terracotta headpiece.

'One . . . two . . . three . . .' and pulled hard.

The force of the tug pulled the pot away and flung Max and Linden across the room into a clumsily stacked rack of golf clubs.

'Aahh.' The man rubbed his head and felt to see if his ears were still attached. 'Not a bad job at all. I was conducting an investigation that went a bit wrong. Well done. I'm Harrison, by the way.

Don't feel you have to stand so far away. Come closer if you like. Never was one for normalities . . . I mean, formalities.'

Max and Linden untangled themselves from the clubs and sat down in two huge leather armchairs in front of Harrison's desk.

As Harrison said nothing.

And still nothing.

Linden was curious. 'Are we waiting for something?'

'Should be here any minute.'

More waiting. Then a knock at the door.

'That'll be them now.' Harrison stood up and clapped his hands together in a grand slap. 'Now that we're all here, we can sing . . . I mean, begin.'

Max and Linden turned in their chairs as someone came through the door behind them. As their eyes ran over the guests, two things happened. Max looked like someone who had just sucked on a lemon and Linden's crooked smile became even more crooked. He may have even blushed a little.

'Ella!'

'Linden! They didn't tell me you were going to be here.'

'Me either.' He blushed even more. 'I mean,

they didn't tell me about you being here. We got here by invisible jet.'

'Invisible jet? I got here by a Sleek Machine. It's a cross between a motorbike and a glider and moves at an oscillation level that makes it and objects that touch it undetectable to the human eye, unless you wear these special goggles.' She pulled a pair of thick-lensed goggles from a jacket pocket. 'So you zoom above the cars and buses, and through red lights and no one can stop you.'

Steinberger stepped behind a transfixed Linden, whose lopsided smile got shoved over by a look of amazement. 'Awesome.'

Max watched it all and was trying to come to terms with the fact that her life had taken a disastrous turn for the worse.

'Have you had the tour?' Linden couldn't talk fast enough.

'Yeah. How about the Vibratron 5000?'

'Felt like a fizz frenzy all over me.'

'That's what I thought!'

'Feels like one giant puke fest,' Max grumbled, unsure how long it'd be before she'd need a lifeboat to save her from all the vomit-gush swirling around her.

'Did you have any Slimy Toadstool?'

'Two helpings,' Ella admitted.

'How'd you go on the Wall of Goodness?'

'Passed through without a hitch. It was like falling through a feather cloud.'

'Of course it was,' Max sneered quietly. 'Bet she'd slide straight through a Tunnel of Terror without a scratch too. And a Halo of Hellfire or a Fountain of Fear.'

'Oh hello, Max. You're here too. How great!'

Finally Miss Perfect has decided I'm not invisible after all, Max thought. 'Hi, Ella.' She didn't put too much effort into trying to muster any enthusiasm.

Steinberger had cleared a pile of terracotta pots from another chair for Ella as Harrison got the meeting under way.

'I thought it was time to bring my three young flies . . . I mean, spies . . . together in London to officially say thank you for thwarting Mr Blue's evil plans to steal the Time and Space Machine.'*

Linden and Ella smiled at each other as Max was thinking of ways to erase the last few minutes of her life and replace them with a different version of events altogether.

*See Max Remy Spy Force, In Search of the Time and Space Machine.

One that didn't involve Ella.

'How is the machine going? Ben and Francis finished it yet?' Harrison asked hopefully.

Max hesitated. 'There's been a small hitch. They're really busy at the moment and it's going to take a little longer than they thought.'

'Never mind. We'll get in contact with him and see what help he needs from us. It will revolutionize the world once it's finished. As long as it stays out of Blue's hands the world will have everything to worry about . . . that is, *nothing* to worry about. We'd also like to offer you something. Steinberger?'

The tall, damp man stepped from behind the chairs and handed them three white scrolls tied with a red ribbon flecked with gold.

'Max, would you like to read yours out cloud . . . I mean, loud?' Harrison invited her.

She unrolled the parchment and read the message. There was a soft click before some official brass band-type music played quietly in the background.

Dear Max Remy,
For your bravery and services to this country and the world, I,
Reginald Bartholomew Harrison, the Chief of Spy Force International

Spy Agency, hereby invite you to be inducted into the Force and to carry out the noble and time-honoured task of fighting crime and other dastardly acts for the protection of humanity and the betterment of the world.

Signed

And following this was a scribbled smudge that looked like a misguided worm had slid through a puddle of ink and left its scrawled mark.

Steinberger reached across and after another click sound, which Max saw was the *stop* button on a tape machine, the music stopped.

'What do you think?' Harrison's eyes lit up like a miniature amusement park and, Max thought, the room seemed to go even dimmer. 'The bravery and skill you exhibited in outsmarting Blue are some of the finest examples of, well, bravery and skill we've seen at the Force and we think you'll make excellent additions to an already highly intelligent network of agents.'

Max turned to look at Linden, but he was smiling at Ella who was looking back at him and blushing like some kind of sunburnt sea slug.

Harrison continued.

'There'll be times when you'll be incognito at

some of the world's richest playgrounds or standing side by side with some of the most sinister human beings to ever get dressed in the mornings. Or times when you'll be facing situations so terrifying, it'll take all your energy just to keep sneezing . . . make that, breathing. Danger will become your closest associate, lurking behind you like a black panther. Quiet and dangerous and ready to strike at any second.'

As Harrison finished, the lights brightened and Max spied Steinberger at the dimmer switch.

She was stupefied. She was sitting in the headquarters of the world's top spy agency, being asked to become a Superspy.

She tried to find a suitable answer to such an important invitation and cursed in her head when all she could come up with was, 'OK.'

Ella and Linden were also in.

'Yeah.'

'Sounds great.'

'Excrement . . . oops, sorry. I mean, excellent. Of course as Spy Force agents, your identity will remain a secret outside these walls and you will tell no one, not even your closest friends and relatives, of your position. Secrecy is the linchpin of our survival. And once you've been inducted as agents of Spy Force, you're members for life. We just need to get you fitted out, give you your spy pack and a few others strings . . . make that *things*, and you'll be on your way.'

Just then a series of ringing sounds was heard.

'That'll be the phone.' Steinberger began looking around the room. 'What was it last time, sir?' he asked Harrison.

'Cricket bat, I think. It was the iron the time before that, which could have been nasty if it'd been left on.'

Max, Linden, and Ella looked on as the two men checked boxes, lifted papers and opened cupboards searching for the phone, and every now and then picking up cups, bells, or rulers before saying 'hello'.

'Here it is.' Harrison picked up a golf ball. He pulled the ball in two halves that were joined by a piece of electrical wire and spoke into it.

'Hello?'

There followed a series of uh-huh's that became more solemn as the call went on.

Steinberger explained the phone situation. 'As a security measure, the Central Response Investigative Safety Patrol or CRISP, which is responsible for the internal security of Spy Force, changes the phone system on a regular basis.'

'I see,' Harrison continued. 'We only have one choice then.'

He clicked the two ends of the ball together and looked seriously at his three new agents.

'Team, you're about to go on your first mission.'

Mission! Max sat up ready to accept her orders.

'As you know, when you courageously uncovered the criminal activities of Blue, he resigned from the Department of Science and New Technologies and went very quiet for a while. Now, if there's one thing we've learnt about Blue over the years, it's that when he goes quiet, you can bet your right shoe he's up to nothing . . . I mean, something.'

Harrison came back to the desk and sat importantly in his chair.

'He seemed to have stopped his evil ways and adopted a new public face as the manufacturer of a range of food for kids. He's marketed his foods with much success. Like the Alien Snot Jelly range, which is the number one jelly in the country. Everything looks innocent enough, but Spy Force has uncovered information which suggests Blue has invented a concoction that when eaten, controls minds. Now that his foods are so popular he is going to include the ingredient in his recipes and begin his domination of the minds of children all over the world. We must slop him! I mean, stop him. And who better than the three of you to do it. You've seen first-hand how Blue's mind works and as kids you will be the perfect undercover agents for this mission. Of course, you'll need to be in disguise. As Blue has seen your faces, he will recognize you instantly if he sees you as you are.'

'We'll have aliases.' Linden pictured himself smartly dressed and walking with the swagger and style of James Bond. Max pictured herself dangling from helicopters, climbing mountains, and parachuting from planes.

'What do we need to do?' asked Ella.

'You will infiltrate Blue's factory, Blue's Foods, and go undercover as . . .' Harrison paused to add dramatic effect, 'BRATTs.'

Max's shoulders fell.

'Excuse me?'

'BRATTs. Bona-fide Registered Authorized Taste Testers.'

'Is that a real job?' Linden became excited.

'It certainly is,' Steinberger leapt in to clarify. 'There are kids who travel all around the world simply to taste new foods. They are accompanied by a parent or guardian who ensures they eat well and study for school as well as complete specified BRATT training courses.'

'Why didn't anyone ever tell me about this before?' Linden puzzled. 'That's it, I'm switching careers. I know I've only been a spy for about five minutes, but I'm not too big a man to say I made the wrong choice.'

Ella giggled as Linden tried for as long as he could to hold the serious pose he'd taken. It didn't last long.

Max stared at both of them wondering what it would take to have their mission treated a little seriously.

Harrison completed his instructions. 'An agent has been placed in the factory as a nude technologist ... um, excuse me, I mean a fully clothed food technologist and will be your point of contact once inside. Sleek will take you as close as he can to the factory where another agent will meet you and declothe the rest of the mission details ... that's, um, disclose the details. For now Steinberger will take you to the lab where Quimby will equip you with all the deer you need ... um, that's *gear* you need, and provide you with your disguises and new aliases.'

He rose and stood at attention. Max, Linden, and Ella followed his lead and only just held back an impulse to salute.

'I believe you're the best team for this job and have no doubt that Mission Blue's Foods will be a swift and successful operation. There's just one thing left to say: all systems are go.' Harrison gave a cheeky smirk. 'Always sounded so good when the *Thunderbirds* said it, so I've borrowed it for Spy Force. Good luck, team!'

With Harrison's words resonating in their ears like the chimes of Big Ben, Max, Linden, and Ella followed Steinberger out of his office to be equipped for their first mission as Spy Force agents.

CHAPTER 15
MISSION: BLUE'S FOODS

After a cramped ride in another terracotta pot, Max, Linden, Ella, and Steinberger arrived at Quimby's lab ready to be equipped for Mission Blue's Foods.

'This is a very special part of the Force. It's the birthplace of many of the inventions that are created here at Spy Force and is run by perhaps one of the most brilliant scientists in this country, maybe the world. Why, there's even . . .'

Steinberger was cut off by the sudden appearance of Dretch stealing out of the lab. 'Ah, Dretch. Good to see you again. Doing a little maintenance work?'

Dretch flinched and spun round, offering the three new spies a prickly stare as if they'd just run over his favourite pet. With one eye peeking out from behind his craggy fringe, they each felt an ice-cold tingle run down their spines that made them want to reach for a long warm coat to stop their blood from freezing over.

'Urrrrr,' urred Dretch as he skulked away, his sagging maroon coat only just managing to cling to his hunched shoulders.

'The Hunchback of Notre Dame stands a good chance of losing his job as long as that guy's around.' Ella shivered, still trying to shake the icy chill.

'Yeah, and if the Hunchback was ever hard up on cash he could earn a few dollars giving Dretch a few beauty tips.' Linden rubbed his shoulders, trying to get some warmth back into them.

Just then, Delilah burst out from behind the lab door and screeched past Max's nose before landing expertly on all four paws and rushing after her owner.

Max wasn't feeling so comical about Dretch's bad attitude or his cat's sudden appearance. She needed to know more.

'What's wrong with him?' she demanded of Steinberger.

'Dretch? Nothing. He's just got a different way of looking at the world from most people.' And then he baulked as if he was trying to work out how to say the next part. 'Sometimes when things go wrong it can leave people quite . . . changed.'

'Did something bad happen to him when he was a spy?'

'Let's just say there's a kind and good man hidden beneath that somewhat rough exterior.'

'Any more rough an exterior and he could double as barbed wire,' mumbled Linden.

Max wasn't going to let Steinberger off so easily. 'But what did he mean when he said others like us have come before and have never been seen again?'

'He said that?'

'Yes. Outside the VART.'

'He has an unusual sense of humour not many of us share. Trust me. He'd never mean that.'

Steinberger turned away, eager to end the conversation, and knocked on the door of the lab.

'Come in,' a small disembodied voice moused from within.

Steinberger led the way inside but Max wasn't satisfied. That was the second time they'd seen Dretch and something told her he may not have been in the lab for Spy Force business alone. And how come he was in there just as they were about to receive their spy packs? He'd made it clear he didn't want them around and maybe he was planning something to get rid of them sooner. She made a note to keep an eye on Dretch and was determined to find out what it was Steinberger wasn't saying about him.

The lab was a shining maze of chrome benches, transistors, resistors, circuit boards, cords, wires, diodes, and electrical gadgets that ticked, flicked, and whirred. There were cupboards with glass doors toppling over with jars, tubes, and bottles. There were fridges, burners, beakers, soldering irons, clamps, safety masks, and an enormous fish tank with seaweed, a little stone castle, and a small tropical fish called Fish.

'Team.' Steinberger referred to them now as 'Team'. 'Meet Professor Quimby, the head inventor of Spy Force. She's a professor of physics, astrophysics, chemistry, robotics and holds the trophy for Spy Force bowling champion three years in a row.'

Quimby looked embarrassed.

'A few lucky strikes, that's all.'

She looked away and buried her burning red face in the long wisps of dark hair that fell around her head like a shower curtain. A bright pink scarf tied in a knot at the back of her head struggled to hold the rest of it in some kind of order. She wore a long yellow coat over baggy dark blue trousers and red and white striped trainers.

'Before each Spy Force mission, our agents are supplied with packs that have been specially equipped for their particular assignment. It's up to Quimby and the lab staff to read the mission specifications and decide what you might need. They're experts at this and have never been wrong yet. Quimby?'

The scientist's head shot up as if she'd just heard a loud bang.

'Would you like to take our new recruits through their packs?'

Quimby pushed another snaking piece of hair out of her face with her latex-gloved fingers. In front of her were three backpacks of differing designs and colours.

'We don't have much time. We've been preparing for this mission for weeks and now that it's happening we've no time to lose. These may look like ordinary bags but they are in fact bottomless. No matter how much you put in them, they will never be full and never heavier than five kilograms. Also, if you open the pack completely, it can be spread out so far it can be used as a coat, a piece of camouflage—it is colour sensitive so that it instantly blends in with your surroundings—or with these strings, even a parachute. It also has a special locking device that is sensitive to your fingerprints. The instant you touch it, the bag will recognize your prints and open only for you.'

She held out a booklet called *1001 Uses for a Super Pack*. 'All the possible uses and functions of the bag are spelt out in this.'

She undid the zipper around one of the packs

and opened the front cover to reveal what was inside and picked up a matchbox-sized device that looked like a miniature TV.

'This is a Substance Analyser Meter, or SAM. It can identify almost any known substance in existence. All you need to do is hold the top end of the SAM to the substance you wish to identify and within seconds a reading of all the components of that substance will appear on this screen along with their level of toxicity or danger.'

'Better not put it near one of your jokes or the thing will explode,' Linden whispered in Max's ear. Max opened her mouth to shoot off a reply but when she heard the tittering of Ella nearby, she pursed her lips so tightly they resembled the rear end of an uptight cat.

'And this,' continued Quimby, blowing an unruly piece of hair from her mouth, 'is a Danger Meter. In the presence of danger, it emits an electronic pulse. The stronger the vibrations, the more dangerous the situation. It's best to wear this inside your clothes, so when there's danger nearby, you'll know it instantly.'

She then picked up a circular metallic disc and held it carefully in her hand.

'This precious thing moves objects from a

distance. Just point the channelling beam at the object you'd like to move and control the movement of the object with this miniature joystick. It's called the RHINO, or the Remote Hauling Infra-nice Operator.'

'Infra-nice?' Ella queried.

'Yeff,' murmured Quimby as her scarf finally failed to hold back her wild hair and fell over her face. 'We decided we liked the name RHINO and we couldn't think of another suitable word that started with N.'

The professor then handed them each a watch and asked them to put them on.

Linden's was a transparent ice-blue colour that showed the components working inside. Ella's was silver with a fliptop cover that revealed a red metallic watchface, while Max's was bright pink with a picture of a pony behind two sparkling watch hands.

'Pink?' she asked in disgust. 'I can't wear pink. And what's with the pony?'

'These are walkie-talkie watches,' said Quimby timidly.

'I'm sure they are,' Max agreed firmly. 'But I can't be seen anywhere wearing this. I'll have to have a different one.'

'I'm afraid you can't,' Quimby reasoned. 'Each

watch has been specially made for each of you and adjusted to a certain frequency that is suited only to the allocated wearer.'

Max knew she couldn't argue against that and wanted to get on with the mission.

'OK. I'll wear the stupid watch. How do they work?'

'Simply adjust the frequency to the person you wish to speak to and press the side button to begin talking. Max, your frequency is one, Linden on two, and Ella, you're on three.'

Quimby reached for another gadget.

'This laser gun cuts through solid metal, this cupcake bomb lets off a silent wall of tear gas, and the truth gum makes the chewer speak nothing but the truth. Everything you have in your packs has been personally checked by me and is in full working order,' she finished proudly.

'What do these lollipops do?' asked Linden.

'Nothing. They're just lollipops. A lot of agents have a sweet tooth so we throw them in as a treat. There are pens and notepads too that are also just pens and notepads. And these,' said Quimby reaching for three covered coat hangers on a rack nearby, 'are your disguises.'

Max, Ella, and Linden took their hangers as

the sound of zippers being unzipped circled around the lab.

Quimby continued. 'From now on you'll be known as Cynthia, Jeremy, and Angelina.'

Max's face screwed into a crunched-up mess as she held out a pink ribboned dress and long blonde wig.

'Don't tell me. I'm Cynthia.'

Ella held out a baggy pair of trousers and a bright T-shirt. 'Which I guess makes me Angelina.'

Linden sifted through his bag to find a pair of trainers, dark denim jeans, and a sports shirt and cap. 'Hello there, Jeremy.'

Max looked at both of them smiling smugly with their new identities. Of course they'd be happy, she thought, since the whole concept of fashion had managed to pass them by their entire lives. The watch was one thing but she wasn't going to take the rest of it lying down.

'I don't want to be Cynthia.'

'Max, it's just for the mission. Happens all the time in the business.' Suddenly Linden was an authority.

'OK, Mr Expert. You be Cynthia.'

'I'm a boy.'

'I'll be Cynthia,' Ella volunteered.

Of course, Max thought. Little Miss Perfect once again acts all nice.

'I don't want to be Angelina either,' said Max, not willing to let Ella win.

All four of them stared at Max.

'After the mission, you'll go back to being Max,' Quimby assured her. 'But for now your identities are fixed.'

Just then Frond billowed through the door, her coat trailing behind her in a red swirling whoosh and her beehive hairdo half-collapsed like a mini Leaning Tower of Pisa. Steinberger's face drained of colour so much he almost disappeared in the white glowing lab except for the beads of sweat that again began dappling his nervous brow.

'Sorry I'm late. I got caught up with an oversized Venus Flytrap who mistook me for lunch. My fault. Should have remembered it was feeding time.'

Frond's coat pocket was torn and her sleeve seemed covered in some kind of milky-coloured goo. In a blurred daze, Steinberger lifted her hand which had a few scratch marks and a tiny trickle of blood. He wiped it against his jacket in a smooth, slow gesture but when he realized his hand was holding hers, he let it go instantly and looked very much as if he was going to faint.

'I think I might wait outside,' he stammered, trying to work out how to make his feet walk towards the door and tripping over them in the process.

Frond was unfazed as she lifted a small cotton pouch onto Quimby's desk.

'I've brought a few Plantorium goodies that may come in handy, like this sneeze powder. It makes people sneeze continuously and, as you know, it's impossible to sneeze and keep your eyes open at the same time. Just throw a little at the person you wish to distract. Great for when you need to make a quick getaway. I've also included a stink bomb for those times when you need to clear a room fast or just leave a nasty surprise for someone evil. You'll find a face mask in there as well to save you from the bomb's smelly wares and there are a few nature bars from Irene in case you get hungry. Packed full of fruit, vitamins, and minerals.'

Then she stopped and smiled proudly. 'Good luck, and may the Force be with you.'

Max, Linden, and Ella were shown to a series of changing rooms nearby where they put on their new outfits. Linden and Ella looked up when Max came out, but before they had a chance to say anything, she stopped them.

'Not one word, OK. Not a smirk, not a giggle. Nothing.'

She led the way, walking a little uneasily in her patent leather shoes and a dress that looked like a giant pink marshmallow. She grabbed her pack, said goodbye, and headed out of the lab where they found a calmer and more colourful Steinberger, happy to see the disguises working so well.

'You look . . .' he began.

'Um, it's best not to mention it actually,' warned Linden.

'Right. To the Vehicular All-Purpose Tower,' he commanded, as if he was leading some kind of cavalry in battle.

After another ride in a terracotta pot that took them on a short cut to the VART, Steinberger stood in front of them on the long metal deck as the lights above them swayed gently in the breeze. Sleek, dressed in brown leather goggles, a cap, and a long, scuffed coat as if he was some Second World War fighter pilot, warmed up the engine on the Sleek Machine below. Max, Linden, and Ella stood ready for their journey, thick-lensed goggles hanging around their necks.

'Good luck, team.'

Steinberger handed them their BRATT

authorization badges and papers as well as a London A–Z each. He also gave them some money and three rather large hankies.

'My grandma always used to say, wherever you go you'll never be lost if you have a hanky, and she hasn't been wrong yet.'

He was sounding a little choked up and tears moistened the corners of his eyes. Max took her hanky and hoped he wasn't going to cry. She hated anyone bawling in front of her. It made her feel annoyingly embarrassed and curious as to why people didn't save their tears until they were somewhere other people didn't have to witness them. Especially her.

Sleek made the final adjustments on his machine and wondered what the hold-up was.

'Remember, use your watches to stay in close contact and make sure each other is safe at all times.'

Sleek revved the machine and eyed Steinberger through his goggles, wanting him to get a move on.

'And this is my private line. In case you get into any trouble. Which you won't. I'm sure of it. It's just that—'

The horn blasted from the Sleek Machine as

Ella took the slip of paper with Steinberger's number and put it in her pocket.

'Thanks.'

'Good luck,' he sniffed as Linden and Ella climbed on the back of the motorbike-like machine and Max sat in the sidecar, pushing her bulging pink dress down to fit it all in.

'May the Force be—'

The rest of Steinberger's farewell was lost in the thunder of the Sleek Machine's departure out of the VART and on to Blue's Foods, where Max, Ella, and Linden would embark on their first Spy Force mission. Apart from the dress, Max knew this would be one of the greatest days of her life but what she didn't know was that deep inside her pack, a small regular pulsing was being emitted from her Danger Meter. The sound and vibrations of the Sleek Machine meant she felt none of it.

As the Sleek Machine left the VART, a small feline cry came from within a shadowy corner as a clutch of pale bony fingers ran the length of its deep black fur.

CHAPTER 16
AGENT 31

After an eventful ride through the skies of London dodging pigeons, swerving around statues, and only narrowly missing being squashed by a double-decker bus as it entered a low level tunnel at the same time as they did, the Sleek Machine arrived with its four passengers in a small park, in a quiet street.

Max unfolded herself from the sidecar where she was squashed down so low only her head poked out above the leather cover. This, along with the constant flapping of a stray piece of pink dress in her face, meant that all of the sites she'd heard Ella and Linden shouting about had been hidden from her.

Sleek flung one leg over the machine and, taking care to avoid a large crack in the pavement, stood before his passengers. Like an airline steward on an intercom, he bid them goodbye.

'One-way ride to somewhere in the vicinity of Blue's Foods of the three new recruits complete. Please leave your goggles in the appropriate compartments and make sure you take all your belongings with you. Your contact will be here directly to advise you of your next move. Have a pleasant mission and thank you for flying with Sleek.'

His serious face flicked into a wide toothpaste advertisement grin before it snapped back into being serious again, as though some time in flying school he'd been advised of the importance of such a grin but hadn't quite got it right. Avoiding the crack in the pavement once again, he climbed back onto the Sleek Machine and flew into the afternoon. Within seconds the machine disappeared as the oscillation level for invisibility was reached.

'Some ride, huh?' Ella was pleased Linden got to try the Sleek Machine.

'Heaps better than I thought.'

'I wonder how far it can go? Do you think it could fly all over the world?'

'That'd be awesome!'

Max looked at the two of them and wondered why whenever Linden was with Ella he started talking as if he was an overacting presenter on some lame kid's show. The ones that are all teeth and no talent.

'Maybe wondering about how we're going to meet our contact would be a more clever way to use the brain capacities you have?'

Max turned away while Ella and Linden threw each other a shrugged look that said they knew they were in trouble but didn't really care.

'And maybe if you sold your brain to science they could work out the missing ingredient in having a sense of humour.'

'What was that?' Max spun round on her shiny black heels, not quite out of earshot of Linden's quip.

'I said maybe if our contact's nearby they could work out where we'll be sitting by our professional demeanor.'

He whipped into his bag, pulled out his Danger Meter and began clipping it to the inside of his shirt. He concentrated on redoing his buttons to make sure his meter was properly concealed, but mostly to avoid Max's deadly gaze. Ella clipped hers on to the inside of her waistband, also eager to avoid the Maxvibes that were coming their way.

Max was sceptical and turned away abruptly to sit on a bench nearby. She looked up to see Ella and Linden talking and laughing as the bright sunny day lit up everything around them. She attached her Danger Meter to the satin pink lining of her dress so that it sat just above her heart. As she made sure it was firmly fastened she again felt that dull, familiar ache she felt whenever she moved houses and knew she was losing a friend. She looked at the two of them laughing and joking together and wondered why she couldn't be the one standing with Linden having a good time. Ella seemed to have everything: a nice mother, a good sense of humour, and Linden liked her better. If only—

'Psssst.'

Max's self-pity was interrupted by what sounded like the hissing of a punctured tyre. She held her head still as her eyes roamed the park, trying to spy what it was.

'Psssssssst.'

This time the sound was louder plus it sounded as if it was coming from the garbage bin beside her.

Linden and Ella continued chatting, oblivious of the hissing bin.

'Down here.' The hissing had turned into a real voice. Max leant down into the bin to come face to face with a person looking back at her.

'Cynthia Gordon?'

For an instant Max was going to say no, but then remembered her ridiculous pink outfit. 'Yep, that's me.'

'I'm Agent 31. Your first contact for Mission Blue's Foods.'

'What are you doing in the bin?' she had to ask.

'I'm Spy Force's secret hidden agent. It's my job to relay information to agents from discreet places. On the last mission I was posted in the steampipe of an ocean liner. Got a very warm bottom on that assignment, I can tell you. The one before that I was in a fish tank. Good thing I can hold my breath so long. Costs a fortune in dry cleaning bills but it's a steady job and I'm pretty good at it, if I don't say so myself.'

'How can you fit your whole body in such small places?' Max eyed the barrel-sized bin.

'I studied the ancient eastern art of Physical Origami for ten years under one of the Grand Masters. You should see what she can do. Once she got in and out of a teapot in ten minutes flat. The tea tasted a bit funny after that but it was amazing to see.'

Max wondered if Agent 31 had mashed a few brain cells out of existence and whether his squashed up experiences had left him a bit loopy.

'And I'm not loopy. I know that's what you're thinking because I also study mind-reading by correspondence. The ancient wisdoms of the world are mysterious and wonderful.'

Ella and Linden noticed Max leaning into the bin and hurried over.

'Are you OK, Cynthia? Are you feeling sick?' Ella looked concerned.

Max disliked Ms Perfect even more because she could still be nice even after Max had been rude to her.

'This is Agent 31. He's our contact.'

Ella and Linden stared at each other, seeing no one around except Max.

'I think you're getting a little too much sun,' Linden suggested.

'Just look in the bin.'

They leant over the rim and spied a crumpled man.

'Pleased to meet you. Thirty-one's my name and information's my game.'

There really was a man in the bin.

'What do you have for us?' Max had her notepad ready to take down everything she needed to know. Agent 31 began his instructions.

'In the last three months, Blue's Foods has come to dominate the kids' food business with his fancy new food flavours and marketing campaigns. His latest promotion even offered a trip to the moon to a lucky consumer of his Man in the Moon Cheesy Nibbles. You can imagine how many people bought those little fromagey treats. Anyway, now that so many kids are hooked on his foods, he is planning to add a secret ingredient over the next few months that will slowly take over the minds of kids everywhere, leaving him in control. Your mission is to enter Blue's Foods as a BRATT—a Bona-fide Registered Authorized Taste Tester—find out the ingredient he is planning to use and stop him before he can have his wicked way. But remember, it's not certain when Blue will start putting his plan into action, so whatever you do, don't eat the food.'

Max busily scribbled down all that 31 was saying.

'Your next step is to go to the lawns of Blue's Foods where you will be ushered along to the food-tasting area. Here is the address and a map of the factory layout for each of you. We believe Blue's office is located here.' He reached past an empty chip packet and a half-eaten sandwich to point to a particular location on Max's map.

'Once settled into your position, you will contact an agent who has been working undercover as a food technologist. She is of medium build, has long dark hair, and is expecting your arrival. When you see her you need to say this line, "The bluebird sings a happy song," and she'll reply, "Only when the sparrow farts."'

Ella and Linden stifled their giggles as Max quickly scribbled the message.

'Good luck and may the Force—'

'Be with you . . . We know.' Max stood up from the bench and took the London A–Z from her pack.

'Thanks, Agent 31,' Ella said, trying to make up for Max's rude behaviour.

He smiled warmly. 'Call me 31.'

'Will we see you again, 31?' asked Linden.

'Perhaps.'

'Got it.' Max had her finger on the location of Blue's factory. 'Let's go.'

'Remember,' warned 31 before they left. 'Watch out for Blue. No matter how nice he may seem, he's one of the meanest characters in the business. And even though you're the perfect agents for this mission, he'll have his eye out for you so don't do anything that will draw attention to yourselves.'

The three of them moved off with the agent's warning circling in their heads. As their feet sank into the soft green carpet of grass beneath them, Max and Linden remembered the vulture-like look of satisfaction on Blue's face as they dangled perilously over his vat of jelly. He was a man who'd stop at nothing to get what he wanted and they'd have to watch every step to keep out of his way.

CHAPTER 17
MEETING THE UNDERCOVER AGENT

Alex Crane looked over the rim of her thick tortoiseshell glasses and held up the Substance Analyser Meter, or SAM, in front of her.

'Just as I thought.'

The reading was the final piece of proof that Blue was up to no good and if she didn't act quickly, he'd begin one of the most evil plans of mind control the world had ever known.

'Now to get this back to the lab.' But before she could take a step, Blue's snivelling henchman, Kronch, snatched the SAM from her and threw it to the floor, smashing it into a million pieces.

'I knew there was somethin' fishy about you. The head technologistician said she wasn't convinced you were just any food technologist, and guess what, she were right.'

Kronch paused for effect.

'Ms . . . Alex . . . Crane.'

Alex flinched on hearing her name punctuated by this meat-brained, no-necked, half giant. Kronch was twice her size but had the brainpower of a rock. In a one-arm swoop he picked up Alex and strode towards the boiling cauldron of Vampire Blood Syrup.

'In just a few seconds, Ms Crane, you'll turn from Superspy to super dessert. Kids all over the

world will be slurping you up with their favourite
vanilla ice cream and not even know it.'

Kronch held Alex over the boiling copper tub as
the bubbling, sugary heat rose up and stung her
nose and eyes. Kronch wasn't smart but he was
every inch as mean as his uncle Theolodious Blue.
Every inch as—

'Oooph!' Alex Crane was jolted from Max's
thoughts and was replaced by the back of Ella's
head right up against her nose.

'Oops. Sorry, Cynthia.'

Max boiled.

'Don't stop so suddenly next time and maybe
we'll all manage to get to where we're going in one
piece.'

Max was her own mini-storm as she thundered
past Ella towards the factory.

'Don't worry about Max,' Linden tried to comfort
a downcast Ella. 'She has a really nice personality,
she just sometimes forgets to bring it with her.'

There was no doubting who the factory
belonged to. The building was a blazing modern
kaleidoscope of glass and curves and colours gleaming
in the sun like a mirage in a desert. Outside the

factory was like a circus ground with splashes of red, blue, pink, and yellow snuggled among leafy green trees filled with exotic birds and colourful butterflies buoyed on a calm, gentle breeze. Dotted around like giant marbles were statues of rounded chefs holding cartons of custards, stirring pots of puddings, and juggling jars of jelly beans. Towering above everything was a fountain of fake juice spilling from a gigantic mouth and a bold and friendly sign that read, 'Blue's Foods . . . So good it's almost criminal'.

'I'll bet it's criminal.' Max stood under the sign and thought about Ben, Eleanor, and Francis and what Blue had done to them. 'We'll get you yet.'

A sprawl of kids were arriving for the taste testing and after hugs and goodbyes and adults wiping corners of eyes with hankies, the BRATTs drifted into two lines. Ella waited in one as Linden stood behind Max in the other.

'The food tasting title they gave us is just a name, you know. You don't actually have to live it out.' He leant towards her.

'I'm not being a BRATT, but thanks for pointing it out. I just think she shouldn't have stopped so suddenly.'

'Ella's really nice and if you'd just give her a chance you'll find that too.'

Max spun round. 'Who said anything about Ella? It's not Ella I'm worried about. I've hardly even noticed Ella. It's the mission I'm worried about, not Ella.'

By the amount of times Max said Ella's name he knew the problem was definitely Ella. Linden sighed. One day he'd understand girls, but today he wasn't even going to get close.

A large truck of a man sitting behind a desk at the front of the queue lifted his head to see what the commotion was. He eyed Max closely as she approached the desk and stepped into his darkened shadow. She felt her Danger Meter tingle inside her dress as her eyes rose warily up his bulky frame. He had stubby sausage-like fingers, arms as thick as an old armchair, a crumpled orange shirt stretched over his bulging belly, and a bucket-sized head rimmed with a motley black and grey beard that was so thick you couldn't see his lips.

'Badge and papers?' the beard rustled.

Max reached in and took them out of her bag. The way the man was looking at them she wasn't sure he could read. Then she saw something else. Her eyes flung open like roller blinds as she read his name tag: 'Kronch.'

'Kronch?' She didn't realize she'd said it out loud.

'Hmm?' Kronch hmmed grumpily.

'Nothing.' Max felt as if all the words had been sucked out of her head as she remembered her Alex Crane story.

'First-timer, eh? Just do as the other BRATTs here do and you won't get into any trouble ... Cynthia.' He said her name as if he wasn't convinced it was hers.

Kronch looked down at a list in front of him. 'Room B for you.' He gloated as if it was some kind of punishment. Before he let her go he groaned, 'Wait, let me see that bag.'

Max stiffened. If Kronch saw what was inside her backpack they were done for. She tried to think of how to explain her way out of it.

'There's not much in there, just a few—'

'The bag.' This time it wasn't a request as much as a quietly spoken threat.

Max took her bag off her shoulders and handed it over. Linden's mouth went dry as he felt his temperature go up.

Kronch was enjoying every minute of their squirming, but when he tried to undo the bag, he got nowhere. He pulled at the zippers, tugged at the straps and then used his teeth to try and tear it open. Max made a mental note not to touch the bag where his slobber would have sunk in. The security system worked. It seemed the backpack really was meant for no one except Max.

Unable to open it, Kronch threw it to the floor. He moved his beard closer to Max so she could feel his warm, stale breath pouring all over her.

'I'll be keeping a careful eye on you, missy. Make one move out of line and I'll be on you quicker than a rabbit trap.'

Max stepped aside and picked up her pack, unable to take her eyes off the hulking man. Linden stepped up and handed his papers over. He felt his Danger Meter shiver inside his shirt as well. There was something about Kronch that was like rolling black storm clouds after a hot and humid day. Everything was calm now, but any minute the skies were going to open up and come crashing down all over them.

'Room F.' Max was sure Kronch was smiling underneath his beard as he ordered Linden to a separate room.

They sidled away from the desk eager to get away from him as soon as possible. Kronch kept them in sight and spoke slyly into a mobile phone that looked like a domino in his baguette-like fingers. Ella met them on the neatly manicured lawn near a statue of a large jolly chef holding up a can of whipped cream.

'I'm in Room B,' she announced, hoping Linden would be there too.

'Room F,' he said disappointedly. 'You're with Max.'

Ella's smile faltered a little.

'We'll have to make sure we keep in touch with our watches.'

Max did her best to ignore Ella's disappointment and turned to walk towards the factory entrance, but as she did, a strap on her pack got hooked on the thumb of the jolly chef and she was flung back into him like a ball on a piece of elastic.

Linden and Ella did their best not to smile but worried they were going to burst out laughing, moved off quickly. Behind them, Kronch finished his phone call, stood up and ambled through an oval side door painted as a giant strawberry.

Once inside, Linden said goodbye as he was led down a long polished corridor with glass floors. He could see down into the level below to a network of benches, stools, charts, and bowls of brightly coloured foodstuff everywhere.

Ella and Max were led in the opposite direction. Max's Danger Meter was only now quietening down after her encounter with Goliath. Ella saw her anxious face and guessed what she was thinking. 'I don't like being separated from Linden either.'

That was exactly how Max was feeling but she wasn't going to let Ella know she was right. 'The reason I'm worried is that my Danger Meter doesn't like the hulk we just met one bit. I think it's good we've been split up. We'll cover more area that way.'

'Oh.'

'For now let's concentrate on not doing anything that attracts attention.'

Just as Max finished saying this, she tripped over another BRATT who had bent over to do up his shoelace. She rolled over the top of him and landed on a skateboard that sped down the polished glass floor, past a forest of kid's legs before she crashed head first through the door of Room B straight into the boots of Kronch.

'Can't you use a door like everyone else?' His nostrils flared like a crazed horse about to bolt. 'Now find your seat and do the job you're here to do.'

The door opened and other BRATTs giggled as they stepped over Max. She struggled to her feet, rubbed her sore head, and walked to her allocated desk.

Three food technicians in long white coats with clipboards and pens were pushing carts with different coloured bowls of food. Red, yellow, aqua, and fluorescent pink mousses, custards, jellies and breakfast cereals. As they approached each desk, they handed over a few bowls and a piece of paper for each BRATT to fill out once they'd tasted their samples.

'Do you think one of these is our contact?' Ella breathed quietly.

'Not sure.' Max tried to catch the eyes of each of them. One technician was a short squat man with no hair and a moustache so thin it looked as if he had drawn it on with a pencil. Another was a tall woman who chewed gum and wove through the desks nodding her head as if she had a radio playing inside it. The final one was very serious, wore thick-rimmed glasses, and her long brown hair was tied back in a ponytail. Max had the feeling they'd met before. But how could that be? This was only her second time in London. Just then, the technician looked up and caught her eye. Then she pushed her cart towards Max and stopped alongside her to pick up several bowls and place them in front of Max. There wasn't any obvious sign she was their contact, but something told Max she was the one. She looked down, started to fill out her form and decided to give the signal.

'The bluebird sings a happy song.'

The technician finished placing Max's bowls on her desk and stepping between the two new spies, did the same for Ella. Max was disappointed. She was sure the contact was her.

The technician held her clipboard up in front of her face and whispered towards Max, 'Only when the sparrow farts.'

Max pressed so hard on her pencil she snapped the lead.

'Cynthia?'

Max and Ella looked at each other.

'That's me.'

'I'm your contact. Crane. Alex Crane.'

Alex kept looking at her clipboard and marking off the food samples she'd given them as Max was dealing with a serious case of shock.

'Who?'

'Alex Crane,' she repeated softly, barely moving her lips.

Max couldn't believe it. Alex Crane really

existed! And she was standing beside her! On the same mission!

'I'm Max!' she almost yelled, plunging her overexcited hands across the desk and sending several bowls of blue and red food samples dribbling onto Alex's coat and trousers.

Kronch's head spun towards them.

Max's embarrassment made her heart beat faster and her face fire up as if she was sitting way too close to a heater.

'Yes, I know . . . Cynthia,' replied Alex, annoyed at Max's clumsiness and at revealing her real name. She took a cloth off her trolley and wiped the gunk from her clothes. Max was mortified and desperately wished there was some way she could rewind the last few minutes of her life and start them all over again.

Alex handed out new samples and leant into them both, pretending to explain the food-tasting process. Kronch stared at them. His eyes like hungry sharks.

'Harrison's hunch was right. Blue is planning to add a secret ingredient to his food products. One that isn't marked on the packet. Which isn't surprising. Half the time you read the ingredients on products and you still don't know what you're eating. Flavour enhancers, colourings, preservatives.'

Alex was starting to sound like Max's mother.

'What does this secret ingredient do?' asked Ella, not suffering from any of Max's shock or embarrassment.

'It's called T3-35A. It surrounds the part of the mind that determines good from bad and stops it from working, much like an antibiotic around bacteria, leaving the evil side of a person's mind to take over. It can make an ordinarily good person become evil almost instantly.'

Kronch was getting suspicious at how long Alex had been with Max and Ella.

'Meet me in Lab X in an hour and we can take a reading with your SAMs. I couldn't bring mine because of the rigorous search procedures for employees.'

'Any problems here?' Kronch's breath floated over them like blackened smog. Max's Danger Meter vibrated inside her dress even harder than before.

'No. They're all set now.' Alex put her clipboard on her trolley and walked away.

'Hurrumph,' Kronch hurrumphed as he walked back to his desk.

'We've got to tell Linden,' Ella whispered.

'Yep,' said Max, managing to speak again. 'But

we've got to get Igor off our backs first. When he's lost interest in us, we'll sneak out of here, get a reading of the secret ingredient and head back to Spy Force.'

Max and Ella pretended to go about their tasting, careful not to put the food in their mouths. In her head Max saw herself knock over the bowls again and again and each time it happened, she became even more angry at herself for being such a klutz. She looked up and saw Kronch speaking furtively into his phone, as if he was planning something devious. Something that probably was going to be bad for her. She hoped he would leave them alone, but with the impression she'd made on him so far, she knew that wasn't going to happen easily.

CHAPTER 18
A TERRIBLE DOUBLECROSS

After half an hour of food testing, the BRATTs were given a short break to refresh their tastebuds with Blue's Foods Fresh-from-the-Spring Mineral Water. The glass-floored corridor filled with a frenzied clutch of kids drinking water and talking food samples as Max and Ella stood as far away as they could, trying to work out what to do.

'Kronch is watching us so closely there's no way we're going to be able to sneak away and meet Alex,' Ella deduced.

'You noticed.' Max was chewing a fingernail and not trying one bit to be nice to her.

'What do you think we should do?'

'I think you should be quiet, so I can work that out.'

Max skated over some ideas in her head, wondering why of all the places in the world she had to share the part she was in with Ella.

'I've got it! *We* can't sneak away, but Linden might be able to.'

Max put her hand to her chin, adjusted the frequency on her watch and began talking.

'Come in, Lin . . . I mean, Jeremy. It's . . .' Max could hardly say it, 'Cynthia. Can you hear me?'

'Loud and clear,' came a tinny, wire-thin voice from her watch.

'Good. We've got a plan—'

'It's no good,' interrupted the voice.

'What do you mean it's no good, you haven't heard it yet?'

'It's me. Angelina.'

'What?' Max turned around and saw Ella with her watch to her mouth.

'Jeremy is frequency two.'

'I knew that.' Max hated being wrong and hated even more being *told* she was wrong. 'My frequency button must be stuck.'

Kronch came out of Room B and stood at the door, his eyes carving into them like chainsaws tearing through wood.

Max tried to ignore her Danger Meter and turned her back on Kronch as she spoke into her watch as discreetly as she could.

'Jeremy, are you there? We've got proof that Blue is up to no good. Jeremy? Can you hear us?'

Nothing. Max tried again.

'Can you hear us, Jeremy? We need your help.'

'Ah, how I've missed that voice. So lovely to hear from you again.' Max's heart jolted in her chest as if it momentarily forgot how to keep beating. 'I was just on the phone to Kronch who was telling me how lucky we are to have you with us . . . Ms Maxine Remy.'

It was Blue.

And he had Linden's watch.

Which meant he must have Linden.

'Your little game, Maxine, while brave, has unfortunately come undone and as you know, in this business, that sadly comes with unpleasant consequences.' He paused. 'And perhaps some bad news for your little friend Linden.'

At the mention of Linden's name, Max felt a wave of fury crash through her. If Blue hurt him in any way she'd do everything she could to make him regret it. Her finger pressed hard on the talk button to let him have it. 'Now listen, Blue—' but before she could say anything further, the watch went dead.

Hearing Blue's voice again struck deep fear into her as if she was sailing towards a hidden iceberg lurking dangerously in frozen waters. When she tried to swallow, it felt as if an icy lump was stuck in her throat and, what was worse, when she looked up, she saw Kronch heading straight for them.

'Quick! Run!' she yelled.

'Where?' Ella asked.

'Not sure. Just run.'

They raced along the corridor followed by a lumbering Kronch. He pushed past a group of BRATTs sending them hurtling into fake jelly baths and gloopy mountains of imitation cheese. People below looked up as Max's and Ella's legs hurled them as fast as they could across the glass floor towards a huge twisting banana slide which connected their floor to the one below. They looked behind them and saw Kronch gaining on them.

'Down there,' Max instructed before leaping onto the slide and plunging round the yellow twists and turns and landing headfirst in the soft belly of an armchair shaped like a chef.

Max just managed to get out of the way as Ella nose-dived into the pudgy chair.

'Lucky you were here,' she breathed at the chef, pulling her curls out of her face.

'Urrrr.'

Ella's eyes rocketed wide open as she thought the chair spoke back to her, but looking up, they saw it was Kronch, trying to lift his oversized body onto the banana slide. They considered each of the four corridors around them.

'Which one do we take?' Ella thought they all looked the same.

Kronch had managed to get one leg on the slide.

'This one,' Max decided and they sped off down the closest one.

They flew past noticeboards filled with posters of happy kids eating and laughing and cabinets filled with award-winning Blue's Foods products. They ran so that each step was faster than the one before, until they came to an abrupt stop at a solid steel door.

Kronch's broken cry foghorned behind them as he toppled down the slide.

Gulping big draughts of air, Max tried the door. 'It's locked.'

A bellowing cry sounded behind them as Kronch missed the armchair and whacked straight into the concrete wall behind it.

'My Danger Meter is going crazy,' Ella breathed.

Then Max had an idea.

'The laser!' She reached into her pack, took the device from its hold and pointed it towards the lock. She pressed hard on the detonator button knowing this would be their only chance to get away from the fast approaching Kronch, but when her finger came to a stop, she stared at the small grey gadget trying to believe what she saw.

Nothing had happened. She pressed the

detonator button again and again but still there was nothing. Quimby's words zigzagged in her head. The ones that told her all their gadgets had been checked and were in full working order. What were they going to do now?

Ella inhaled a quick fear-filled breath as Kronch got closer and closer. She took her laser from her pack and aimed it at the door.

'It's worth a try,' she explained, wishing as hard as she could that her laser would work.

She pressed the button hard and a sharp line of red light blasted a high-powered beam at the lock.

'It works!' she cried.

Kronch's plodding footsteps got closer and closer as the smell of melting steel filled their noses.

'Quick,' Max pleaded as the laser drew a heated line around the lock, leaving a puddle of liquefying mess at their feet.

Kronch was so close they could hear his laboured grunting as his stale breath clamoured to escape his lungs.

Ella held the laser firm, aiming it directly at the lock as Max's mind raced back to when they collected their packs and to the last person she saw just before they entered the lab. Dretch! Of course. It was obvious he hated them and would get rid of them if he had the chance. He must have slipped into the lab to sabotage her laser before she picked it up. Which means he must be a double agent. That would explain why he flinched when he heard Harrison's name. They were in deep trouble now but if they didn't get back to Spy Force soon, the very existence of the agency was in serious danger.

'Please!' Just as Max said this, the lock fell to the floor and the door creaked open.

'All right!' they cheered before Kronch's thumping footsteps cut their celebration short.

Max took off through the door and skidded around a corner where she spied a goods lift in the shape of two bulging red lips.

'In here!' She parted the lips and Ella ducked inside with Max following quickly after her. She pressed the *down* button and pulled her hand quickly inside as the machine began its descent just as an enraged Kronch reached the top of the shaft and shouted down to them.

'You won't get away from me that easily, you brats.'

The words rained on them like a volley of poisonous darts.

Max took the map of the factory out of her

pack. 'If my guess is right, Linden is being held in Blue's office.'

'According to the CTR, he's somewhere much closer than that.' Ella held the device in her hand and tried to estimate his position.

Max rolled her eyes. 'Or somewhere nearby, which I was going to say before you interrupted.'

'What will we do when we find them?' Ella was still nervous about Kronch's menacing threat.

'I don't know. We can work that out on the way.'

Ella wasn't so sure that was the best thing to do. 'Don't you think we should work out a plan before we sneak up on one of the most evil masterminds in the world?'

Max looked up from her map and offered Ella a stare so icy it could have kept a packet of peas frozen for a month. 'We've got to get moving now or there'll be none of Linden left to save.'

Then, just because she could be nasty, she added, 'Unless saving yourself is more important.'

For the first time ever, something snapped inside Ella and she decided she'd had enough of Max's constant bad attitude.

'You think you're always so right, don't you, Ms Expert dot com? I don't know who told you your

brain is superior to everyone else's but if I was you
I'd trade it in for a new one because the one you've
got is a real reject.'

Max's head jerked back, not sure she was
hearing right.

Ella was just getting warmed up.

'And another thing, Miss Crabby, it's obvious
you don't have many skills as a people person but
you could at least try and scrape together a little
decency so you're a bit more pleasant to be around.'

Max was dumbfounded. She'd never heard Ella
speak like this before. Part of her was stunned that
Ella could get so angry but the other part of her had
to hand it to her. That was a good piece of insulting.

'Linden's right.' Ella stuck her chin out and
raised one eyebrow. 'You need to take yourself
shopping for a badly needed dose of humour.'

The lift came to a halt and the hatch opened
before them.

Max knew Linden didn't think she had such
a great sense of humour. That was OK. She could
handle not being very funny, but there was something
about hearing it from Ella that really hurt. When
she tried to think of something to say, the only
thing she could come up with was, 'Oh yeah?'

'Yeah,' Ella said defiantly.

She bent her head and walked through another set of lips into a large, brightly lit basement. It was crammed with shiny metal cylinders mounted on tall, spindly legs that looked like gigantic, overweight insects. Steam was rising from their heads and the sound of bubbling echoed from inside them like hunger pains.

Ella crossed her arms in front of her and stared at Max, daring her to say more.

'At least I'm taking this mission seriously,' Max began. 'Unlike you, who are so caught up with looking pretty that you—'

'What's going on?' a voice nearby asked.

'Wait your turn,' Max snapped, resenting the interruption and continuing with Ella. 'You're so caught up with looking pretty—'

Max stopped and spun round.

'Linden!' she squealed as she threw her arms around him in a very unMax-like manner. 'We were so worried about you. Where have you been? Are you OK?'

Linden laughed and prised Max's tight grip from his neck.

'There's no need to get all gushy. I was only in a different lab.'

Shocked at her over-emotional reaction, Max

straightened her dress and tried to find something else to do with her hands. She lowered her voice a few semitones. 'We thought you were with Blue?'

'Why would I be with Blue?' he asked.

'He was speaking on your watch,' Ella told him.

'I must have dropped it somewhere,' Linden said a little sheepishly, patting down what was for him an immaculately neat hairdo.

'That's weird,' Max puzzled. 'My Danger Meter is buzzing.'

'The whole place down here is full of bad energy. This is where Blue is planning to add the secret ingredient,' Linden added a little too quickly.

'How do you know that?' Ella questioned.

'Well, where else would they do it? This is the main food preparation area if you look on the map.'

While Linden looked like Linden, except for the hair, there was something very unLindenish about him.

'Guess who our contact is?' Max suddenly remembered.

Linden seemed annoyed. 'You've met her already?'

'Yep. It's Alex Crane!'

She expected a big reaction but got none.

'You know. Alex Crane. From my book.' She

was disappointed. Linden was the only one who'd read the Alex Crane adventures she'd written. Apart from Toby and the kids he'd read to at school while she was in the mud.

She checked her watch. 'We've arranged to meet her in Lab X in five minutes.' To try and hide her disappointment at Linden's lack of enthusiasm, she concentrated on the map. 'According to this, it's on the second floor—'

'Don't worry about the map. I know a short cut,' Linden cut in, not showing the least bit of curiosity at the fact that Alex Crane was real.

Ella threw an inquisitive glance at Max, who for the first time since they'd met, felt the same way as she did. They walked warily behind him through the spindly insect legs, beneath the rumbling metal stomachs and onto a conveyor belt that wound its way up and over, in and around the whole churning super kitchen. It then began a steep climb high into the extractor-fan-filled ceiling.

Max was worried. There was something very slippery about the way Linden was behaving. Normally he would have been excited about meeting Alex. He wouldn't have minded her throwing her arms around him. He would have asked more questions about where they'd been.

Especially of Ella. And the final clue that made her think something was wrong: he hadn't made one joke since they'd found each other.

'Here we are,' he announced as he hopped off the conveyor belt in front of a furry blue door surrounded by blue frosted windows.

'Are you sure this is it?' Max was expecting something very different of Lab X.

'Yep. Come inside,' Linden offered as if he was inviting them into his own home.

He opened the door and stood aside as they moved into a dark, silent room.

'I'll get the light.'

They heard a click followed by the gentle infusing of soft light that revealed a totally blue room. Blue beanbags, blue floor covered by blue rugs, blue televisions, a blue fridge, and a blue desk. There were even blue plants growing out of blue soil.

'This doesn't look like a lab.' Ella's Danger Meter was going berserk.

'That's because it isn't.' They turned to see a figure at the top of a blue staircase with a thick, blue snake coiled around the railing.

It was Blue.

He moved down the stairs with catlike grace.

Kronch stood at attention beside a moulded blue desk swathed in the light of a blue, jelly-bean-shaped lamp.

'Welcome, little ones. We're so happy to have you with us.'

'Well, don't get used to it,' Max warned him, 'because we aren't staying.' As she turned to go, the door slammed shut courtesy of a remote control clamped in Kronch's lumpen hand.

'What'll we do now?' Ella whispered to her friends. Before anyone could answer, something happened that even today can still make Max's blood turn to ice.

Linden looked at them, smiled, and walked slowly over to stand next to Blue.

'Linden?' Max wasn't sure what was happening but deep inside her she knew it wasn't good.

'Mr Blue and I have been chatting.' Linden's voice was slow and deep, like a talking doll when the batteries are running low. 'He has convinced me that what he is doing here at Blue's Foods is for the good of humanity and Spy Force is only trying to stop that.'

A smile crawled up Blue's face like a spider climbing towards a fly trapped in his web. Slow. Dangerous. Ready to devour.

Normally Linden had a body that leant with a kind of slouch and wild hair that even heavy-duty cement couldn't tame. The Linden standing next to Blue looked as if he'd been stretched out on a rack, made ten centimetres taller, and had hair so smooth and slick it looked like one solid, glistening piece.

'You now have two choices,' he continued, as if he was some overpaid businessman about to bankrupt a small country and enjoying every minute. 'You can join us and help the struggle of Blue against the unprogressive and selfish workings of Spy Force, or . . .' and at this he paused, sneaking Blue a devoted glance, 'you can enjoy the one-way thrill ride of the Moons of Mars confectionery room.'

Kronch let out a strangled snort.

Max and Ella felt as if someone had wrenched them out of their lives and dumped them into a world they didn't understand.

Nothing was familiar.

Nothing made sense.

Linden not only agreed with Blue, he was now one of his most loyal supporters.

CHAPTER 19
A STICKY END

The Moons of Mars confectionery room was filled with a highway of bright red conveyor belts going in all directions and large, rounded cauldrons filling the air like oversized silver balloons. The cauldrons were labelled 'choc-biscuit mixture', 'toffee-caramel', and 'hundreds and thousands'. Each of the machines was churning away, like a mechanical army, pouring, sprinkling and slicing to a rhythmic, ordered beat, busily making the confectionery delights. The machine that had everyone's attention was the one in the centre, where two securely bound prisoners were about to become part of the biscuity process.

Max and Ella hadn't accepted Linden's offer of joining the ranks of Blue's Foods. In fact, Max had been so opposed to it, she suggested Linden take the offer and put it somewhere that sounded really painful. As a result of her blunt suggestion, Max's and Ella's backpacks had been removed and they'd been tied up with rope and tossed onto one of the conveyor belts like sausages on a barbecue.

Framed by stacks of large cotton bags filled with choc-biscuit mix and hundreds and thousands, industrial ovens, mixers, temperature gauges, rising steam, and pipes that ran around the room like long fingers hugging the walls, Linden picked up a finished biscuit from a rack nearby and took a small bite. Again this was unlike Linden, who would have finished the chocolate mound in one swift munch.

'At the moment, with everyone having minds of their own, the world's in a complete mess.' He took another careful nibble. 'I mean, look at it. We've got wars, famine, poverty, environmental collapse. If only we had one unified way of thinking, the world would be without chaos and hatred for the first time in the history of mankind.'

'Humankind,' Max corrected.

Blue stood behind Linden, his hands held snugly across his chest, proud of his newest recruit and enjoying every minute of the crumbling friendships before him.

Linden finished the last of his biscuit. 'You're too cute, Maxine.'

He knew Max hated being called that. She clenched her teeth so hard she only just avoided chipping them.

Ella stared at the boy who was once her good friend but who was talking like someone she normally tried hard to avoid.

'You don't really believe that, do you?' she

asked quietly. 'What about all that stuff we found out about Blue last time?'

'Ella,' Linden said with as much condescension in his voice as it could hold. 'At your age and with your intelligence, have you never heard of bad press?'

'Bad press!' Max shouted. 'Spy Force are the good guys and you know it.'

'Don't talk to me about Spy Force!' Blue shouted, his hands falling from his chest into two closed fists. 'They're the ones who can't recognize good from evil.'

Max stared at the unusually flustered and rouge-coloured Blue.

'It is they who walk around pretending to be the good guys and pointing fingers at the bad guys when they haven't the least idea.'

Max watched Blue's chest lurching in and out as if he'd just run a marathon. A sprig of normally perfect hair fell in front of his face that had become distorted with anger. Max frowned as she tried to work out what she'd said that had upset Blue so much. Then she had it. It was something Steinberger had said to her at the Wall of Goodness.

'You were the Spy Force agent who went bad, weren't you?' She said it through a small, quiet gasp.

Blue pounced forward and slammed his fist onto the conveyor belt beside Max's head. He was so close to her, she could feel his rage trembling inside him.

'It wasn't me who went bad. It was them!' The fury in his eyes lit the edges of his face with a dangerous glow. 'It was I who had the ideas to turn Spy Force into an organization to reckon with. We could still do the good deeds they wanted but with a few clever deals of mine, they could have had vast reserves of money to solve any crime they'd wanted. But they wouldn't listen.' Blue's face crumpled into an ugly sneer. 'Harrison's do-gooding ways prevented him from seeing that what I was saying made perfect sense. We were a good team, Harrison and I, before he threw it away.'

Max knew she should have been scared but couldn't hold back a widening grin.

'So they threw you out of the Force?'

Blue's eyes fixed on her malevolently as if she was a target he was lining up. 'They didn't throw me out, I quit,' he said in a voice that moved over her like a cold wind.

Just then the door of the confectionery room crashed open and a bound, gagged, and struggling

Alex Crane was hauled in by the bumbling, lumpish Kronch.

'Alex?' Max's head spun round to see her hero being bundled in like a bag of potting mix.

'Ah, you found her, Kronch. Well done.' Blue straightened himself up, pushed his momentarily unruly hair into place and went back to being his usual composed and evil self. 'Where was she?'

'On her way here, looking for these kids. But I nabbed her before she got too close.'

Alex flinched in his grip, desperate to release herself from his leaden hold.

'That's the most intriguing part about most humans,' Blue puzzled, now back in control of his behaviour. 'They have this terrible weakness for other people. They build up all these emotions and loyalties. Terribly icky stuff that just gets in the way of life. It's such a design fault. If I was in charge of designing humans, that would be the first thing to go.'

Kronch hardly moved as Alex squirmed and moaned through her gag. Linden smiled as Blue continued with his devilish plan.

'Don't worry, Ms Crane. Kronch is about to help you get your wish of joining your young friends. Kronch?'

The oversized oaf nodded his bucket head and dragged Alex to the conveyor belt. After a brief struggle, she was securely tied to the belt between Max and Ella.

'Take her gag away,' Blue ordered. Kronch did as he was told as a smile filled with meanness etched into Blue's lips. 'Comfortable, Ms Crane?'

'I've never been comfortable in the presence of snakes,' she shot back.

Max smiled. Her hero was every bit as clever as she'd written.

'Now now, Ms Crane. I don't think there's any need for insults.'

'That was no insult, Blue. It was the best compliment I could give you.'

Blue's smile slipped a little, then he quickly resumed his composure.

'Now that the whole gang is here, the Moons of Mars coating process can begin and we can be rid of three very pesky obstacles to making the world a better place. And this time I am going to stay and watch,' he said, remembering the time Linden and Max had given him the slip. 'Linden? Would you do us the honour?'

Linden walked past Blue and Kronch towards a large green button secured under a plastic cover.

Max and Ella watched him lift the cover, unable to believe their friend was about to have them turned into life-sized, sugary sweets. He looked across at them and smiled.

'It's for the best,' he said, and lifting his hand he rested it on the button.

'Once Linden has started the machine,' Blue began with an air of delight surrounding every snivelling part of him, 'the conveyor belt will transport you under a delightful flow of choc-biscuit mixture, before you're given a coating of warm toffee-caramel. You will then be covered in the multi-coloured sweetness of hundreds and thousands. Soon after that, you will come face to face with the sharpened blades of the slicer which will carve you up into tasty, mouth-sized mini agents. That's my favourite part.' He looked across at Linden who reflected an evil grin back. 'You will have roughly two minutes to do all you'd like to do with the rest of your lives. Mind you,' and at this he gloated even more, 'in this position, your options are somewhat limited.'

Ella remembered all the times she and Linden had emailed each other and spoken on the CTR. Her heart drooped as she watched one of the kindest, funniest people she'd ever met prepare to bring about her end.

'Linden!' she cried. 'You aren't really going to do this, are you?'

He stared at her as if he was in a trance.

Max looked up at the metal cauldrons and the shining blades of the slicer waiting at attention for the order that would spell their doom. As much as she tried to deny it, Linden seemed to have been totally sucked in by Blue's cockamamie story about being the good guy. She looked at his blank face and struggled with the realization that she was being betrayed by the one person in her life she thought was her friend.

'Linden, what about our pact?' For one instant she thought she saw a hint of hesitation in his eyes, but it was no good. He pressed his hand down on the button and the conveyor belt jerked to life, beginning the process that would take Max, Ella, and Alex to their premature demise.

She frantically searched her mind for what they could do. When her backpack had been taken, she'd managed to sneakily grab a small sachet of sneeze powder. How could it be helpful?

Blue stared at his three bound prisoners like a hungry fox standing before a chicken coop.

'Bon voyage, ladies, and farewell to your last attempt at foiling my brilliant plans.'

CHAPTER 20
UNDER THE MOONS OF MARS

The clanging, whirring noise of the conveyor belt droned beneath Max, Ella, and Alex as it transported them towards the cauldrons of the Moons of Mars confectionery machine.

Max swallowed nervously and shifted inside the snug-fitting ropes as she got closer and closer to the tilting vessels and the best friend she'd ever had stood nearby and watched. Her stomach twisted into a ball of sadness and fear. She spoke to Alex.

'I liked what you said to Blue before. You really showed him,' she stammered, still a little nervous about being so close to her hero.

Alex didn't reply. She was deep in thought, trying to sort out a way to save them.

'It was really brave of you to risk your life to find us.' She blushed. 'I always knew you would.'

Alex looked around as if she'd only just heard Max's voice. 'Sorry?'

There was something about Alex's tone that made Max feel she had it all wrong. 'It was good of you to try and save us?' she tried again uneasily.

The glooping, oozing, sprinkling, and slicing got closer as the conveyor belt carried them ever dangerously forward.

'I didn't come back to save you. I came to get the SAM so I could take the reading of the new ingredient to send to Spy Force. I'm on a mission to save the world, not make new friends.' And with that Alex went back to her thinking.

If Max felt sad before, she now felt as if her heart had been tipped over and emptied of all the happiness it ever had in it. Her Danger Meter was going crazy while Blue, Kronch, and Linden blissfully lapped up the prospect of their imminent demise at the hands of Blue's Moons of Mars confectionery machine.

Ella hadn't heard what Alex had said to Max because she'd noticed something strange about Linden.

'Alex, Linden's eyes are a bit weird looking.'

Alex turned her head towards Linden and focused on his eyes. They looked glazed with a slight blue tinge.

'He's been given the secret ingredient,' she surmised. 'Blue instructed his technicians to make the side effects of the ingredient as minimal as possible, so they created a substance that is side-effect free except for a slight blue colouring to the eyes.'

The sound of the slicer was getting louder and louder, like a hundred sharpened, plunging guillotines. But as they continued to look at Linden, another strange thing happened.

'Look,' Ella gasped.

Linden was slowly reaching into his pocket.

'What's he going to do?' Max's eyes widened, thinking perhaps Linden's evil side had something else in store for them.

She looked over at Blue and Kronch. They hadn't noticed a thing. Blue's face was alight with a twitching, sickly smile and Kronch was indulging in a gross display of sniggering that was sending little balls of slobber spraying into the room. In fact, they were so preoccupied with the biscuity process that neither of them saw Linden pull the Spy Force RHINO from his pocket. He kept his eyes firmly pinned on the machine, looking as if he too was enjoying the show, while, barely moving, he aimed the device at a large cauldron above Blue's head labelled 'toffee-caramel'.

'What's he doing?' Max was confused, unsure of who or what to trust any more, including what she was seeing.

'He's directing the RHINO towards that cauldron,' Ella said as they edged closer to the squirting choc-biscuit mixture.

'And he's going to try and save us,' Alex added without emotion.

Linden's eyes swept discreetly across to Max and sent her a small wink. For an instant she was bewildered about what it meant until she realized he needed her to distract Blue for the next part of his plan to work.

'Hey, Blue!' she shouted above the mechanical noise. 'You're not as smart as you think you are, you know that?'

Slowly, she slid her fingers into the pocket of her pink dress.

Blue gave her a quizzical look, which made him turn his back on Linden.

'Now, Maxine, what can possibly make you say that? I've had you tied up and placed on a conveyor belt where you have barely a minute left before you will be no more.'

With his finger on the miniature joystick of the RHINO, Linden was manoeuvring the cauldron so it tilted towards Blue's head.

'And what makes you think you're going to succeed?' Max asked, reaching for the sneeze powder and carefully taking it out of her pocket.

Blue let loose a laugh just as a clump of choc-biscuit mixture blobbed right next to her ear.

'You're a feisty one, aren't you, Maxine? Even when you're beaten. I admire that in you.'

'It's Max,' she shot back, sick of people calling her that. 'If you're as smart as you think you are,' she challenged, seeing Linden's cauldron tip even further, 'you'll look up right now.'

Ella's eyes widened as a large blob of biscuit mixture landed on Max's chest.

'Now, Max, what would I possibly want to look up for?'

'A final request?' she said sweetly, her Danger Meter vibrating so hard it was almost pounding through her ribcage.

'I guess it can't do any harm,' Blue said. And as he did, the cauldron of gooey toffee caramel poured over him in one gluggy spurt.

His cries were muffled as he quickly became enveloped in the hardening mixture. He tried to pull it off but it stretched around him like gluey brown pieces of chewing gum. Kronch stood rooted in the same spot as his pea-sized brain grappled with what was happening, and just as he worked it out, Max hurled the bag of sneeze powder at him in a mini-explosion of white, nose-irritating dust.

'Ahhchoo! Ahhchoo! Ahhchoo!' Kronch sneezed and, stumbling backwards bumping into machines, he landed head-first in a fresh batch of toffee-caramel biscuit goo.

Linden picked up a biscuit-mix bag and pulled it over Blue's head, causing him to fall in a sticky, mumbling heap. He then headed over to Ella and began untying her as another blob of mixture clomped on Max.

'Ahhchoo! Ahhchoo! Ahhchoo!' Kronch continued to sneeze.

'What happened?' Ella wriggled in her loosening ropes. 'I was worried that you really believed all that stuff you said before.'

Linden untied the last of the knots and helped her off the moving belt. He then moved across to untie Alex.

'I didn't realize at the time, but I'd been given a drink that had the secret ingredient in it. When it began wearing off I realized what was happening. Ahhchoo!' Some of the sneeze powder had worked its way into Linden's nose.

'Mmmm mmmm mmm,' Blue mmmed from inside his biscuit-mix bag as he spun around like a miniature tornado.

Linden struggled with the last of Alex's knots before he moved across to help Max.

'Ahhchoo! Ahhchoo! Ahhchoo!' Kronch sneezed.

'When did it start to wear off?' Max flicked her

head as the brown toffee goo began falling on her.

'Mmmm mmmm mmm,' Blue mmmed and spun around some more.

'Around the time I took you to Blue's office.' Linden's hands became covered with toffee caramel as he tried to undo the last of Max's ropes.

'Ahhchoo! Ahhchoo! Ahhchoo!'

There was a pause.

'Blue's office? Ahhchoo!' Max had inhaled some of the powder as well.

'Yeah.' Linden was almost through the ropes as another glob of toffee landed on both of them.

'You mean all the time we've been here, thinking we were going to die, you were pretending? Ahhchoo!' Max could feel her temper rising.

Linden realized that his plan, which had saved their lives, may not have sounded too good.

'I can't believe you'd do that!'

'Ahhchoo! Ahhchoo! Ahhchoo!' Kronch's sneezing attack continued as he bumped into Blue who mmmed as if he was in pain.

Max was totally covered by toffee caramel as the hundreds and thousands made their way towards her.

'It was the only way I could get close enough to you to try and save you. Ahhchoo!' he explained.

'Wait until I get off here. Ahhchoo!' Max warned, the sprinkling process falling on her like coloured snow.

'Do you want to be freed or not?' Linden asked, a little of the evil-inducing ingredient making him unusually impatient with Max.

Ella noticed the blades of the slicer getting closer and closer.

'Maybe you two should talk about this later?' she suggested anxiously.

'Ahhchoo! Ahhchoo! Ahhchoo!' Kronch sneezed as he stumbled into a bag of flour which powdered over everyone.

'No. I'd like to talk about it now,' Max insisted, before sneezing again.

'Mmmm mmmm mmm,' Blue mmmed again from inside his biscuit-mix bag.

'Max!' Alex shouted.

'And another thing—' Max began.

'Max! The blades!' Ella cried.

Max looked up and saw shafts of glistening steel fall just centimetres in front of her face. The next slice was meant for her. Just before they fell, Linden lunged forward and, grabbing her arms, dragged her off the conveyor belt and onto the floor.

'Ahhchoo!' Max and Linden sneezed together.

Ella and Alex breathed a deep sigh as the Moons of Mars confectionery machine continued to whirr on as if nothing had happened.

CHAPTER 21
BACK AT
SPY FORCE

Max, Linden, and Ella stood in front of Harrison's desk holding fresh tropical juices Steinberger had made them. Actually, Ella and Linden were holding theirs while Max's drink perched on a high stool near her face with a long straw in it because the Moons of Mars toffee mixture made it hard for her to move.

They each sipped and watched as Steinberger tried to help Harrison unhook his sling from a rack of fishing lines he'd become entangled in. He was wearing a sling because of an accident he'd had that morning, during a meeting with the Brazilian Foreign Minister, when he was reaching for a rare garden gnome that was perched a little too high on the mantelpiece. He stretched up to the gnome, grabbed its foot, but unable to get a proper hold stumbled backwards. He only just managed to catch the gnome with one hand as the other became twisted behind a marble carving of himself that was given to him as a present from the people of the Congo.

If Max could have moved or made any facial gestures, she'd have firmly folded her arms across her chest and be scowling at having spent the entire journey from Blue's Foods to Spy Force bent into Sleek's sidecar, while Linden and Ella chatted incessantly like a pair of parakeets at sunset. They were all gush and froth as they talked about the mission and what was even more sucky was Linden saying some of it in French which he'd started studying at school after Ella had told him she lived in Paris as a kid.

Blah blah blah, they went on and on. Ooh-la-la and big deal, thought Max. She was still angry with Linden for lying to her during the mission and making her feel as if he'd turned his back on her. She'd never felt so alone in her whole life and here he was laughing and talking to Ella as if it was nothing.

Finally, after a tricky struggle, Steinberger freed Harrison from the fishing rods and left him to make his way to his seat behind his desk.

'Team,' he said importantly, straightening his tie with his one good arm. 'Well bum . . . I mean, well done. On behalf of Spy Force I'd like to thank you for helping uncover the evil plans of Blue. Linden, the drink sample you brought back for us to test was put through the SAM and came up exactly as we thought. The special forces have been sent in and we hope to have Blue behind bars where he belongs.'

Ella sent Linden a warm smile that Max would

have called 'soppy' if anyone had asked her. Which they didn't.

'Awesome! Aaachoo!' Linden still had traces of sneeze powder in his system.

'Oh, and Max?'

Max's heart tripped over itself.

'Yes?' she asked eagerly, hoping perhaps he had something special to tell her.

'Sorry there isn't time to let you get cleaned up but Sleek has got the plane fired up and you know how he is about keeping to schedules.'

'That's OK,' she lied, thinking her journey home couldn't be any more uncomfortable. She was still wearing that stupid pink dress while the other two stood around in their own clothes.

'Spy Force is so proud of you three and would like to take this opportunity to officially declare Mission Blue's Foods a success.'

Harrison held his juice aloft as Steinberger pressed the *play* button on the tape machine and a chorus of celebration music sounded throughout the room. He then burst into an impulsive and hearty round of applause. Ella and Linden clinked their glasses together while Max sucked on her straw and felt an itch on her nose start up.

But that wasn't the only thing bugging her.

'Mr Harrison? Where's Alex?'

'Alex doesn't like to hang around for the festivities. Never has. She's an elusive one, our Alex.'

Max tried not to sound obvious. 'Did she leave any messages?'

'Once a mission is finished, she just takes off. She's not too fond of goodbyes.'

Max was disappointed. She knew she and Alex hadn't got along too well but she was sure they'd be brilliant friends if they got to hang out a little more.

For now, though, there was something else she had to tell Harrison.

'There's one more thing I need to tell you about the mission, sir. One of your Spy Force officers is a double agent.'

Linden and Ella looked at each other.

Harrison's face clouded over.

'Tell us what you blow . . . that is, what you *know*.'

Max knew what she had to say was going to shock everyone and she could hardly wait to tell them.

'It's Dretch.'

Steinberger frowned.

'I thought we'd been through this already, Max.

Dretch is one of our most loyal members and has been with the Force since its inception.'

Harrison took the accusation very seriously.

'Let her speak, Steinberger. Tell us how you know this, Max.' Harrison put his sling on the table and prepared to listen.

'When we arrived he made it clear he didn't like us and warned us we may not make it out of Spy Force alive. And his cat, Delilah, is his spy. Turning up to gather information just when it is needed. Dretch always flinched when he heard your name and he sneaked into the lab and tampered with my laser so that it failed during the mission.'

Steinberger and Harrison exchanged a solemn look.

'Steinberger. Ask Dretch to come in, will you?'

The tall lanky man did as he was asked. Max stood by and contemplated how proud Harrison would be of her now that the mission was completed and she was about to uncover a double agent.

'You have made a very grave accusation, Max.' Harrison's voice was low and measured. 'Let's hope you're not jumping to conclusions.'

'I have no doubt, sir.' But hearing the tone of Harrison's voice made Max's certainty falter.

Within a few short minutes Dretch was standing among them.

'Max tells us you might be a double agent.' Harrison got straight to the point.

Dretch spun his head so fast towards Max she stepped back.

'Did she now?' His voice was full of anger. 'And what makes her think that?'

'Max? I think it's best if it comes from you at this point,' Harrison invited.

Max swallowed to moisten her suddenly dry throat.

'Every time Harrison's name was mentioned to you, you'd flinch, almost as if in disgust.'

Dretch dug his hands deep into his pockets.

'I never knew it was a crime to feel loyalty towards someone who is one of the most clever and brave men I know. We've worked on many missions together and Harrison always thought about others before himself. It will take my whole life to repay the kindness this man has shown.'

Max swallowed again.

'And what about you sneaking into the lab just before we got our packs and my laser not working when I tried to use it during the mission?'

Dretch fixed her with a iron stare.

'Quimby asked me to fix some equipment of hers. She was present every second I was there and can vouch for everything I did.'

'And what about the threat you made to me about not making it out of here alive?'

Max suddenly became more confident, remembering the venom in his deadly warning.

'If you must know I think it's dangerous to have kids working on missions when they aren't trained and can't make proper judgements. I was just letting you know that what you were stepping into wasn't fairyland but real and dangerous work.'

If Harrison hadn't been present, Max was convinced Dretch would have jumped across the room and flattened her toffee-coated body into a million sweetened pieces.

'I'm sorry for the interruption, Dretch. You can go back to what you were doing.'

Max felt about five centimetres tall.

Harrison fixed her with a stern eye.

'Max, what just happened must never happen again. It's pleasing to see you are keeping so aware of your surroundings, but a good agent is sure of all their facts. Dretch is as fine and loyal an agent as any I've met. In fact during our last mission together, he saved my wife . . . I mean, life.'

A tear pricked the corner of Max's eye as she realized she'd gone from hero to sugar-coated idiot in the space of about ten minutes.

Beep, beep, beep, beep!

Steinberger looked at his beeper.

'It's Sleek. He's got the jet ready for Australia and another pilot to take you home, Ella.'

Steinberger saw Ella's face fall.

'But maybe you could walk us to the VART and we can say goodbye together?'

Ella smiled. 'I'd like that.'

Harrison beamed at all three of them. 'Your mission is done and I'm proud of all three of you. Until bed time. We'll be in fudge,' he said before wincing and correcting himself. 'I mean, until next time. We'll be in touch. Au revoir.'

On their way to the terracotta ride, Max lagged a little behind the others as she struggled with her extra sweet, toughened layer and her sadness at disappointing Harrison. As she turned a corner towards the elevator, she ran headlong into the sallow features of Dretch.

'I told you to keep out of my way,' he sneered.

'I . . . I . . .' Max stammered as the others moved ahead.

'I'm not interested in excuses and if you

ever try to muddy my name again, you might just find yourself adrift in some gooey mess you won't be able to get out of so easily. Just stay away from me, got that?'

He disappeared as Steinberger reached the elevator and turned around to see how she was doing.

'You OK, Max?' he asked jovially.

'Sure,' she answered, again feeling the icy chill customary with meeting Dretch. She'd really earned his anger in Harrison's office and now he hated her even more, but there was something in her that knew he wasn't telling the whole truth and she was sure going to keep an eye on him next time they met.

After a brief terracotta ride they arrived at the VART, where Sleek had the jet ready and waiting.

Steinberger walked a little slower to stay with a slow-moving Max. He thanked them a million times for their work and recounted over and over again how successful the mission was and what it meant for the world. He told her not to feel bad about Dretch. He was a good guy; not the easiest to get along with, but he wouldn't hold any grudges about her mistaken conclusion. He spoke so fast it was a wonder his lips could keep up. What he said made her feel better, but suddenly Max wasn't worried about his lips or what he was saying or about Dretch, she was more concerned about trying to overhear what Linden and Ella were whispering about in front of her.

She missed most of it and what she did hear was all in French.

Why did she spend most of her life looking silly and feeling as if she was the odd one out?

When they reached the end of the ramp, it was time for Ella and Steinberger to say goodbye. Sleek, as usual, had the invisible jet prepared for take-off.

'There's a jet there?' Ella exclaimed.

'Sure is, and you should see inside,' Linden answered.

The engine sounded out an eager jet thrust.

'Maybe next time.' Steinberger was well aware of Sleek's need to keep schedules.

'Max?' Linden asked, hoping she'd get the hint and move away so he could say a quiet goodbye to Ella.

'Yes?' she said innocently, knowing full well what he wanted.

'Maybe you should get on the jet first. Make yourself comfortable,' he suggested.

'No, I'll wait for you,' she offered kindly, not wanting to leave them alone for a second.

All four of them stood in heavy silence as Sleek climbed out of the cabin.

'Everyone ready?' he asked. Then seeing Max's sweetened layer he broke off a piece of toffee and plonked it in his mouth. 'We leave in one minute.'

Linden and Ella tried to cover their smiles as Sleek climbed back in the jet.

'Bye, Ella. I'll call you when we get back to Australia.'

'That'd be great. Bye, Max.'

'Bye,' Max mumbled.

Steinberger hurried them along. 'Sleek has been known to leave without any passengers,' he warned.

'Bye, Steinberger. Thanks. For everything,' Max managed through toffee-stiff lips.

Max followed Linden as he climbed into the jet and found his seat. As they buckled up, the hatch closed and they waved goodbye.

'We did it,' said Linden warmly.

Max tried to smile.

'Yeah we did,' she said feeling a little better as the invisible jet taxied out of the VART and carried them away from their first successfully completed Spy Force mission.

CHAPTER 22
AU REVOIR, MINDAWARRA

'When were you working for Spy Force?' Max and Linden had arrived back on the farm and after a very long bath that dissolved her toffee coating Max was now sitting at the table facing Ben and Eleanor over banana sandwiches and orange juice.

'Most of the time we were in London,' Ben said matter-of-factly, taking another bite out of his sandwich. 'In fact, once you've been inducted you're members for life, but I guess Harrison told you that. They've got great fringe benefit offers too.'

'Why didn't you tell me?'

'They're a secret organization, Max, you know that. We can't tell anyone.'

'Even me?'

'Even you,' Ben said, taking a slurp of juice as if he was telling just another everyday story.

Eleanor leant across and held Max's hand. 'We knew you'd been recruited and that you'd gone to London to be inducted into the Force. We got an email from Spy Force before you left. They are a world class operation and take very good care of their spies. It's a good career. As long as in your everyday life you act just like any other kid. We're so happy for you.'

This was so bizarre. Ben and Eleanor not only knew about their London mission—minus the details, of course—they were once spies themselves. A few times they were involved in missions, but mostly they worked in the labs.

'Does Mum know?'

'No,' Eleanor answered gently, trying to soothe Max's shock.

'Another sandwich?' Ben asked, reaching for his third.

'No thanks. I think I might just go to bed.'

It was the last day of Max's visit to the farm and she was waiting in the front room for her mother. She hadn't seen much of Linden over the last few days because he was busy helping his father. And also because she was doing her best to avoid him since she was still upset with him for lying to her during the mission.

And for liking Ella more than her.

Trouble was, as she rested her chin on her arms and stared out of the window, feeling small in the long, sinking sofa, she missed Linden and was feeling sad that he hadn't come to say goodbye. She heard the back door slam and Eleanor's voice drifted down the hall.

'She's in the lounge room packed and ready

to break our hearts by leaving us to our quiet lives again.'

There was a short moment where Max heard nothing before she turned to see Linden standing next to her.

'How do you do that?' she asked.

'Do what?' He frowned.

'Just turn up behind people?'

'Not sure. I guess it's the angelic side of me kicking in before its time.'

Max didn't smile.

'Can I sit with you until your mum comes?' he asked.

She moved to the end of the sofa, leaving him heaps of room to sit down, then she stared at the carpet in front of her.

There was this annoying silence that sat between them like a stranger.

'Ella called.'

Just the name made Max clench her fingers.

'She said Blue's Foods is being shut down and there are TV reports that a big Japanese firm is going to buy the company and keep making all the favourite foods as they were originally.'

Max pretended not to be too interested but was hanging on Linden's every word.

'By the time the police reached the factory,' he continued, 'all the evidence had been destroyed and Blue had disappeared leaving no trace that he was even connected to the company except for his name.'

'They didn't lock him up?'

'Nope. Couldn't find a trace of him.'

'That means it won't be long until he plans another scheme.'

'Yeah,' Linden agreed, happy Max had started to talk to him.

There was another one of those long silences. Max had so much she wanted to say to Linden but nothing would come out.

'Max,' Linden began uneasily. 'I know you're still mad at me for what I did at Blue's factory, but I was only doing what I thought best.'

Max didn't budge. Sometimes she could be so stubborn Linden was sure if he looked up the word in the dictionary it would say, 'See Max'.

'Besides. We did it. Our first official Spy Force mission.'

No response.

'And I still think we make the best team there is.'

Max smiled reluctantly.

'If you hadn't understood why I'd winked at you, we'd all have been in big trouble,' he said. And dropping his head a little he added, 'And I would have lost a really good friend.'

Max smiled even more as she tried to find the words to tell Linden the reason she was angry was because she thought he didn't care.

'It's just that—' She was interrupted by the crunch of gravel beneath tyres as her mother's car drove towards the house.

Great, thought Max. When I want her to arrive she doesn't and when I want her to stay away she's here.

'That's my ride back to paradise,' she joked.

Linden smiled. 'When are you coming back?'

'Not sure,' she answered, feeling as if she wanted to say something nice but couldn't think what. 'Maybe you could come and visit me in the city.'

Linden's face turned into one of those big smiles that took over his whole body.

'That'd be great! You could show me all your favourite places.'

The car pulled up in front of the house and the engine was turned off.

'Yeah,' Max said, walking over to pick up her bags.

Linden got up off the sofa and pushed a strand of hair out of his eyes, but just as quickly it flung back.

'It's good to see you're back to your normal self.' Max never thought she'd be so happy to see his uncontrollable hair. 'I got worried too that you really meant all those things back there.'

'I might think you're a bit difficult at times but not enough to want to turn you into a giant biscuit.'

Max smiled. Linden really did have a way of making things seem OK again.

She heard a car door slam and looked out of the window.

'Oh no,' she moaned. 'She's brought the kid with her.'

'Who?' But before he needed an answer Linden remembered. 'Aidan. Let's watch,' he said, jumping onto the sofa and thinking this should be fun.

'Yeah,' Max gasped excitedly, preparing to watch another awkward family reunion.

After a quick check in the mirror and applying more lipstick and other face goo, Max's mum got out of the car, straightened her tight skirt and adjusted her overdone salon hair. The kind where they spend hours making it look as if you spent no time on it at all. She giggled and preened herself as Eleanor and Ben said hello and shook hands with Aidan. Ben was holding a well-behaved Ralph on a leash but when Aidan stepped closer, Ben had to hold him back.

'Grrrrr,' Ralph growled.

'Ralph,' Eleanor scolded, 'you don't do that to guests.'

Ralph went quiet but they could tell he didn't like Aidan and was only being good for Eleanor.

Aidan nervously stepped around Ralph and bunged on one of those Hollywood grins that was so fake it looked as if he'd been practising it in front of the mirror for weeks.

Again Eleanor did her best to invite them in but after a short desperate look from her mother, Aidan made some smarmy excuse that was so slick Max could just picture them rehearsing the answer in the car. Then there was silence as they could think of nothing else to say.

'Another famous family moment,' said Max.

'These hellos and goodbyes are fun,' Linden cracked. 'But then I always have a good time when you're around.'

Max blushed. 'Thanks,' she said quietly, feeling the same. 'I—'

'Max, honey? It's time to go, sweetie.' Her mother's timing was terrible as usual.

'That's our cue.' Max got off the sofa and picked up her bags.

Outside there was a stilted series of hellos and 'darling' pecks on the cheek.

Ben kept a tight hold of Ralph and looked at Max.

'He promised he'd be good this time.'

Ralph sat up even taller just to prove it. Max had to admit that was cute.

'Thanks for everything. Can I come back soon?'

'Any time you like.' Eleanor folded her up in a big, duvet-like hug as Max's mother looked on, a hint of jealousy on her face as the hug continued a little longer than she thought necessary.

Ben handed Ralph's leash to Eleanor and gave Max a hug that was just as warm.

'Don't take too long about it, that's all,' he said, and he scooped her up and twirled her around like she was a rag doll. Max giggled as the farm dipped around her feet.

All the hugging and twirling made Max's mother uncomfortable and she tried to hurry things along.

'We should be going then.' Her smile was a

mixture of anxiety and muscles trying to keep up a fake smile.

Max turned to Linden. 'See ya.'

'See ya. We'll do it all again soon.' And with that he winked.

Max laughed. 'Yeah, let's do that.'

Max's mother looked at Aidan, smiling an apology at how long this was taking.

Ben and Linden packed Max's bags away and Max opened the back door of the car. Just as she was about to climb in, a crescendo of screeching and a flurry of feathers and dirt burst in front of her. She lost her balance and toppled onto the ground.

Geraldine. Max should have known she wouldn't get away without a goodbye from her.

'You'll get yours,' she warned the chicken as it innocently strutted away.

Eleanor lunged towards Max and helped her up.

'I'm so sorry, Max. Geraldine's normally so quiet. Are you OK?'

Max's mother stood nearby watching Eleanor fuss. She moved in before Max had a chance to say anything and took her out of Eleanor's arms.

'Of course she is. Aren't you, sweetie? No use fussing, you're still alive and we're late.' She brushed Max down and just as quickly stepped around to the driver's side and got in the car.

'Thanks, Eleanor. I'm fine,' Max whispered to her aunt who she'd miss more than anyone.

Max climbed onto the back seat and Ben closed the door after her. Then they took off in a storm of dust in her mother's hurry to get back to the city.

'Yeah. We'll do it again,' said Max. She leant her head against the window. She was Max Remy Superspy, and she was going to be back.

'NOW, IF YOU'LL EXCUSE ME, I MUST GO AND
SUPERVISE THE END OF SPY AGENCIES THE
WORLD OVER . . .'

Evil Mr Blue is back. And this time he's wriggled his
reptilian way right into the heart of the Academy of Spies.
The world's greatest spy agency is holding its annual awards
dinner, which means that the world's greatest spies are all in
one place.

Also in that place is a huge dormant volcano. And Blue's
managed to wake it up. If Max, Linden and Ella can't calm
things down, the whole thing's going to go sky high.

Will their super spy training help them save
the day? Or will Max's fear of heights spell the
end for Spy Force . . .

ISBN 978-0-19-275420-2

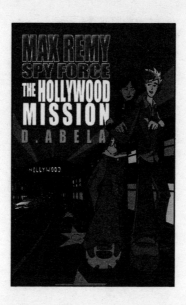

'BIGGUS FARTIE IS ONE OF OUR BEST SCIENTISTS.
I WANT YOU TO SAVE HIM BEFORE A FOUL-
SMELLING PLAN IS LET LOOSE ON THE WORLD.'

Lights! Camera! Action! Max and Linden are on a Spy
Force mission in Hollywood—but it's not all films and fun.

Somebody has kidnapped Dr Fartie and is forcing him to
encrypt movies. Now, top-secret security information is
being passed to baddies the world over. Worse, it looks as if
someone Max knows has infiltrated Spy Force.

Who can the pair trust? How will they find Fartie? And will
Max's bad mood finally lead to somebody's sticky end?

ISBN 978-0-19-275421-9

'I THINK I'LL PASS ON BEING
POISONED FOR TODAY.'

Something toxic has got into the world's top spy
organization. Spy Force agents are falling like flies. At the
same time, a venomous villain has stolen the agency's
manual, the key to all of its secrets.

Could the two things be linked?

Is Spy Force's brilliant botanist involved?

Only Max and Linden can uncover the truth.
But first it's up to them to find the antidote deep in the
Amazon rainforest. Oh dear . . .

ISBN 978-0-19-275422-6

'BLUE WILL NOT REST UNTIL HE
GETS HIS REVENGE . . .'

Evil Mr Blue is safely locked behind bars.
But the team at Spy Force don't trust their
old enemy an inch.

And with good reason. First Max's mum is kidnapped. Then
Spy Force agents are attacked. Even Chief Harrison is
trapped.

Max and Linden set off on a rescue mission. But can they
survive the Pulverizing Cell and the deadly world of the
Portal Room? Or will Blue finally settle old scores?

ISBN 978-0-19-275423-3

Photograph by Todd Decker

When Deborah Abela was a small child, she spent most of her time imagining she was on great adventures all over the world. When she grew older, she bought a backpack and a plane ticket and actually went on them. After three years she came home and worked for seven years on one of Australia's most popular children's TV programmes, before leaving to write novels about a small girl who goes on lots of adventures all over the world.

Deborah grew up in Merrylands, a western suburb of Sydney, but now lives in inner-city Glebe with her partner Todd, who is almost as nice as Linden.